MURDER IN THE CATHEDRAL

MURDER IN THE CATHEDRAL

Cora Harrison

**SEVERN
HOUSE**

First world edition published in Great Britain and the USA in 2022
by Severn House, an imprint of Canongate Books Ltd,
14 High Street, Edinburgh EH1 1TE.

Trade paperback edition first published in Great Britain and the USA in 2023
by Severn House, an imprint of Canongate Books Ltd.

severnhouse.com

British Library Cataloguing-in-Publication Data
A CIP catalogue record for this title is available from the British Library.

ISBN-13: 978-0-7278-5052-2 (cased)
ISBN-13: 978-1-4483-0761-6 (trade paper)
ISBN-13: 978-1-4483-0760-9 (e-book)

All Severn House titles are printed on acid-free paper.

MIX
Paper from
responsible sources
FSC® C013056

Typeset by Palimpsest Book Production Ltd.,
Falkirk, Stirlingshire, Scotland.
Printed and bound in Great Britain by
TJ Books, Padstow, Cornwall.

This book is dedicated to my friend of many years, Patricia Hawkes.

Our children played together and now we share news of grandchildren.

Thank you for your interest in my books – the fruits of my retirement.

Cora

ONE

Reverend Mother Aquinas often thought that Christmas Day was probably the most sociable day of the year in the life of the convent and its nuns. No school, no crises, no visits from the police, no weeping children, nor distraught mothers, no terrible stories of evictions, of brutal assaults. Her community of hardworking nuns and lay sisters relaxed, enjoyed good food and sociable visits from their families. The Reverend Mother herself went from room to room, greeting everyone, exclaiming at the Christmas presents brought by excited children and turning a blind eye to the surreptitious racing of toy cars on the long smooth expanse of the back hallway, and even to a new baby doll being brought on one occasion into the convent chapel by a crowd of little girls enthusiastically planning to perform a surreptitious christening at a real font.

She herself had long ago prohibited visits from her own family on this morning, so she was surprised when, as she was displaying the convent hens and their neat nests of straw to a couple of lively ten-year-old nephews of Sister Bernadette, a breathless novice tracked her down to tell her that she had a visitor.

'There's a bishop waiting to see you in your study, Reverend Mother,' announced the young lady. 'Not the real bishop,' she said hastily, seeing the Reverend Mother's startled face. 'It's the Protestant bishop,' she added primly.

'Dr Thompson! Really?' The Reverend Mother quickly removed a few pieces of straw from her black habit, straightened her veil, sent the novice flying for a basket so that the boys could have the fun of collecting eggs for Sister Bernadette and went hastily indoors to see what had brought Dr Thompson, bishop of Cork's Anglican Church of Ireland, to her door on the morning of St Stephen's Day. An amiable man with a large family of pretty girls, she was acquainted with him only to the extent of greeting him in the street and once listening to him with interest as he explained the history of the beautiful Gothic cathedral over which he reigned and of the cathedrals and monasteries that had formerly occupied the site.

That this was no casual social meeting was immediately apparent to her when she saw his white face and realized that he was under considerable strain. She shut the door firmly on Sister Bernadette, ignoring her usual offers of hospitality, and sat down quietly beside the distraught man and prepared to listen to what he had to say.

'Something terrible has happened,' he said gravely and then stopped. 'It's about one of your pupils,' he began again. 'I have to see the mother, but Inspector Cashman thought it best if I were to see you first and Tom Hayes, my sexton, knows the woman and he felt the same.'

'One of my pupils,' echoed the Reverend Mother.

'A very tiny boy with red hair.' He winced visibly and then swallowed hard. 'My sexton says that his name is Enda, Enda O'Sullivan.'

The Reverend Mother sighed heavily. It would be Enda! The most troublesome small boy that the school had ever encountered. He was aged seven, but so small that he looked like a four-year-old; sang like an angel but behaved mainly like a little devil. A lot of her time was spent dealing with irate shopkeepers and stallholders who had found by experience that it was of little use to tackle the child's mother.

'What's he done now?' she asked and waited calmly to hear, but her mind went instantly towards the donation box which probably stood conspicuously in the Anglican church where mainly rich citizens would go to worship God in a manner laid out by those who had conquered Ireland hundreds of years ago. Undoubtedly that would attract Enda, but how would he have got into the cathedral? Tom Hayes, the sexton, would have sent him away with a clip around the ear if he had ventured to present himself at the door. The Protestant cathedral, in a city renowned for its strong IRA and Sinn Fein presence, would ensure strict security, even on Christmas morning.

He did not answer immediately. A nice man, searching for words. Reluctant to alarm or to offend her. She suppressed a moment of impatience. Why was he making such a fuss about this? Small boys, hungry small boys, would steal, and she didn't suppose that the boy had made a fuss about being grabbed, probably by the sexton. Enda would be well used to this and would know that his age, his size and his adoring mother would probably protect him from any serious punishment. No one knew who the boy's father was; perhaps even the mother herself did not know. An enormously fat, elderly woman, she had cheerfully admitted that she had no idea that she was pregnant, had been 'on the lash' – out drinking – for days, had thought that she would have been far too old, until, according to accounts which the Reverend Mother had heard, 'it was too late to do aught'.

Little Enda was her first and undoubtedly her last child – a freak of nature, but a gift from heaven according to his adoring mother.

'So, Tom Hayes sent you to see me.' The Reverend Mother thought she might move the conversation on. 'He's got Enda, has he?'

She knew Tom Hayes. Not very well paid by the affluent Protestant community, but he dug their graves, stoked their coal boiler, and rang their bells for a wage sufficient to pay his rent in Barrack Street and to feed himself. He had been born and christened in the Roman Catholic Church, had even attended the Christian Brothers' school on George's Quay, but when faced with the choice between emigration and taking a good job at the Church of Ireland cathedral, he had instantly chosen the latter, and though neighbours might mutter about burning in the flames of hell, he seemed happy and reasonably well-dressed whenever the Reverend Mother greeted him in the street.

'Yes, I know Tom Hayes; a kind man,' she said aloud.

Dr Thompson suddenly buried his face in his hands and the Reverend Mother started in alarm. The man's face was half-hidden, but she could see red patches behind the outstretched fingers, and she hoped that he wasn't having a stroke or something. She glanced quickly at the bell rope which hung over her desk, but before she had a chance to take matters further, he mastered himself and removed the hands.

'Reverend Mother,' he said, in a voice which shook with emotion, 'the little boy is dead.'

The Reverend Mother allowed a silence to lengthen for a few seconds and then resorted to a question. 'What happened, Dr Thompson?' she said and with an effort kept her voice steady.

'Dr Scher, the police surgeon, thinks that he was poisoned.'

'Dr Scher is there.'

'And Inspector Cashman. You see the archdeacon, Dr Hearn, he's dead. He dropped dead in the middle of the service. It was only after the church was emptied that we found the boy. We thought that the archdeacon had succumbed to a stroke or a heart attack. Dr Babington, my dean, thought it best to clear the church immediately. I'm afraid that I felt paralysed, just didn't know what to do. Heard a shriek from the Dean's Chapel just before the celebration of communion. He was conducting a quick service for some elderly people and others while I was on the high altar, of course, conducting the usual Christmas service for the children, visiting the crib and finding presents under the tree, and apparently, he dropped dead, quite suddenly and without warning and . . .'

Dr Thompson broke down and wept.

'And Enda?' The Reverend Mother spoke as gently as she could but, nevertheless, she could hear a stern note in her voice. The bishop, she thought, must have led a sheltered life.

'The sexton, Tom Hayes, found him. Just behind the font.' The bishop took a large white handkerchief from somewhere in his robes, mopped his eyes and shook his head with a look of disbelief. The Reverend Mother thought about the hospitable Sister Bernadette and how she would minister to the needs of this overwrought bishop, but she had more important matters to think of. She got to her feet decisively, unhooked her cloak and pulled the bell.

'I'll walk back with you to your cathedral,' she said. And then, when Sister Bernadette arrived at the door, beaming at the prospect of showing hospitality to the Reverend Mother's unexpected guest, she said crisply, 'I'm going out, Sister, would you kindly let Sister Mary Immaculate know.'

He followed her obediently as she went down the corridor as rapidly as possible and in his gentlemanly way managed to pull himself together to open the hall door for her. She would ask no more questions, she decided. He had said that Inspector Cashman and Dr Scher were at the cathedral so she would get all relevant information from them. Neither did she indulge in any small talk but, with her veil shielding most of her face, she confided the soul of little Enda O'Sullivan to God and then prayed for the unfortunate mother that she might be given the strength to bear this terrible loss of her greatest treasure on earth.

There was, she speculated, little fear that the news would be spread prematurely to Barrack Street. Cork was not a large city, but the division between the people of both faiths, Roman Catholic, and Church of Ireland, was wide. The Anglican cathedral illuminated the skyline between her convent and Barrack Street, but its worshippers came, in their expensive cars, from the more salubrious dwelling places upon the hillsides of Montenotte, Douglas and Bishopstown. Nevertheless, she walked as fast as she could and left it to bishop as to whether he matched her pace or lagged a few yards behind. It did occur to her that he was probably not so used to walking as was she – her glimpses of him in the street were usually of him sitting in an expensive Mercedes Benz car behind his chauffeur, but she rejected the thought impatiently, her mind fixed upon poor Mrs O'Sullivan and the necessity of seeing her as soon as possible. She would, she thought, send Sister Bernadette to fetch her, and once she had seen the body of her son, they would bring her to the convent and keep her there during the first violence of her sorrow. Sister Bernadette had related the piece of gossip that Mrs O'Sullivan's insistence that Enda could do what he liked and without sanctions had alienated his mother from near neighbours, but had added that she was a nice and a kind woman. Yes, Sister Bernadette would be the best person to help to console the grieving mother.

The Reverend Mother's busy mind planned the breaking of

the news as she waited impatiently for the bishop at the door
of his cathedral, noticing the presence of Sheehan's Undertakers,
their van parked discreetly and very neatly at the side of the
magnificent building.

She saw a body as soon as they emerged from the gloom
of the porch. It was in a small chapel to one side of the high
altar, illuminated by dozens of candles and small lamps. Not
Enda. This was a man, a clergyman, the body encased in a
coffin and lying on the red velvet carpet that covered the step
to the altar, clothed in flowing white garments, the gold stole
carefully arranged around his neck, and draped symmetrically
from shoulder to waist. Two men, one dressed as a clergyman
and the other in a three-piece suit, knelt side by side in the
front row.

'The dead man's two sons,' murmured the bishop in her
ear. 'One is the rector of Midleton, the Reverend Mr Adam
Hearn and the other, Mr Owen Hearn, is a music teacher.'

'A music teacher,' echoed the Reverend Mother. When was
he going to talk about Enda?

'Yes, the young man went very much against his father's
wishes,' said the bishop, mistaking her automatic repetition
of his last words for an expression of surprise. 'They were, I
fear, quite estranged as his father had planned that he, like his
brother, should enter the church. In fact, it was I who persuaded
Owen to come to church today and meet his father, hoping
that the Christmas spirit would heal the breach. Little did I
know!' The old man caught his breath in a suppressed sob.
The Reverend Mother turned away from the bishop impatiently
and began to scan the cathedral, looking up and down and
around the tall, narrow space. Where was little Enda?

Then she saw a figure at the back of the church. Not a
clergyman. A short man with wide shoulders and worn, rather
dirty clothes. As she turned towards him, he passed his hand
over his face as though to wipe away the tears. The truth
flashed through her mind. The half-listened-to and then
forgotten observations of Sister Bernadette, prefixed usually
with the words: 'not that I like listening to gossip'. The neighbours didn't like Mrs O'Sullivan, not just because of her lack
of control over the mischievous Enda, but because of some

other 'goings-on' which Sister Bernadette hinted at but 'would not sully her tongue with repeating' and yes, there had been something about 'him working for Protestants'.

A relationship between two lonely people.

It must have helped her, thought the Reverend Mother. Tom Hayes, the sexton, probably earned a decent sum from his work as gravedigger and bell ringer at the cathedral. But, of course, there would have been gossip. The Reverend Mother turned her back on the scene of the dead body of the clergyman, laid out with such care, mourned by two sons, illuminated by the glow from the magnificent stained-glass windows, and went to where the shabbily dressed man stood, just beside the baptismal font at the back of the cathedral. The font was almost hidden away, but ornate like everything else in this magnificent cathedral. Made from the almost crimson-coloured Cork red marble, it was decorated with a carving of the head of John the Baptist, a marble shaft of sculpted capitals, and an octagonal base with the well-polished brass lettering reading: 'We are buried with Him, by baptism into death'. Between the font and the open door of a cupboard lay a small figure, his dirty, torn clothes stained with gobbets of vomit, his eyes open wide and appearing to stare up at the wooden beams of the roof.

'The police think that he came in through that window.' The bishop pointed upwards, his voice hushed and slightly hoarse.

High above their heads was the magnificent rose window with a broken pane of glass. The space seemed exceedingly small, and the Reverend Mother looked with pity at the tiny body at her feet. Could he really have fitted through that small opening and managed to climb down to floor level?

A certain measure of cold and well-contained anger suddenly came upon her. This child should not lie here unattended, while the archdeacon was clad in all the pomp and ceremony that money could ensure. Even if she had to pay for it herself out of God alone knew which fund, she would not show that pathetic stinking corpse to his mother.

'Where is Inspector Cashman? And Dr Scher?' she demanded of the bishop and allowed her voice to sound imperious. He did not reply, but raised a finger and sent a minor dignitary scurrying towards the top of the church, doubtless to fetch them. The Reverend Mother turned her attention back to Enda.

The boy lying there was undoubtedly dead, but no one had seen fit to bestow any care upon the body. His face and limbs were convulsed in a death agony. His dirty, ragged clothes were stained with vomit, his small hands clenched in agony and his eyes wide as though with terror. The Reverend Mother took in a long breath, calmed her anger, and then consciously turned her charm upon the bishop.

'I would not wish his mother to see him in that state,' she confided to him. 'Is there anything that we can do? Would Inspector Cashman permit the body to be moved, to be washed? What do you think?'

Of course, she told herself, there could be no possible objection from the police since the other victim had been cleaned and dressed and was now lying with all the pomp and ceremony that the Church of Ireland could command. However, she had long learned the value of a question rather than a demand and so she waited while the bishop sent another messenger after the first and they all stood and waited for the inspector, who was hurrying down the aisle towards her.

Patrick Cashman had once been a pupil of hers, had been such a boy as Enda, not so small, not at all so talented, certainly not so mischievous, not so sure of himself, either, but hard-working and reliable. Nevertheless, he and Enda had shared a poverty-stricken childhood, and both, like so many in her care, had lacked a father. She looked at Patrick with pride every time she saw him, watching him tread a difficult path through a city where terrible poverty existed side by side with considerable wealth; where the life of the citizens was constantly disrupted by political assassinations and where crime and retribution followed each other as surely as night followed day.

'This is sad, Reverend Mother,' he said now, respectfully bowing his head and holding his cap close to his chest. 'Dr Scher will be with you in a minute, but he is doing a few tests. We are fairly sure, though, that both the child and the archdeacon were poisoned with the same drug.'

Patrick hesitated for a few seconds, and then added in a low voice, 'We think that the child was used to gain entry to the cathedral through the broken window in the roof, in order to poison the wine in the chalice and then was poisoned himself so that he could not bear witness.'

'I see,' said the Reverend Mother. 'I am concerned that his mother should not see him in such a state. Is there anything we can do?' The bishop, she guessed, would be shocked at her apparent lack of emotion, but almost sixty years of dealing with the deaths of children, from disease, lack of food and violent criminal acts, had taught her to keep her feelings under control and deal with what she could achieve. The police would deal with the crime. She would endeavour to help the mother endure this terrible death.

She had addressed her remarks, not just to Patrick, but to the bishop and to another tall, thin clergyman who had just joined them. The newcomer was the first to answer.

'Yes, surely,' he said eagerly and quickly. 'Surely, my lord, the undertakers can see to the boy also. We must remove those clothes. I'll find a choir surplice for him; that will be appropriate. He sang like an angel, God have mercy on his soul, poor little child.'

The Reverend Mother gave him an approving nod and the bishop hastened to make the introduction. 'Reverend Mother, this is Mr Flewett, our precentor, in charge of our music and of the choir. Mr Flewett, Reverend Mother Aquinas.'

'You've heard him sing, then, have you, Mr Flewett?'

'Yes, indeed, our good friend, Tom Hayes, here, introduced him to me. I must confess,' he went on pleasantly, 'that I committed the sin of envying your church a voice like that.'

The Reverend Mother bowed her head but did not express the opinion that their parish choir, which consisted mainly of middle-aged and most respectable women, would be horrified if young Enda O'Sullivan had even come into their presence. She doubted whether either he or his mother went frequently, if ever, to Sunday mass.

'He's an only child,' she explained, 'and his mother lives alone and appears to have no relatives and, as far as I can tell, no friends, either.' The man was about forty, she reckoned, but despite the grey hair, his face was fresh, and he had a look of youth about the slightly flushed cheeks and the very bright, very blue eyes. His face was deeply sympathetic as she explained about not wanting his mother to see him like that.

'And the burial?' he enquired.

The Reverend Mother tightened her lips. Funerals of children were many and from what she could make out, were financed by a joint effort from neighbours. She wondered whether this community spirit would operate in the case of Mrs O'Sullivan.

'Don't you worry about that, Reverend Mother; I'll pay the priest and dig the grave, too,' said Tom Hayes gruffly. 'I'll bring him into the doctor now and we'll get him cleaned up before I go and get his mother. There's one thing, though, Reverend Mother.' The man hesitated and then said in a lowered voice, 'She'll expect a funeral, Reverend Mother, a good funeral, like – well, you know, Reverend Mother.'

The Reverend Mother knew what he meant, but she said nothing until Tom Hayes, having folded the proffered surplice carefully and placed it into the pocket of his jacket, lifted the small light body in his arms and went off towards the top of the church. Only when he was out of hearing did the Reverend Mother look from one sympathetic face to the other and then heave a sigh.

'In confidence,' she said, 'no matter what the men do, deserted wives in the parish are expected to be . . .' She hesitated for a moment, but an innate dislike of hypocrisy as well as the church's teaching on the importance of telling the truth, made her substitute the more forthright word 'celibate' for her initial choice of 'discreet'.

She saw the bishop blink at her outspokenness but ignored his embarrassed expression. 'Children's funerals,' she went on, 'are big affairs in the parish, no matter how poor the family. All the neighbours, almost everyone in the parish, will attend and there are long lines of children, a whole school, almost, sometimes marching behind the coffin. I fear it will break Mrs O'Sullivan's heart if that does not happen; she'll expect that procession of mourners,' she finished and then, as was her wont, she turned from the matter that seemed insolvable, to a matter that might be arranged.

'Would it be possible for Mrs O'Sullivan to come here to see her son?' she asked. 'I presume that Dr Scher will want both bodies for the post-mortem, but if she can see him first, I think it might be best for her, poor woman. Tom Hayes could fetch her. She lives quite close by.'

She expected the bishop to agree, and, indeed, he nodded his head almost immediately, but she did not expect the very enthusiastic response from the choirmaster. 'We'll make a little place for him,' the precentor said to her. 'Let me have a word with the canon. Mr Wilson,' he called as a thin, red-headed man came through the door. 'Mr Wilson,' repeated the precentor, 'just a quick word, if you please. You remember the old manger that we thought was oversized, have we still got it, by any chance?'

The Reverend Mother left him to his errand and turned back to the bishop. 'This is not going to put you out, is it?' she asked and endeavoured to suppress a perfunctory note in her voice.

His answer, though, was quick and reassuring. 'Not at all,' he said immediately. 'Mr Flewett will manage everything. The poor woman. She is very welcome to come here. I have a grandchild, a very beloved grandson, of about the same size, and I can hardly bear to think how my daughter and the whole family would suffer if anything happened to him. But you are still worried, aren't you?' he added, looking with concern into her face. 'Do tell me. A trouble shared – well, you know the old proverb.'

The Reverend Mother was taken aback. It seldom happened to her that someone asked her about her own state of mind or to share her worries. 'I'm somewhat concerned about the funeral, but one thing at a time,' she ended, trying to sound more cheerful.

'I see,' said the bishop. His face was sympathetic, but she knew that this was her problem, not his. The child had to be buried by the parish and in the parish graveyard. The mass in the South Chapel, as it was always known, would be easy to arrange, especially if the sexton, Tom Hayes, was willing to pay the priest and to dig the grave, but the funeral party that set out to walk to the graveyard in St Mary's of the Isle, would have to be of a respectable size or the unfortunate mother would be broken-hearted.

She turned her attention to the precentor who had arrived back in the church carrying a rather beautifully made manger. He stood for a moment, looking around the church and then went hesitantly towards the aisle on the south side of the nave. The early morning sun poured in through a beautiful stained-glass window on the wall of the side aisle and cast a kaleidoscope of blues, greens and deep crimson on the mosaic floor beneath. The precentor carefully placed the manger in the exact centre of the medley of colours, rapidly mounted the altar steps, took a deep-purple velvet cushion from the bishop's throne and arranged it carefully on the wooden manger.

The Reverend Mother stole a look at the bishop. She had not moved her head, but he spoke to her in an undertone. 'A very artistic man, Mr Flewett,' he said in a low murmur. It was left to the canon, Mr Wilson, to protest.

'My lord,' he exploded and then lowered his voice. 'The reverend lady must excuse me, but I think this is all most unseemly and most unnecessary. The child, a tool of some burglars, doubtless, was not even of our flock. Our responsibility is to the archdeacon. He would have been the first to say that those who used the boy as a tool must now be the ones to reclaim him.'

The bishop surveyed him rather sternly, but when he spoke it was to the precentor. 'You chose a good place for the child, Mr Flewett. He shall lie beneath my favourite window in the church, the portrait of the loving Jesus who, the Bible tells us, admonished his apostles, saying: "Suffer little children to come unto me, and forbid them not: for of such is the kingdom of God". You know the quotation, of course, Reverend Mother?' he said to her, turning away from the canon.

'You use the King James version, do you?' asked the Reverend Mother with interest. There was much that she did not know about a fellow religion, holding a ministry only a few hundred yards away from her own church. 'I'm a Latinist, I fear, and my version would be "*Jesus vero ait eis: Sinite parvulos, et nolite eos prohibere ad me venire: talium est enim regnum cælorum*",' she said lightly, anxious to deflect attention from the angry red face of Canon Wilson. Why was the man making such a fuss? Perhaps he had been a close friend to the murdered archdeacon and resented attention being taken from him. But if so, why was he not kneeling in front of the altar of the side chapel and joining with the prayers there? She dismissed the matter from her mind and went forward, up the side aisle to where Tom Hayes was carrying the dead body of the poor child, now clothed from top to toe in a dazzlingly white miniature surplice with his pale-gold hair combed in a way that she had never seen on any of her boys, and certainly not on this particular boy. The hair had been dampened with water and swept back from his brow as though he were a little choirboy. Slightly trimmed, also, she thought, and looked with gratitude at the kindly precentor.

'Put him here, Mr Hayes,' she said and felt tears prick her eyes as she indicated the manger which the precentor had lined with the splendid cushion. 'Now, go as quickly as you can to fetch his mother. You need to see her before the word gets around.' Luckily, she thought, it was Christmas morning and hopefully most of the neighbours and their children were indoors. The Vincent de Paul charitable society had been collecting in the streets of the city for money to buy toys for poor children and had also run a most successful door-to-door collection of toys that were outgrown or not wanted. She, herself, had gone through the list with an idealistic young solicitor who was giving up most of his Christmas holiday to this charitable deed. He had even volunteered to dress as Santa Claus, with some attendant elves, and to knock on all the doors on Christmas morning, after early masses were over and before the solemnity of High Mass at twelve o'clock. Yes, she thought with satisfaction, the children from the streets in the vicinity of the school would be happily occupied at this time on Christmas morning.

When he had gone, she looked hesitantly at the bishop. Morning services were over for him, just the one, she had gathered, but he was a family man. His wife, his daughters and even a little grandson might well be waiting for him.

'Don't feel that you need to stay,' she urged him. 'Close neighbours, as we are, don't need to stand on ceremony. I'll

wait for Mrs O'Sullivan and then take her away before the
bodies are removed. I'm sure your family are waiting for you.
Mr Hayes, your sexton, will look after me.'

The bishop was hesitant, but she pressed him. The dean, the
canon and Mr Webster, who had been introduced as the deacon,
were all hovering with the expectant air of those who are
eager to depart. As was the clerical son of the dead man. The
other son, she noticed, stayed in the background.

'I'll look after the Reverend Mother,' said the precentor
cheerfully. 'That's the best of being a bachelor! No one wants
me to show my face until dinner is ready to be served at my
father's house. I'm a nuisance in the kitchen, so my sisters
tell me. I'd like to meet Mrs O'Sullivan, also,' he said somewhat more seriously. 'She may be too upset to listen to me,
but I would like to say to her that I thought her son was gifted
by God with the voice of a little angel.'

The poor mother would cherish these words, thought the
Reverend Mother and she smiled at him. 'The words will stay
in her memory even if she is too upset to reply,' she said to
him. Then, to keep the conversation going as Dr Babington
whispered to Mr Webster some query about his interview with
the police inspector, she enquired about who would be cooking
Mr Flewett's Christmas Day dinner. He gave her a lively
account of his sisters and the number of clergymen in the
family, all stemming from the rural dean of the town of
Fermoy. She encouraged him to talk as the deacon and the
dean seemed to be arguing about something, raising their
voices occasionally and then dropping them in response to
the bishop's raised finger. There would, she thought, be no
awkward pauses in the conversation if she were left with Mr
Flewett. Already he was hauling out an enormous gramophone
– a heavy box with a horn attached – and offering to play
her a recording of his choir. She agreed hastily as she saw
the bishop trying to mute the raised voice of Dr Babington,
who was almost spitting the words: 'Totally incompetent,'
and she walked over to stand by the gramophone and then
listened with the assumed enthusiasm of an almost tone-deaf
person to the high-pitched voices of his choir of small boys.

TWO

' I would have fetched the poor woman, Reverend Mother. You knew you had only to ask,' said Dr Scher reproachfully.

The Reverend Mother knew a moment of compunction. Dr Scher had, obviously, finished what he could achieve here in a back room of the cathedral and was anxious to get back to his workplace to conduct the autopsy on both bodies. Inspector Cashman had arrived back into the body of the cathedral, was glared at by the deacon, Mr Webster, who had immediately and rather hurriedly made for the front door and slammed it rather hard, leaving the Reverend Mother to face two overworked officials who were now forced to be idle while the precentor played his recording machine quietly in the background.

'I know,' she said. 'And I do apologize for keeping you waiting. I don't know why there is the delay. I expected that the child's mother would have been here by now.' That, she thought, was one of those white lies which she sprinkled through her everyday conversation and mentioned in a rather perfunctory fashion into the deaf ear of the convent chaplain during the weekly confessional rite. She did, of course, know the reason for the delay. The unfortunate sexton, Tom Hayes, would have been faced by a mother who, once she had been convinced of the reality of his words, would have descended into floods of tears and probably a full-blown attack of hysteria. She did not envy him his task, but she was sure that she had done the right thing in sending him to break the news. He was probably the only one who could bring any consolation to the mother of a murdered seven-year-old and they would just have to wait until he was able to soothe her a little and until she managed to regain some control and was able to face going out into the street and down to the place where her small boy lay dead.

'What killed them?' she asked in a low tone, relying on the high-pitched voices from the gramophone to mute her words.

'Cyanide, I'd say,' he said briefly. 'I'll check when I get back, but that is what I think. Some fast-acting poisonous substance, anyway. There were traces of chocolate around the little fellow's mouth. The archdeacon, I suspect, may have been poisoned by the communion wine. He fell down soon after drinking it, so we've been told.'

'I see,' said the Reverend Mother. Her eyes went to the broken window above the western door. Such a magnificent window, a rose window it was called; she remembered seeing one like that in the Cathedral of Chartres which she and her cousin had visited in France when they were girls. The circular, rose-shaped window showed God as the creator resting on a rainbow and in the act of blessing, surrounded by eight compartments, each inspired by the scenes from the Book of Genesis, beginning with the creation of light, and ending with the birth of Adam and Eve and the naming of the animals. The stained glass depicting the fourth day of creation, when God had made the sun, the moon and the stars, had been smashed and the Reverend Mother looked at it sadly. Her patron saint, Thomas Aquinas, had written a long and scholarly article about the creating of light on the fourth day, based on the words from Genesis. She had recently re-read it with interest, but now her mind's eye saw only the tiny body of the undersized, underfed little boy who had been tempted by some devil to insert himself through that space, to open the front door and then to find his chocolate.

Dr Scher's eyes followed her gaze. 'A few shards of glass on the clothing, poor little fellow,' he said with an air of compassion. 'Used to have a picture of something like that, of God creating the world in seven days, in the synagogue that I attended as a boy,' he said. 'Never believed it myself, but it makes a beautiful story and I suppose that you do believe it all . . .'

The Reverend Mother wondered whether she believed anything as strongly as she had done once. There were dark moments when she even wondered whether the biblical story of a merciful and all-seeing God was true. Could there be a justification for all the evil in the world? And could a merciful God permit the corruption and the murder of a child?

'I suppose that he was inveigled into putting the poison in the communion wine,' she said after a minute. 'I don't suppose that he would ever have been an altar boy, but he is, was, quick and sharp. He wouldn't have needed much instruction. I'm not certain of the procedure here, but in our church the altar boy brings the wine in a cruet and the priest pours it into the chalice. No doubt, Patrick will find out the details of the service from one of the clergymen. Enda was clever enough to follow instructions and so he did,' she finished sadly.

'And he was told that there was some chocolate for him in the cupboard by the font,' said Dr Scher. 'Patrick's sergeant found a packet of Rolo chocolates on the shelf. Patrick thinks that the boy was told that he would find his reward in the cupboard at the end of the church. Only one had been eaten, but that one would have been enough. It takes less than a teaspoon of the powder to kill the strongest man. I'll explain to the mother that he was poisoned by a fast-acting poison. No need to go into any more detail. Leave it to me. People always have this strange idea that doctors know what they are talking about and don't usually question them.'

Mrs O'Sullivan was strangely silent when she arrived. The recording of the hymn, 'Jesus, Friend of Little Children' was playing when she came in and she was quite bewildered by the high-pitched voices coming from the side of the church. The Reverend Mother, holding out her hands, went down the aisle to meet her, but Mrs O'Sullivan seemed numb. The Reverend Mother retained one cold hand within her own and took the woman up to where her small son lay, swathed in the white surplice and lying upon the magnificent purple velvet cushion. The precentor went to the gramophone and bent over it. The high sweet voices were muted, and a ray of winter sunshine shone through the eastern window above the altar, sending a kaleidoscope of colours down upon the figure of the child. It was indeed almost as though it were a vision of heaven.

This was almost too much for the mother. With a passionate outbreak of almost hysterical sobs, she knelt upon the cold, hard, marble cubes of the mosaic floor and placed a hand tenderly upon the golden hair. The Reverend Mother knelt on the opposite side of the little crib and without hesitation embarked upon the prayers for the dead and followed it with the rosary. After a few minutes, Mrs O'Sullivan joined in timidly with the Hail Marys and though the Reverend Mother had a moment's compunction for the Church of Ireland clergyman who was listening silently to this alien prayer, she herself kept her voice clear and loud and supported the woman's broken utterances along the familiar path of the rosary. The terrible sobbing stopped as the rhythm of the prayer carried the woman along and so the Reverend Mother finished with a hasty: 'Glory be to the Father and to the Son and to the Holy Ghost.' Quickly she reached over, took the woman's hand and said decisively, 'Now, come and meet Dr Scher who has been looking after Enda. He will tell you what happened.'

In a moment, Dr Scher was with her assisting the weeping mother to rise and bringing her over to a chair by the altar. The precentor slightly raised the volume of the music. The Reverend Mother crossed over and went to stand beside him, and the dark-suited, bespectacled young man, Mr Owen Hearn, joined them. His brother, the rector from Midleton, remained kneeling in front of the side chapel where his father lay in splendour.

'I'm so sorry to hear of the death of your father, Mr Hearn,' said the Reverend Mother in an undertone. Quite respectably dressed and a sober-looking young man, she thought and wondered, with her ingrained insatiable curiosity about humans and their motivation, why his father had cast him forth from the family. A music teacher, the bishop had said. There had been a note of regret in Dr Thompson's voice as though he had bewailed the decision of his archdeacon.

'Thank you.' The young man bowed his head politely, but said nothing about his father, not even the conventional: 'he will be sadly missed!' Instead he looked pityingly across at the dead child. 'I knew Enda, you know. I heard him sing,' he said to her. 'It was Ariel's song in *The Tempest*. He flew across the stage and sang "Full Fathom Five". I've seen the play in London on many occasions, but never have seen it so beautifully done as in The Loft, up there in Shandon Street, above the sweet factory. I don't think I'll ever forget that child's voice.'

And with that, the young man bowed his head politely to the Reverend Mother, gave a quick nod to the precentor and then left the church. The Reverend Mother registered that he had not taken leave of his brother, nor had he knelt once more beside the body of his father, but had marched straight towards the porch, slipped a coin into the hand of the sexton, and then closed the heavy front door with a decisive click. The Reverend Mother was left feeling bewildered. Who, on earth, had trained Enda to sing Shakespeare's most celebrated song? This young man, this violin teacher, heard him sing – and fly across the stage. She was quite puzzled.

Nevertheless, there was more to be done now. The bodies had to be moved for a post-mortem. Already the rector from Midleton had risen from his knees and was now talking with Mr Sheehan, the undertaker.

'Come with me to the mother and talk to her about Enda's singing voice,' she said hastily to the precentor. 'Just keep talking, use any words, praise him to her.' And then she went down towards Dr Scher and decisively she took Mrs O'Sullivan's hand within both of her own.

'Come back with me to the convent,' she said to her. 'Sister Bernadette will be glad to see you. She's got a cup of tea waiting for you. Dr Scher will take care of Enda. But first, you must meet a man who admired his voice immensely.'

The precentor, she was glad to see, went instantly to the other side of the woman and began to talk in an animated way, using a lot of technical terms such as high C and treble, but introducing Enda's name into every sentence and was so convincingly warm in his praise of the boy that the poor mother mopped her face with her shawl and allowed herself to be drawn down toward the porch and shepherded through the door. Here he warmly shook the Reverend Mother's hand and patted the grieving mother on the shoulder, before making his way back into the cathedral to deal with the undertakers.

The news had got out. The Reverend Mother could see that instantly as they stepped onto Bishop Street. And by the time that they reached Sharman Street, little clusters of women eyed the bereaved mother in the respectable company of the Reverend Mother Aquinas and murmured a few words, blessing themselves and praying aloud. No one, though, approached with the usual spontaneity of commiseration and the Reverend Mother told herself that she would have to do something about the funeral. It would break the poor mother's heart, once again, if she had to walk in solitude behind the coffin.

But how on earth was it to be done? She mused upon it even while being welcomed warmly back into the convent by Sister Bernadette who informed her that dinner would be in half an hour and that all the visitors had now departed.

Her mind full of the problem of the funeral, it took her a few minutes to register that there was little warmth in Sister Bernadette's acknowledgement of Mrs O'Sullivan, and she began to wonder whether she had made a mistake to bring the grieving mother back with her. Christmas dinner was such a tradition for Sister Bernadette. Visitors were hustled out a good half hour before the goose was ready to be taken from the oven and it was a tradition that no one, except the sisters and their reverend mother, would partake of the festive Christmas dinner. Once the words of commiseration were uttered, there was a silence. No invitation to come into the kitchen.

To the Reverend Mother's distress, Mrs O'Sullivan must have sensed the hostility, or perhaps the sound of merry voices singing, 'Oh, the Holly and the Ivy' and the bustle and the glimpse of the beautifully laid table in the best parlour, were all too much for her, but she stopped at the threshold, and shook her head.

'I must be going now, Reverend Mother. I have a visitor coming.' And with those words she turned and almost ran back towards the gate. The Reverend Mother watched a group of women cross the road to the opposing pavement so that they did not meet her and grieved within herself for the lack of charity, though perhaps it was just embarrassment. Not that she could find it within her to blame Sister Bernadette. Even in the open air, there was a strong, unwashed smell from Mrs O'Sullivan and her garments were torn and filthy, and her presence in the kitchen would not have enhanced the festive atmosphere. She hoped it wasn't a sin to desire intensely that Tom Hayes, the sexton, had already made plans to spend Christmas Day with the sorrowing woman and even that they might leave the squalid decaying basement where she and Enda had lived and spend their Christmas in one of those warm and uncritical public houses where sorrow might be drowned by the expenditure of Tom Hayes' Christmas silver bestowed upon him by the bishop and his clergy as well as by kind-hearted worshippers.

With that pious thought, the Reverend Mother closed the door decisively and turned as festive a face as she could manage towards the hard-working Sister Bernadette.

'Goodness,' she said, 'what an absolutely delicious smell from the kitchen! Is that the goose?'

Sister Bernadette's face lit up. 'It is indeed, Reverend Mother, and I'd better get back and make sure that these girls are turning it. Oh, and I nearly forgot. Eileen is here. She's promised only to stay a few minutes, so I've left her in your room.' And with that, Sister Bernadette bustled back into the kitchen from where the Reverend Mother, busy rearranging her features with the aid of the looking glass belonging to the hallstand, heard her shrieking a mixture of praise and admonitions to her young assistants. The sound did her good and she watched as a smile crept over her lips and a slight tinge of colour warmed the very pale face. With a conscious effort, she widened the heavy-lidded green eyes that looked back at her from the mirror and swept down the corridor, opening her door with a flourish as she said, 'Happy Christmas, Eileen!'

The Reverend Mother had always claimed that she had no favourites, but deep within her she had to acknowledge that Eileen, out of all the thousands of pupils who had passed through her hands, was the one who was dearest to her. A clever child who had learned at the speed of lightning; a rebel who had left school early in order to join the illegal organization, the Irish Republican Army; a girl who had then pulled herself together, won a university scholarship, managed to graduate with first class honours and the extension of her scholarship and now was studying law; the Reverend Mother smiled upon her visitor and resolved not to spoil the day with sad news.

'Happy Christmas, Reverend Mother,' said Eileen demurely. Then a smile came over her face and she produced from behind her back a tiny but carefully wrapped parcel.

'Open it, Reverend Mother,' she said eagerly.

Originally it would have been the lid of a Beamish beer bottle, guessed the Reverend Mother, but it had been fitted with a pin to turn it into a miniature brooch and on its surface a snow-capped mountain had been painted and below in tiny letters had been printed the Latin words: '*Festina Lente*'.

'Do you remember? Do you remember writing that on my homework a few weeks after starting to teach me Latin?' Eileen's voice was eager, and the Reverend Mother nodded.

'I do, indeed,' she said. She gazed upon the little brooch. 'And now the roles are reversed,' she said. 'The pupil is telling the teacher to "make haste slowly", isn't that right?'

'No, no!' Eileen flushed with embarrassment. 'It was just that the last time that I met you, I thought that you seemed a bit depressed – well, not depressed, exactly . . . well, I'm not sure what I mean – you were saying . . . you seemed . . .'

'*Frustrated* is the word you are looking for, I suppose,' said the Reverend Mother placidly. 'And I should not allow myself that luxury. I should be content to "make haste slowly" and thank you, Eileen. I shall treasure this little brooch, and yes, I shall wear it. Goodness knows what the bishop will make of it, our bishop, I mean,' she added with a hasty memory of the easy-going cleric whom she had met on this sad Christmas morning. With an effort she banished the image of the small boy from her mind and smiled upon her erstwhile pupil. 'Where shall I put it?' she asked.

Eileen put her head on one side and surveyed the black habit with the snowy white bib. 'What about on the inside of one of your sleeves?' she suggested. 'They are so full that it won't bother you in least, but whenever you fish in your pocket for your watch, or for your keys, you will feel it and, if you like, you can look at it and—'

'And say to myself: "*Festina lente*",' said the Reverend Mother, trying to sound cheerful, but then she thought of how Eileen supplemented her university scholarship and helped her mother by writing articles for the local newspaper, the *Cork Examiner*. She had long since squared it with her conscience that she made use of any material that came her way and so now she had an inspiration of how Eileen could help her.

'I've just come back from St Fin Barre's Cathedral,' she said hesitantly.

Eileen's face changed. 'I thought you might have. I've heard the news. Poor little Enda O'Sullivan!'

'And Archdeacon Hearn,' said the Reverend Mother.

'He's old,' said Eileen rather sharply. 'He's got a son that's older than myself. I know him and I've heard his side of the story. His father threw him out of the house because he didn't want to be a clergyman. Shows what kind of man that archdeacon was. What business of his, was it? His son is a grown man. It was up to him to choose what he wants to do with life, and he wants to play the violin, not sing hymns, and play the clergyman. And he's very good at playing the violin. I've no patience with people who bully their children.'

'You know young Mr Hearn, then?' said the Reverend Mother with surprise.

'I've met him once or twice. And I know someone who taught him and who thinks that he is gifted. She's a professor in the university. She's the first woman to ever have a doctorate in Music,' said Eileen. And then, a little shyly, she said, 'I'd like to be the first woman judge in Ireland, Reverend Mother, but, of course, that probably sounds silly.'

'Not at all,' said the Reverend Mother firmly. 'It sounds very sensible to me.' She fingered the little brooch with its motto: '*Festina lente*!' A good maxim for an elderly woman like herself, but, perhaps, not always the best for the young, the talented and the ambitious. 'Judge Eileen MacSwiney,' she said aloud. 'Has a good ring to it. *Ad astra per aspera*!'

'I remember that, too,' said Eileen with a smile. '"Through hard work, to the stars", isn't that right? I'll take that as my new motto. We'll see if it leads me to become a judge.'

'Now Judge Eileen,' said the Reverend Mother, 'I think you'd better go. Sister Bernadette is almost ready to dish up the Christmas dinner.'

'And my mam has a chicken roasting over the fire,' said Eileen, getting to her feet. 'She's jumping up every few minutes to turn it. She's never cooked a chicken in her life before. I bought it from the English Market with my earnings from the *Cork Examiner*, and a bottle of wine, also,' she added with a proud smile as she got up from her chair. 'Happy Christmas, Reverend Mother!'

'Happy Christmas, Eileen, and thank you for my brooch. I shall treasure it,' said the Reverend Mother.

Eileen went towards the door rather hesitantly and then stopped, and turned. 'You look worried,' she said. 'You shouldn't be worried on Christmas Day!'

'Well, I am a little. Mrs O'Sullivan wants a good funeral for Enda, a long line of mourners; I don't quite know whether that is possible to achieve,' said the Reverend Mother. Her voice, she knew, had lost its usual briskness, and sounded depressed and anxious. It was, she thought, unfair of her to burden Eileen with a matter to which the girl could offer no solution, but she felt worried, and the words had slipped out.

Eileen made an involuntary grimace but said nothing for a moment. Growing up, thought the Reverend Mother. A year ago, a hundred solutions would have come flowing out, none of which would have taken into account that the world of Cork city was not filled with idealistic, self-sacrificing and impulsive people. After a minute, though, her face brightened, and the frown disappeared from her forehead.

'I know,' she said. 'I'll have a word with Father O'Flynn. He was rehearsing a funeral for Ophelia with a pack of kids, his choir, all dressed up, when I dropped in last night. His Shakespearean company are putting on *Hamlet* on St Stephen's Day.'

'But . . .' the Reverend Mother began to speak and then stopped. Father O'Flynn, the choirmaster at the Diocesan

College in Shandon, was famed for teaching boys and girls to appreciate Shakespeare and to play him enthusiastically, in high-pitched Cork voices, just as though they were arguing in the city streets. Men and women all over Cork came to these Shakespearean performances in The Loft, which was over a sweet factory in a back lane near Shandon. But Father O'Flynn had a thousand calls upon his time. It was asking too much of him to expect him to solve her problem.

'Oh, he knows, knew, the little fellow,' said Eileen, guessing her reason for hesitating. 'Didn't you hear? Last month they put on *The Tempest* and Enda sang "Full Fathom Five, Thy Father lies" – just one verse, but because he was so tiny, they were able to suspend him on wires and fly him across the stage while he was singing. Mr Hearn, the music teacher, the son of the archdeacon, played the violin and Enda sang. Not scared at all. It was fantastic. I've never seen anything like it. I wrote an article about it in the *Cork Examiner*. I'm surprised that you didn't read it, Reverend Mother,' said Eileen, finishing on a slightly puzzled note. 'Still,' she said more cheerfully, 'I'd say that Father O'Flynn would be willing to do that for Enda. Make sure that the funeral is in the afternoon, after school, Wednesday or Saturday half-day might be best. But of course, it's school holidays, lucky little beggars, so there will be no problem. Now that I come to think of it, the little sweet factory has a van. I bet I could talk the owner into bringing the boys from the college and the girls from St Vincent's down to the South Parish for the funeral. I'll tell him that I'll mention him in an article that I will be doing. These people will do anything for publicity,' said Eileen cheerfully. 'I won't forget to see Father O'Flynn and fix it up with him,' she added as she went towards the door, and opened it to find Sister Bernadette hesitating on the threshold in the hallway. 'Happy Christmas, one and all,' she sang out cheerfully and then shot through the front door, vibrating with youth and energy.

'Oh, Sister Bernadette,' said the Reverend Mother. 'I'm so looking forward to your dinner. What delicious smells from the kitchen!'

THREE

'The bishop is gone.' Joe had put his head in through the door where Patrick sat, surrounded by richly coloured and profusely embroidered church vestments. 'I'm sorry,' he said, coming through the door, shutting it after him and then reverting to his normal voice. 'The poor old fellow looked so ill and so shocked that I didn't have the heart to stop him. As soon as the Reverend Mother went, he cleared off. I knew you wanted to interview them all, and I've managed to catch the rest of them and tell them that you would be as quick as possible, but I just had to let him go, couldn't go running out into the church yard after him. Didn't want him to have a stroke, or something. Most upset about the little boy – more so than about the archdeacon, oddly enough.'

'That's interesting,' said Patrick. 'Don't worry, Joe. I'll pop into his house and see him. There's probably not too much that I can ask him that I can't find out from the others at this stage. Just want to go through their routine. Did you think to ask him who held the keys to the cathedral?'

'Yes,' said Joe. 'It was the sexton and himself, just these two. Apparently, all of the clergy used to have a set and then the archdeacon decided that was not a good idea since there was so much valuable stuff in the cathedral and so they all handed them back to the bishop, including the archdeacon himself. He said he had them safely locked into the safe.'

'Strange,' said Patrick. 'I'd have thought that they would all have a set. Or at least the archdeacon himself. Still, it makes our job easier, I suppose.'

Joe nodded. 'Apparently up to a couple of weeks ago, everyone had a set, but then the canon, Jack Wilson, accidently left his on the edge of the pulpit all night; an absent-minded chap – always doing that sort of thing, apparently, but this time the archdeacon made a big fuss and insisted that the bishop locked all sets into his safe and the archdeacon gave up his also. Made quite an affair about it, according to the Reverend Wilson. Insisted that all should come over to the palace and each person should place their keys in an envelope, label the envelope and place it into the safe, themselves. If ever they needed it for any purpose, then they had to go to the bishop and sign out their set. The choirmaster told me that he didn't bother. Just arranged to have choir practice while the sexton was cleaning the boiler or doing some jobs around the cathedral. I got the impression that this idea of the archdeacon was very resented by the rest of them.'

Patrick thought about that for a moment, made a note to check the safe in the palace and then said, 'Well, I'd better see them all as quickly as possible and then allow them to go home.'

'How do you want them? Order of seniority?'

'That should be as good as any other. Who is it first? Oh, the dean, is that right?' Patrick looked down at the list of clergymen that Joe had left upon the small table which he was using as a desk. 'Send him in, then. Tell them all that I won't keep them too long.'

Patrick looked at the man who had just come in and then back quickly at Joe's list, with its neat headings: name, position, date of birth, address. Dr Babington, the dean, was older than he looked, he thought. Despite the very grey hair there was something rather young about the fresh colouring in his cheeks and the traces of the summer bronze over his face and on the backs of his hands. Carefully Patrick took him through a brief description of his duties in the church and of the personal details of his home and his family.

'Sorry to be asking all of these questions,' he said, the words coming out fluently. By now, after all his years in the police, these sorts of phrases tripped easily off his lips and were a good preamble to extracting as much information as he could.

'Not at all.' The man was pleasant and well mannered. 'Yes, I get people muddled with my large family. The older boys are from my first marriage and the little fellow from my second marriage. My first wife, very sadly, died, and I remarried a few years ago and now I seem to be starting all over again.'

There was something rather engaging about his light voice
and cheerful manner, but Patrick always took care to present
a neutral face to all the details. Criminals, he had often thought,
tended to be particularly skilled at interpreting reactions to
their words so he never allowed himself to approve or disap-
prove of any piece of information presented. His job was to
accumulate as much information as possible and then to sift
through it with assistance from Joe.

'You live in Bishopstown,' he commented, looking at the
address.

'That's right, Inspector. When first married, I had the luck
to buy a nice, large house there with the assistance of an
opportune legacy in the form of a lump sum and an annuity
from a kind relative.'

'An annuity – for life?' asked Patrick. He had never been
much good at Latin, had barely scraped a pass mark when he
had sat his Leaving Examination at school, but *anno domini*
meant 'in the year of our lord' so an annual legacy must mean
a sum paid every year. But for how many years?

'Just until my eldest son reached the age of twenty-one,'
said the dean, answering the question readily. 'He gets the
money then, a lump sum. It was meant to launch him on a
career, help him to buy a house and things. Quite a good
arrangement, I suppose, except that his younger brothers are
still costing me quite a packet what with university fees and
all the other things that young men seem to need. So, I'm
afraid, that in a mercenary way, I am going to miss that
nice little annuity.' There was, now, a slightly forced note of
cheerfulness in his voice.

Hard up, thought Patrick and wondered how much the
university fees were. Joe's family were quite comfortably off,
but they had decided they could not afford university and so
Joe had joined the police force. 'Bishopstown,' he said aloud,
'that must be about four miles outside the city. It would be
quite a journey from the cathedral to your home. What time
did you leave the cathedral on Christmas Eve?'

'Oh, I have a car,' said the man still quite cheerfully. 'Not
too far, Inspector, especially once you get onto the Straight
Road. What time did I leave? Let me see. Did the usual Happy

Christmas wishes to everyone, slipped a bob into the hand of the sexton who was waiting conveniently with keys in hand by the front door. I suppose it was after eight o'clock but not long after. I was anxious to get home, put on the Santa Claus costume that my wife had made for me and slip the stocking and presents into my little boy's room. Well, you know what it's like at Christmas, Inspector?'

'Can you remember who was still in the cathedral when you left? Were the altar boys still there?' Patrick ignored the question by replacing it with two of his own.

'Yes, they were. But the bishop had gone and so had the archdeacon, which was a bit of a nuisance as he usually makes sure that the altar boys have everything right. Not like him to leave early, but he did that night. And, of course, the little beggars took advantage. They were larking around, running between the two altars, pretending to drink wine, staggering around as though they were drunk, but I told myself that the precentor could see to them and so I slipped out.'

'Wine,' said Patrick, suddenly alerted by the word.

'Oh, not really drinking, not even real wine. The bottle hadn't been taken out of the cupboard yet,' said the dean reassuringly. 'They were just fooling, as boys will do. Holding the silver cups to their lips, passing them to one another as they were laying out the table by the high altar and the table by the side altar. No harm in them: a nice set of lads. I didn't see anything wrong in it. They were just joking. And as I say, I thought the precentor could handle it, especially as the choir had all gone home and there was nothing left for him to do except get out the wine from its cupboard and pour it into the cruets. The two sets of silver had been taken out of the locked cupboard by the bishop before he had left, and the white-and-gold vestments were ready in the vestry. The archdeacon had already checked the vestments before he left. We were to have two services going on at the same time on Christmas morning. One at the main altar, conducted by the bishop and the other at the side altar to be conducted by the archdeacon.'

'And who would normally pour the wine into the jugs?' Patrick had already had an answer to this question, but it never did any harm to ask the same question of a different witness. He awaited the answer and noted with interest that it took a while to be uttered.

'Do you know, I don't think we have any set duties for Christmas Day,' said the dean in the end. 'I suppose everyone helps. It's a big day for us. We don't have the large congregations that you have in your churches and, of course, attendance is purely voluntary. Normally we have just one service and it would be the responsibility of whoever was on duty to see that everything was ready for the first morning service on Sunday and feast days. Christmas Day is a big day for us,' he repeated, 'and after the Christmas Eve Evensong, we all stayed for a while in the cathedral, admiring the decorations put up by the ladies and making sure that everything was ready for the next morning. The bishop and the archdeacon were going to take the first service and I and the deacon were going to assist with handing out the communion and the wine – of course, as you know, that part of the service did not take place due to the sad death of the archdeacon, but that was what would have happened normally.'

'I see,' said Patrick, rising to his feet, 'Well, you have been most helpful, Mr . . . Dean,' he amended and wondered whether it was the same as in the Catholic Church and that he should be called 'Monseigneur'. The bishop was all right. 'My lord' worked for both churches, but he had an impression . . . Suddenly Patrick pulled himself together. He had called the man 'Dean' and it had been accepted. It would do and if it were wrong, that was just too bad. He had two murders to solve, one of which sickened him to the heart, and he didn't have time to waste on unimportant matters. 'Thank you, Dean,' he repeated and went to open the door for the man.

Joe was lurking in the space by the altar talking with the precentor about church music and he quickly ushered him into the vestry and made the introductions. He seemed to be on good terms with this precentor, but didn't refer to his title or how to address him, much to Patrick's disappointment. He should have checked with Joe about titles. After all, his assistant was a Protestant and should know about all these things.

'What should I call you?' Patrick asked, hoping that he sounded at ease. To his relief, the precentor laughed at that.

'Call me Tommy,' he said in a friendly fashion. 'Not my name but everyone calls me that, for some reason. I think I said it once, by way of a joke, as I think Arthur is a pretentious sort of name and then everyone took it up. Even the boys call me that, behind my back, of course, and I have to pretend I don't hear. It's a sort of joke between us, I suppose.'

'I see,' said Patrick. He was somewhat bemused. Wondered how a choirmaster could keep the boys under control when he allowed them to call him a nickname within his hearing. The Christian Brothers, from his old school, would never have permitted such a thing. Of course, they had nicknames, but these were used very carefully by the boys when the masters were out of earshot.

'Tell me about Christmas Eve night,' he said. 'I understand that all was got ready for the service on Christmas morning. The vestments in the vestry and the wine and the jugs. The altar boys were under your supervision, I understand.'

The man was slightly taken aback at that.

'I don't think that they were under my supervision,' he said. 'Strictly speaking they were none of my business. It was my business to get the choir in good order and make sure that they were properly rehearsed for the service on Christmas morning. I did that, then got them off, by sending them out with a Christmas present in their hand, but the altar boys and the preparing for the communion sacrament was nothing to do with me as I wasn't a celebrant on Christmas morning. There were going to be just two services, one brief one, conducted by the archdeacon in the side chapel and then in the main section of the cathedral was the official Christmas service conducted by the bishop himself. Of course, that was the one where I would be busy conducting the choir and so I was in the church early on Christmas Day, seeing to the organ. You may have noticed, Inspector, that our organ is below floor level, in its own little room, and so damp can be a problem. I put sheets of blotting paper over the keys on the night before an early morning service and so I had to take them off and make sure that the organ was in tune, and then the boys were coming in and I had to make sure that they were properly dressed, check the three soloists – I choose three because you never know when a boy will get a cold or be off form and I bring a packet of sweets in my pocket to console the two who are not chosen so . . .'

'But you saw nothing amiss?'

'No, everything seemed fine. The boys were all in good form. Excited, but sensible. It's their big day, you know.'

'And the communion wine?'

'I assume that it was all set out as usual, but it wouldn't have been my responsibility. On a day like Christmas, everyone takes it for granted that I will have my hands full with the choir and the organ mistress.'

'And the archdeacon?'

'To be honest, Inspector, and *de mortuis* et cetera, but I generally keep a bit of distance from the archdeacon on these occasions. He tended to be very much in earnest about everything and I used to find that he was ruining Christmas for myself and the boys and so I used to close the door to the choir and start playing the organ if he made an appearance. Not a man who liked music, Inspector.'

Not a man who was liked, this archdeacon, thought Patrick but he did not utter his words aloud, but escorted the choirmaster, or precentor, to the door.

'Canon Wilson, Sergeant, please,' he said to Joe and went back to writing up his notes until a knock came to the door and it was pushed open by Joe, with the canon behind him.

'Come in, Canon!' Patrick stood up respectfully, but the man just laughed in a friendly fashion.

'Just call me Jack, Inspector, everyone does.'

That, thought Patrick grimly, was all very well, but it seemed to put an onus upon him to reciprocate and to offer his own first name. And that would never do. And so, he would have to spend the interview dodging the use of names. It was time that he stood up for himself, he thought. It was for him to conduct the interview in the way that he wanted. 'Sir' would do well for all these men.

'Thank you, sir,' he said, endeavouring to sound at ease. 'Police rules, you know.' He'd stick to 'sir' for them all, he thought. Made life easier. 'Could you just tell me a little about the time on Christmas Eve before you left the cathedral after the evening service. Just describe the scene for me, sir.' He wrote 'Canon Jack Wilson' on the top of a new page of his notebook.

'Compline, that's what we call it, Inspector.' So, the man had taken the hint. That would work well. He would call each clergyman, except for the bishop, 'sir' and would be called 'inspector' in return. He felt a slight rush of relief, nodded his head, repeated the word 'compline', even wrote it down and then turned an attentive eye upon the canon.

'You see, Inspector, I'm not too sure,' said the man in an easy-going fashion. 'Well, to be honest with you, I wasn't taking too much notice, just thinking how soon I could slip away. I'm not too musical and get a bit bored with the choir, though I'm sure that they are excellent. I had been invited to a Christmas Eve party by some neighbours and I was looking forward to it so I was just waiting until the bishop left and then I could slide out.'

'Who left first?' Patrick put a series of neat figures down the side of the notebook page.

'Oh dear!' The man shut his eyes in an exaggerated panto-mime of recollection. 'Well, Arthur Flewett got rid of the choirboys pretty quickly. They must have been first. Went to the door with a Santa sackful of presents – he does this every year and the boys line up, close their eyes, put their hand in and pull out a present. They are not allowed to open it until they go outside the cathedral, that's the rule so they go straight off. Spend some time out in the churchyard, swapping presents, shouting, and even singing, until their parents take them off and we all get some peace. He's good with the boys, is Arthur. They'd be bored if they all got the same thing and jealous if names were written on presents and they fancied someone else's present more than their own, but like that it's all a bit of fun and we get rid of them quickly.'

'And the altar boys?' Don't make a big, long story out of everything, thought Patrick, writing choirboys opposite the figure one.

'Oh, they were busy laying out the communion vessels.'

'And can you recollect who was still there at this stage? As well as the altar boys.'

'Well, the bishop left just after the choirboys, I think. I know he was at the door shaking each by the hand, but he went while they were still around outside. He likes to see the choir parents, wish them a happy Christmas and all that sort of thing.' Patrick made a note and then looked enquiringly at the canon.

'Oh, I think it must have been the archdeacon next. So, he'd be number three. I remember waiting while he went through the door, giving him time to get clear. Yes, he had definitely gone when I came out! He lives just across the road from this cathedral, you know, and I heard the door of his house slam when I went to my car, so I'm probably number four. I don't know about anyone else.' There was a note of slight impatience in the canon's voice and Patrick occupied himself with writing the other names at the top of the page and then rose to his feet.

'There is something else, Inspector, something that I feel I should mention. It may be of no importance, but . . .'

Patrick sat down again hastily. 'Any small details may be of importance,' he said, the oft-spoken words tripping easily from his mouth. Some piece of gossip, he guessed, but fixed his eyes attentively upon the canon and opened a new page of his notebook.

'It's just that . . . well, let me tell you how it came about. You see, Inspector, I am a very keen bird watcher, belong to a society of bird watchers. I love all birds, am interested in them all, but owls are my great love – a bit of a night bird, myself!'

Patrick did not bother to write down that little joke but waited patiently.

'Now last year, in the spring, I was working late at the cathedral, and when I came out and went towards my car, I heard a sound, a snoring sound. At first, I thought it was a tramp sleeping in one of the little niches around the cathedral, but then I realized that it was coming from the top of the apse, from the little roof over the altar, Inspector, and I knew what it was. I had never had the luck to hear it myself, but when a barn owl has chicks, she makes this snoring sound. As you can imagine, I was hugely excited and I kept on looking out for her and the chicks, haunted the place! But I had no luck. Never saw a sign of them. But then, one evening last autumn, just about five o'clock in the evening I saw the little fellow, little Enda O'Sullivan, up on the roof, just beside the statue of the angel, the golden angel with two flutes. Well, I must say, Inspector, I had my heart in my mouth, watching him come down, but he was incredibly sure-footed, no bravado, or showing off, he was just as though he were coming down the stairs in a house. So, I said nothing, but from time to time I watched out for him and saw him scramble all over the roof of the cathedral, just like it was a playground for him, and then this autumn, I asked him if he could climb up onto the top of the apse and tell me if there were any remains of a bird nest there. I was thinking, you see, that I would talk to my society about it, and we could mount some sort of surveillance on the nest, make sure that the chicks were not disturbed. I described an owl nest to him, told him to look for a layer of old pellets, regurgitated pellets, which is what barn owls use to create their nest. He was an intelligent little boy, and he was quite interested when I told him about that, and I explained to him that they didn't weave a nest but used a cavity that was already there so that I reckoned that it would be in the gap between one of the spires and the roof.'

Patrick's pencil scribbled fast, and his mind worked as quickly. This was most interesting.

'Did anyone hear you with the boy, sir?' He had another question in his mind, but he did not need to ask it as the canon read his mind.

'I'm not sure, Inspector, but there is something else that has been very much in my mind. I knew I had no coins in my pocket, just notes and a cheque book, but I took out a packet of Rolos, sweets that I had bought for one of my nephews, and I gave it to him. He seemed so pleased, poor little fellow.'

There was a moment's silence while Patrick stared at him, and the canon stared at the table. But then, he raised his head and said earnestly, 'I can assure you, Inspector, that nothing in the world would have made me poison a small child.' There was another silence before he continued in a low voice, 'But it may be that I put the idea into a person's head. I established that the child could easily climb on the roof to perform an errand – he brought me back a very exact description of the nest and even had a soft breast feather from the mother owl stuck into his pocket; he performed the errand very quickly and in a sure-footed way. Anyone watching could have seen that and could have seen his delight when he was rewarded with the Rolo sweets. He told me Rolos were his favourite sweet, poor little fellow, called it back over his shoulder as he went off.'

'Did you think at the time that anyone else did hear you or see you give the sweets to Enda O'Sullivan?' Patrick asked the question as he finished writing the word 'Rolos', but the silence that followed made him raise his head quickly.

'Not that I can be sure,' said the canon slowly. 'Not anyone that would be perhaps guilty of doing the deed, but I didn't hang around for long. To be honest I cleared off very quickly, because after I had given the packet of Rolos to the child, I saw the archdeacon looking out of his window and I thought I'd get out of the way before he came down and read me a lecture.'

'Did he?' asked Patrick hopefully. If there had been a big fuss some other person might have overheard, and the germ of an idea might have been sown.

The canon smiled. 'No, he didn't, and I don't mind telling you, Inspector, that I was quite relieved to have been spared that lecture. In fact, knowing the archdeacon, I feel sure that he could not have noticed anything or otherwise he would have lectured me about encouraging the boy to climb all over the precious roof of the cathedral. However, someone else might have overheard, and I do feel extremely sorry about that. Especially since I may have given the murderer the idea that the child was enthusiastic about Rolos.'

'I wouldn't worry too much about that, sir,' said Patrick, getting to his feet once more. 'I think that any packet of sweets would have been welcome.' He said no more, though. There was nothing else to say. It was probably quite true that the murderer had got the idea of sending the boy into the cathedral to poison the wine by witnessing how easily he climbed the roof at the bidding of one of the clergymen, and by remembering the fondness expressed for the packet of Rolos. He would have a word with the Reverend Mother about this, though. She and the nun who taught the infants might have overheard some conversation about Rolos, or even about owls, between Enda O'Sullivan and some other little boys or girls in his class.

'You've been most helpful, sir,' he said as he shook hands and opened the door for the man.

His efficient sergeant had Mr Webster, the deacon, all ready for his interview, and was discussing rugby with him. They both looked around when the door opened and Joe immediately said, 'Here's Mr Webster, Inspector!' and that was a relief and in the bustle of getting the man into the vestry and pulling out a chair for him, Patrick was able to ignore the silly schoolboy talk about the headmaster's study and 'six of the best' that the other two men went on with. There was something about clergymen, whether Roman Catholic or Church of Ireland, that seemed to keep them all in the land of boyhood, thought Patrick scornfully. He was glad of the thought because there was a superior look on this young man's face. Every year that he spent in the police force had increased Patrick's confidence in himself, but the marked, almost-English accent and the supercilious air of this young man made him feel his origins.

'Your full name, sir?' This routine always helped. He wrote it down, quickly, pausing only to query whether 'Bob' meant 'Robert'.

'And you are a deacon, Mr Webster. Perhaps you could explain to me the duties of a deacon.' He was slightly irritated by the laugh that greeted his question.

'I believe that a piece of paper that I have somewhere says that my responsibilities involve assisting at worship, setting up the altar for the Eucharist and reading the gospel. Oh, and pastoral care and upholding and manifesting the church! How about that, Inspector?'

'Thank you, sir.' Patrick had finished his rapid shorthand by this time and the first question lay ready for the asking.

'So, you set up the altar for the Eucharist – that would mean putting out the communion wafers and pouring the wine into the jugs, the cruets,' amended Patrick.

Bob Webster held up his hands. *'Mea culpa,* Inspector. I am an idle dog, and I don't believe that I did a thing that Christmas Eve, except talk to Jack Wilson about golf. You see, the thing is, none of us have much to do. It's a small congregation – all they ask of us is to hold two services every Sunday and there are five men employed in this cathedral, six if you count the sexton and, poor devil, I'd say that he's the only one of us who does a decent day's work. He looks after this old building, cleaning and feeding the furnace and then there are the grounds – lots of graves to be dug in the wintertime with our elderly congregation and mowing the grass in the spring and planting bulbs in the autumn and pruning the bushes and sweeping up the leaves. Yes, he works a hundred times harder than the rest of us. I always give him a good tip at Christmas – and so do the rest of us. Guilty conscience, I suppose.'

Patrick wrote all of this down and then reflected for a moment. 'Who do you think undertook the duty of setting up the Eucharist, sir?' he asked.

'Well, it wasn't me, Inspector. I didn't do a thing after the Christmas Eve service, wished all the parishioners a happy Christmas, of course. No, as I said, I just chatted with Jack Wilson.'

'But you must have checked that it had been done,' persisted Patrick. 'It was, after all, your responsibility.'

'Funnily enough, I've never thought of that, but now that you remind me, Inspector, I shall make a habit of checking in the future. Especially now that the archdeacon . . . Yes, of course, it was the archdeacon. I remember now. In fact, I think he was the one who always did that sort of thing. He was fussing around, shouting at the altar boys to be careful with the best silver, reading them a lecture about how rare Cork silver like that was, and how it was made in the seventeenth century and how the bishop just used it at Christmas and at Easter. Looked in need of a good clean, I thought to myself, but I didn't interfere. He was wasting his time anyway. The boys were too excited about Christmas to take any notice of him so I just left them to it and went off to have a chat with Jack Wilson about Lahinch Golf Course and the way the wind can affect your drive on these links.'

'But the silver was all out on the tables before you left.' Patrick thought to himself of the long hours that he worked, of the number of nights when he was roused from his bed because of a riot on the docks, of the murders, the assassinations and robberies that came his way almost every week of the year. And then he wondered how much this man was paid for doing nothing.

'Yes, Tommy – the precentor, you know – was telling the altar boys to make sure that the good silver was for the high altar, but, of course, the archdeacon had already made a big fuss about that. The altar boys were probably thoroughly confused but I decided that no one was paying me overtime for working on Christmas Eve when all my friends were off having a good time. No good looking at me like that, Inspector. You'd be surprised if I told you how little I am paid, not like your priests with their huge congregations, all shelling out for the collections.'

'I'm not sure if I know how much our priests earn,' said Patrick cautiously.

'Well, I'll tell you how much I earn. It will give you a shock.'

And it did. Patrick felt quite taken aback. About quarter of his own salary, he thought.

'Why do you do it?' he asked, almost without thinking – and very much to his own annoyance. This was not a professional question, and he wouldn't blame the young man if he showed annoyance. But he didn't; just shrugged his shoulders.

'Got talked into it by an elderly aunt, you know. Just like Frank Babington. He's another clergyman subsisting on legacies. You get a lot of those wealthy and most religious spinsters, only one left from a well-off family. All the brothers killed off in the Great War. They end up with the family money and they love the power of it. Like having the control over their nephews. At least Frank got a good lump sum to help him

buy that lovely house of his out in Bishopstown and then a
yearly stipend until his son reaches the age of twenty-one, but
I got nothing, nothing but promises from that aunt of mine.
And now, I suppose, she'll live for ever and I'm stuck in this
dreary life.'

'What would you have liked to be, Mr Webster?' Patrick
excused the question on the grounds that he needed to get to
know all possible details about these five men in the cathedral
on Christmas Eve. Nevertheless, he had to admit that he was
intrigued.

'I'd have liked to be a rocket scientist. It's the future and,
I can hardly believe it of myself now, but I used to be a
genius at maths when I was in school – all sorts of maths,
but especially geometry and trigonometry. I would have
loved to go on studying – something like . . . Robert
Hutchings. I don't know whether you have ever heard of
the American, Robert Hutchings Goddard, Inspector, have
you?' Without waiting for an answer, he went on eagerly.
'He was an American engineer, professor, physicist, and
inventor, a wonderful fellow. What I wouldn't have given
to have gone to America and studied under him. He has a
dream that he will build a rocket that will reach the moon.
He has, already, made a rocket, think of it, the world's first
liquid-fuelled rocket. Launched it a few years ago, on March
sixteenth, 1926. And here was I stuck in this dead-end job
that doesn't even pay more than a pittance, just because I
was a fool enough to give into an old woman who wanted
her nephew to be a clergyman!'

'Perhaps you will climb the tree, become a bishop at some
stage,' suggested Patrick.

'Well, if you are suggesting that I murdered the archdeacon
as a preliminary to climbing the tree, as you call it, well,
then I'd better get on with murdering the bishop, and the
dean, and the canon and, of course, the precentor. Quite a
list, Inspector.' There was a bitter note in the young man's
voice and Patrick decided not to reply.

He allowed a short interval of silence and then said thoughtfully, 'We're talking about the archdeacon, but, of course, a
child was murdered also. A little boy who was barely seven

years old and who was probably hungry and would do anything for a packet of Rolos.'

'Yes,' said the deacon after a minute. 'You do well to remind me. The archdeacon may be no great loss to those who knew him, but that child's death was a dreadful thing.' And with that, he rose from his chair, and without a word more, he left the room.

Patrick stared after him meditatively and made no effort to recall him. He had plenty of notes and his mind was overflowing with ideas. He gave the deacon a few moments to get clear of the outside room and then went to the door. Joe was there, but he was alone. Mr Bob Webster, he guessed, would have stalked out of the cathedral, furious, perhaps, that he had betrayed himself to a police officer as discontented and frustrated. The man had given him plenty to think about. Men like that can sometimes become focussed upon their own troubles to an extent that nothing else in the world matters too much to them. The sort of man, he thought, who might end up committing suicide.

'Do you want to see the sexton?' Joe asked the question twice before Patrick pulled himself together. His mind had gone back to his own school days and to the long hours at night which he had spent in memorizing the solutions to Euclid's theorems so that no examination question could throw him. He found it hard to imagine being the sort of person who enjoyed that sort of thing. Geometry, like all the other subjects he had studied, was just a means to an end, part of passing his Leaving Certificate and doing his best to get a job so that his mother no longer had to scrub floors to put food on the table. He wondered what it might be like to have the sort of mind which enjoyed finding the area of a triangle and other such useless skills. He must have nodded, because Joe was back with the sexton, his hands and part of his face smudged with coal dust.

'Come in, Mr Hayes, I won't keep you long,' he said.

FOUR

The Reverend Mother, to her embarrassment, fell fast asleep after her Christmas dinner. Not that she had eaten too much. She had long perfected the strategy of looking around the loaded table and asking eagerly for a taster of this and taster of that. With a plate covered in spoon-sized portions she was able to prolong the tasting procedure for the entire meal. Her enthusiastic comments would, she knew, be carried to Sister Bernadette's ears, and repeated when the lay sisters had their own sociable dinner. No, she thought. Not over-eating. It's just that I am growing old. And then, with a rueful smile, she contradicted herself: *I am old*!

How much longer would the bishop allow her to carry on? He was known to be quite ruthless with elderly parish priests who endeavoured to cling to their posts but were eventually banished to a dreary retirement. She dreaded retirement. She had too much to do. Too many ideas and projects crowded into her brain every morning as soon as she got out of bed. Realist as she was, she expended no false modesty on declaring that another could carry out her work. At this moment, within her own convent, or even within the order in Ireland, she knew of no one who had such a burning determination to improve the lives of poor children and give them a chance to rise above the misery into which they had been born. The fact that she failed, failed often – more often than she allowed herself to consider – never meant that she should not keep on striving.

I'm old, she told herself, but I'm healthy and so I must keep healthy, must fit in a walk every day. She got to her feet, conscientiously covered the burning coals of her fire with some of what Sister Bernadette called 'slack', which was peat mould mixed with coal dust. Then she took down her cloak from its peg and went for the door. A glance through the window showed the usual mist, but it did not deter her. 'Our family all have strong chests' used to declare an elderly aunt, and there was no doubt but that was a valuable inheritance in this fog-filled city where most of the inhabitants seemed to suffer from asthma and bronchitis, as well as the dreaded tuberculosis.

The Reverend Mother pulled her watch from its pocket and examined the time. A walk by the river would do her good. Having recently noticed that, imperceptibly, she had slowed down, she now made a habit of timing her walk from the convent door to Parliament Bridge. Ten minutes, she allowed herself and was grimly determined to keep to her schedule. Ten minutes to the bridge. A few minutes to relax, look down at the river, and then ten minutes for the walk back. A twenty-minute outing did not take too much from her busy day, but was, she thought, as she edged through the front door and shut it quietly behind her, useful to maintain her health. The streets and the quays were empty and so she made rapid progress. The tide was full when she arrived at the bridge. There had been days of heavy rain and so the river flowed fast, ensuring that the air above it was not tainted by the usual unpleasant smells. The seagulls swooped and dived with high-pitched screams into the ruffled water, and she stopped on Parliament Bridge to watch their progress before returning to her convent. She was absorbed in a battle between two birds with splendidly white plumage whose bright yellow beaks were stuck into what looked like a loaf of bread, when a gentle note from a motor car horn made her turn around.

'I was coming to see you, but I see that you were on your way to see me,' said Dr Scher, his head sticking out of the window as he drove in his usual carefree fashion along the right-hand side of the bridge. He leaned across and swung open the door, was about to dismount right into the passageway of law-abiding drivers, so she went hastily around the back of the car and climbed quickly into his shabby old car.

'How much do you pay the police not to prosecute you for dangerous driving?' she enquired tartly.

'You're so out-of-date; there haven't been police in Ireland

for donkey's years. They call them *Garda Siochana*, Reverend
Mother, do try to remember that; inaccuracy sets a bad example
to your pupils,' said Dr Scher as he reversed back along the
bridge and turned onto Sullivan's Quay.

'Where am I being taken to?' enquired the Reverend Mother,
ignoring the jibe.

'You've been invited to partake of Christmas cake with an
old friend and being a well-brought-up woman, of the old
school, you will not dream of causing offence by a refusal,'
said Dr Scher as he drove fast and erratically along the quays
and turned onto the South Terrace where he lived with an
elderly housekeeper who kept him well-fed and tried to look
after his clothes. 'I want to talk to you about the murder
of that poor child,' he added.

She, too, had been wondering about the involvement of
poor little Enda. Why had it been necessary? Was it not a
dangerous move to have confided a secret to a notoriously
mischievous seven-year-old? She turned the matter over in
her mind while he swooped down the empty road and drew
up with a squeal of brakes outside the tall Georgian terraced
house where he had his practice and his living quarters.

The front windows of the beautiful house were hung with
garlands of holly and strands of ivy laced with tinsel and a
small Christmas tree was placed beside the front door. By
the time the Reverend Mother had climbed out of the car, the
housekeeper had the door open and her kitchen maid,
adorned with a silver tinsel crown, was peeping over her
shoulder, so she braced herself to pay the usual compliments
of the season and enthuse about the lovely decorations while
reflecting that Christmas was for children and should be
confined to them. It was a pity that elderly people, especially
an elderly Jewish person like Dr Scher, should have to exert
himself to keep a festival where the day consisted mainly of
overeating and overdecorating.

Nevertheless, she complimented the workers on their
achievement and admired everything. She took her familiar
seat on the window side of the glowing anthracite stove and
made small talk while the housekeeper and her handmaiden
rushed in and out of the room with a pot of tea and another

of coffee and a sizable plate of Christmas cake. The Reverend Mother eyed the small chunks of neatly cut cake with interest.

'Yes, why involve Enda?' she said as she took a large, clean linen handkerchief from her pocket, spread it out upon a plate and built a pyramid of the small cake cubes on top of it.

'Use your head, Reverend Mother; the murderer wanted an alibi,' said Dr Scher, eyeing her with interest as she gathered up the four corners of her handkerchief and made a neat knot at the top.

'An alibi,' she repeated as she carefully inserted the bundle of cake into one of her capacious pockets.

'Do you normally steal cake from the table of your host?' enquired Dr Scher.

'They're just such a perfect size for popping in a child's mouth. I like to keep a few bribes and rewards handy,' the Reverend Mother explained, and then added, 'Tell me exactly how the archdeacon was murdered.'

'Leave those stolen goods on the windowsill behind the curtain,' he advised. 'They might melt in your pocket with that fire. Don't worry; I'll remind you. Yes, the archdeacon is the crux of the matter.'

He got up and went to a cupboard at the back of the room, unlocked it, took a box from the shelf, carried it across and showed it to her. 'This is the silver used at the side altar, where the archdeacon celebrated his Christmas morning service. More ornate than the silver on the high altar, which is older, and to my eye certainly more valuable. I persuaded Patrick to let me have the two sets. You can see the difference for yourself. The cups – a chalice, and, of course, the little cruets, one for water and one for wine – are much smaller, less imposing, less ornate but so much more beautiful to my eyes, stamped with these rare Cork insignia.'

Dr Scher stroked the surface of the old Cork silver lovingly, but then put it down. 'But, of course, you are more interested in the modern silver used on the side altar,' he said. 'This one, here. Someone placed powdered cyanide into this cruet, as I think they call it – just a little jug, really.'

'Added to the wine,' said the Reverend Mother. 'Or was the cyanide put in before the wine?'

'Ah, that's a good question,' he said and leaned back. 'Explain the ritual to me, oh woman of the church,' he said.

'Not my church,' the Reverend Mother reminded him, 'but in our church, and I do believe that the ritual is roughly the same, well before the service, often the night before for the first service of the day, the altar boy usually pours the wine into one of the cruets, one of two cruets in our church, because there is water in one of them, and then during the service, the priest or clergyman, I suppose, holds out the chalice to the altar boy and he pours the wine from the little cruet into the chalice and then a couple of drops of water are added to symbolize . . .' She stopped as he was not listening, not even looking at the jug which she held, just looking meditatively at the other ancient set of altar silver.

'You like that old silver,' she said with a smile. He was, she knew, a dedicated hoarder of old silver and from time to time showed her the small walk-in cupboard where he kept his collection.

'Beautiful old Cork silver,' he said with a sigh. 'This one is not as ornate as the one used every day and on the side altar on Christmas Day, but the bishop is a man of taste and of course this old Cork silver is far more interesting and more valuable and more worthy of being used on the high altar for special occasions. Look at that mark, the engraving of the city arms, the two castles and the ship. That shows it's early work.' Dr Scher lifted the jug with care and held it high. The Reverend Mother nodded. Her eyes were not as good as they had been, and the centuries-old engraving was dull and indistinct. She hastened to change the subject. Once Dr Scher started one of his lectures on antique silver there would be no stopping him.

'Why was Enda used?' she asked. 'Why didn't the murderer slip the cyanide into the jug himself, or herself,' she amended, but she did not believe that a woman had a part in this crime.

'So the little jugs, a matching pair, would have been filled, one with water and the other with wine, made ready the night before and placed, with the silver cup or chalice, on a small table beside the altar, as is always the custom for early morning service, so I understand,' said Dr Scher. 'And, of course, since there were two services on that Christmas morning, then both sets of silver were used. Patrick has been on to me to ask whether I could tell when the cyanide was added, before the wine was added, or after the wine was added, but I couldn't say. It was a powder, not a liquid, that's all I could tell him. Here, look through this.' Dr Scher took a small magnifying glass from his pocket and passed it to her. She peered through it and thought that she could see a crystalline crusting on the rim of the jug which he held, but she could not be sure.

'Without any firm evidence, I would guess that it was after the wine was put into the cruets, but I couldn't be sure. Not enough to swear to it in the court. But it makes sense, doesn't it?' he said. 'And also, it makes sense that it was powder, not liquid.'

'I'll take your word for it,' she said. 'In any case, my own common sense would tell me that it would be tricky to give a young boy some liquid and that it would be easier to entrust some powder containing the deadly poison to a seven-year-old who had to climb up a roof, go through a broken pane of glass and then climb down again.' She passed the magnifying glass back to him and went to the window and peered at the rim of the little jug.

'I'd say,' said Dr Scher, 'though I wouldn't swear to it, but this is my guess, that the wine was already in the jug when the cyanide was poured in. There is a small track of crystals down the inside of the jug, below the handle, which I hadn't noticed before I got my magnifying glass. I'd say that would have been washed down by the wine from the bottle if the goblet had been empty when the cyanide was added. So, yes, I would be fairly sure that the wine was present when the cyanide powder was poured in.'

'If they had a service on Christmas Eve night and then were going to have an early morning service on Christmas morning, there's no doubt that it would be highly likely that the altar boys would get everything ready the night before. But, of course, I can only speak for my own church,' said the Reverend Mother.

'Why did the child do it?' asked Dr Scher curiously. 'Didn't he ask why? There was no money on him so he must have trusted to being paid afterwards.'

'I suspect that the packet of Rolos might have been his payment. A whole packet, all for himself, just to play a trick on the archdeacon. That was probably the way that it was put to him. I'm afraid that Enda would have been delighted to do it for even less. He was a great climber. He enjoyed climbing for the sake of it. Your murderer may well have seen him, caught him in the act. And then thought of him when the desire to murder came into his heart.'

Dr Scher hesitated for a moment and then said, rather tentatively, 'Could it be the sexton? He would have been hanging around. He looks after the cleaning of the cathedral and the furnace and the grounds as well as digging the graves and ringing the bells. Definitely, he would have known the boy well, might have caught him climbing a couple of times.'

'I thought that he seemed fond of the boy and rumour says that he is very fond of Mrs O'Sullivan,' said the Reverend Mother. In her mind's eye, she visualized the tear-stained face of the man and dismissed him from her thoughts. 'Why would he want to kill the archdeacon? It wouldn't do Tom Hayes any good,' she said aloud.

'Well, you know this Archdeacon Hearn was not a very pleasant person. A neighbour of mine played golf with him in Little Island; saw the man this morning when we wished each other a happy Christmas, well he was quite blunt about the late, lamented, archdeacon. "No loss to the city! Nor to the cathedral, either!" That was his verdict. At the risk of shocking you deeply, Reverend Mother, I have to tell you that the man even cheated at golf – would run ahead and nudge the ball into a hole before anyone else could get onto the green. Can you imagine! Had to win at all costs, according to my friend. Bad temper, too. Apparently, a lot of swearing. Flung a glass of whiskey in a man's face once in front of a crowd of people in the club house. And, worse still, was known to be very tardy with paying his club fees and always undertipped the caddies.'

'Doesn't seem like a solid reason for murder, though, does it?' said the Reverend Mother. In fact, she thought that this archdeacon sounded as though he might fit in quite well with the seven-year-old boys in Enda O'Sullivan's gang. Cheating, swearing, fits of temper, throwing missiles and although they had no obligation to pay golf club dues, their views on the ownership of money were decidedly lax and they would steal from stallholders without the slightest compunction.

'And his two sons,' she said meditatively. 'Dr Thompson, their bishop, told me that there had been some sort of falling-out with the younger of his sons, not the clergyman, but the one dressed in a suit.'

'Something about him not wanting to be a clergyman, I think. Remember we have to find a link, not just between the murderer and the archdeacon, but with little Enda, also. I can't see how either the Rector of Midleton or the other son – the layman – could have had much of an acquaintanceship with your little pupil,' said Dr Scher, adding with a look of concern as he saw her wince at the words 'little pupil'. 'My goodness, this is a lovely Christmas cake! Just the way I like it, lovely and moist. Do have some more, Reverend Mother.'

The Reverend Mother pulled herself together and ate an unwanted piece of the cake. 'He may have hung around there in the hopes of having a penny given to him,' she said. 'He was a past master at begging, as well as of stealing, poor child. One of my failures,' she added, but tried to keep the note of sadness from her voice. When you reached her age, she told herself, failures were unavoidable. But there was no need to spread her troubles. Dr Scher worked hard. He had a certain clientele of wealthy clients, many of them belonging to the Church of Ireland, she guessed, but he wore himself out offering free advice and medicine to the poor from the teaming streets and lanes of the city. He should, she thought, be allowed to enjoy his Christmas cake without having to listen to an elderly nun bewailing her failures. Just to oblige him, she took another cube of the Christmas cake and consciously fell into a gossip mode.

'How did your golf-playing friend like Dr Thompson, the bishop?' she asked, and was not surprised to hear that the bishop was considered well meaning, though not very energetic or hard-working. The unpleasant and unpopular archdeacon had been the live wire and the innovator. The archdeacon and the dean, Dr Babington, were both live wires, though not friends, but rivals. The dean, unlike the archdeacon, was very

'High Church', so Dr Scher's neighbour said, and had conspired with the precentor to introduce a sung compline. The archdeacon had stirred up trouble about that, got the parishioners to protest, to get up a petition and send it to the bishop.

'And the canon, Mr Wilson?'

'A great man for raising money, apparently, went around with a begging bowl to all the shops in the city,' said Dr Scher. 'The archdeacon fell out with him because of that. Told the bishop about it. Made the bishop reprimand him as they are trying to keep a low profile and not tread on any Roman Catholic toes.'

'Worried about the IRA.' The Reverend Mother nodded understandingly. It was not surprising that the Anglican Church of Ireland community and its cathedral wanted to keep a low profile and not offend their Catholic neighbours by badgering shopkeepers for subscriptions. 'I would have thought that the Anglo-Irish community would be wealthy enough to look after the upkeep of the cathedral for themselves, and not go looking for subscriptions from local people who are not of their faith,' she said, shaking her head at the proffered plate of cake. She got to her feet and retrieved her parcel, resisting temptation to add a few more to it. Dr Scher enjoyed his cake, and it was, after all, Christmas Day. 'Don't move,' she said. 'I need the walk and your housekeeper will be disappointed if you don't finish up that cake.'

She wanted, also, she thought, when she had made her farewells, to walk quietly by the river and to think about Enda and about boys like him. They needed a father and very few fathers were present. Most of the men, most of the fathers of children in her school who had stayed in Cork, led a precarious existence, hoping to pick up a few hours' labour on the docks or on a building site and many, she regretted to acknowledge, spent very few of the shillings that they earned on their families, preferring to drown their sorrows or celebrate their luck, in the nearest public house. Was there any way that she could inveigle some ordinary men, not priests or brothers, but ordinary men with ordinary jobs, into playing a part in her convent school?

FIVE

The Reverend Mother slept poorly on Christmas night, but she was up at her usual early hour and prepared for another day of merry making. The day after Christmas, St Stephen's Day, was the day for the Wren Boys and the convent could expect lots of small boys to visit. From dawn to noon, knockers were banged on every prosperous-looking house and shrill voices sang a garbled version of 'The Wren Boys' Song':

> The 'wran', the 'wran', the king of all birds,
> St Stephen's Day, was caught in the furze,
> Although he was little, his honour was great,
> Jump up, me lads, and give him a 'trate'.
> Up with the kettle and down with the pan,
> And give us a penny to bury the 'wran'.

Sister Bernadette, though a country woman herself, had instituted some firm rules for the Wren Boys. They had to know the whole song, they had to sing it properly and the wren, or the 'wran' as it was always known in Cork, had to be just a homemade model. She made it known that sweets would not be handed out if a pathetic corpse was exhibited, and that prejudice was well known among the local boys, though their singing often left much to be desired.

And so, on the day after the murder of the child and of the archdeacon, when the Reverend Mother heard the familiar song, she was taken aback by the sound of the piping voices being led by a rich baritone.

'Once again, lads,' came a voice. 'And now don't you be forgetting to lift your voices for the chorus: "Up with the kettle and down with the pan" – the word "up" will pull your voices! Just do the chorus now and then we'll sing the whole thing for the holy nuns, God bless them.'

The Reverend Mother went to her window and peered out from the shelter of her curtains. The usual cluster of shabby boys was gathered around the gate to the convent, but with them was the figure of a bespectacled priest. He led the boys through the chorus twice, conducting with an upraised finger and then started once more on the song. They had to do it twice more before he was satisfied. The Reverend Mother dropped the curtain, took her cloak, and went rapidly to the front door. By now she had a fair guess as to the identity of the visitor. A singer, a teacher, one who took pains with slum children. It could only be Father O'Flynn.

She was just in time. Father O'Flynn had broken off a twig from the convent hedge and had raised it aloft. He turned quickly when he heard the door open and said enthusiastically, 'Well, now lads, it's the Reverend Mother herself. Ye'll do your best for her. I know that. Now deep breath in and get those lovely voices up to the sky where Holy God can hear them.'

It was a revelation, thought the Reverend Mother. The voices which on the first singing had been as ragged as the children's clothes, now soared up, high and sweet, and when they finished, the little crowd of lay sisters and choir nuns crowded behind her in the hallway clapped enthusiastically. Sister Bernadette and helpers bustled out with a mug and a jugful of a hot, sweet raspberry drink – Sister Bernadette's Christmas 'Punch' for which she hoarded some summer fruits – and a basket filled with pieces of cake, saved from the feasting of yesterday, including the small cubes purloined from Dr Scher's hospitality. The mug was filled and refilled, passed down the line in strict order of age by the leading singer and then with lots of shouts of 'Happy Christmas' and 'many happy returns', the Wren Boys took themselves off. Sister Bernadette then took a piece of chalk from her pocket and marked the gatepost with a large cross to indicate that the Wren Boys had visited and no more would be welcome.

The Reverend Mother smiled warmly at her visitor. 'You must be Father O'Flynn,' she said. 'No one else could have turned the Wren Boys into a choir so quickly.'

He shook her hand warmly. 'It's a privilege to meet you, Reverend Mother Aquinas,' he said.

'You've taught me a lesson,' she said as she ushered him into her study. 'My patron saint, Thomas Aquinas, had a saying: "*per aspera, ad astra*". He, like you, believed that the stars can only be reached through hard work. I liked the way that you made them go over it again and again. Perhaps the most valuable thing that we can teach the young is that the two things, hard work and the stars, have to go hand in hand.'

'And support them in the meantime,' said Father O'Flynn. 'And make sure that their particular star is within reach. But, sure, the young have great confidence in themselves, these days. My youngsters, my company, are putting on six different plays of Shakespeare this week. A year ago, I would have thought that they could never manage that. I kept telling them that they'd never do it, would never remember all those words and they just laughed at me. "We'll prove you wrong, Flynnie," one cheeky fellow said to me. The manners of the young these days!' Father O'Flynn shook his head in false sorrow, adding, 'Still, the lad is a great hand at *Richard II* and God knows that's a long part, Reverend Mother!'

At that moment, Sister Bernadette knocked at the door and wheeled in a laden trolley. The Reverend Mother waited patiently while the fire was mended, the cups filled with tea and the plate of cake slices and a few biscuits were carefully placed within reach. Once Sister Bernadette had left, she went straight to the point.

'You've heard about little Enda, Father O'Flynn, haven't you? Eileen told you, didn't she?'

The priest nodded sadly. 'God have mercy on his soul,' he said. 'It's a strange life we lead, Reverend Mother, isn't it? We preach the love of God for mankind and then we are pulled up short when Himself, up there in heaven, allows a thing like this to happen. Sometimes,' he said slowly and deliberately, 'it gets awfully hard to believe in the love of God and sometimes I come near to despair.'

He would be forty to fifty, more than twenty years younger than myself and these things hit harder at that age, thought the Reverend Mother, looking across at the face opposite to

her. She said nothing, though. If asked a question she would
reply, but her own experience was that everyone must find
their own way through the tangled threads of human misery.
He took off his glasses, rubbed his eyes and then cleaned the
lens with the silk lining of his jacket.

'Nice girl, Eileen!' he said cheerfully. 'Tried to get her to
join my troupe once, but Lord love her, she's too busy.
Rushing here and there on that bike of hers. "I'll write you
a play about Cork, one day, Father O'Flynn," she says to
me. "Shakespeare shouldn't have written about Venice; he'd
have been better off sticking to London! So, I'll write about
Cork." "You do that", I told her and when it's as good as
Shakespeare, well I'll stage it!" and off she went, laughing.
Nice girl,' he repeated. 'Good sense of humour. Will make
a fine wife to some lucky man.'

'How did you come to hear about Enda, Father O'Flynn?'
asked the Reverend Mother quietly. The vision of the little
boy, singing in his high, clear, sweet voice, as he was propelled
by wires around and around the roof of The Loft had stayed
with her all through an almost sleepless night.

That took him slightly aback. He stopped to think, and she
watched him patiently, thinking that he was one of the most
interesting men that she had come across. She had heard of
him first when he had organized a huge procession, a sort
of carnival, in and out of the back streets of poverty-stricken
Shandon. Groups of children sang and danced and performed
plays, some falling out of the procession at street corners
and then joining in again when they had finished their act.
People spoke of it for years afterwards, and told the story
of how, when all was over, the sun had come out, had dissi-
pated the fog and it seemed to onlookers as though the
heavens had smiled upon the talent shown by the poorest
children of Cork city.

Father O'Flynn had gone on uncovering talent, teaching the
lame and the tongue-tied and the blind to discover their talents
and to face the world with confidence. Children came and
went throughout his busy life as choirmaster in two schools
and the originator and driving force of 'Shakespeare for all',
whether they dwelt in a slum, or in the palatial-like houses

on the outskirts of the city and on the rich land of the county of Cork.

'Do you know, I think it might have been the choirmaster at the Church of Ireland Cathedral,' he said. 'Flewett is his name. He came to see when we were rehearsing *The Tempest*. I had a very good girl, lovely voice, beautiful high soprano and a great way with the lines of Shakespeare – one of those people who need very little teaching. No particular education – just worked in Dowden's clothes shop – but, by Jove, that girl has a wonderful memory for words and not just that, knows how they should be said, also. Just picked up the rhythm of the iambic pentameters, no fuss about it, just always got the emphasis right. But, of course, like a lot of these girls that are singers, girls with good lung power, well, she was very plump. No way were we going to get her up on a wire – and then I thought about Shakespeare. Well, it was all right for him, I said to myself, Reverend Mother. He had plenty of boys to play the women's parts and so he could have one whose voice hadn't yet broken, who could sing the words the way that they were meant to be sung and who was not too big. And I said to this Arthur Flewett, "You couldn't lend me a choirboy, could you? Just to fly through the air while he sings: 'Full fathom five thy father lies', a nice small one, if you please, Arthur." You see, Reverend Mother, I wasn't too worried about the wires, I could easily persuade one of those lads from the ESB to lend me a good, strong wire for a week, but, you know, most of the old rafters in the building are pock-marked with woodworm and might not be too strong. Wouldn't trust them with a weight too far!'

The Reverend Mother smiled. 'And so, you tried for a choirboy from the Church of Ireland. But I suppose you put the poor man in a dilemma. It wouldn't be too popular with the parents of his choirboys if he lent one of them to a Roman Catholic priest.'

'That's right – sad, but right. So, he told me that he could find a boy for me, that he was a little devil, but that he had the voice of an angel and he thought he'd take to the job like a duck to water. He warranted that the little fellow would pick up a tune quickly as he had heard him, perched up on top of

the golden angel's head outside their cathedral, singing a whole
verse from "Joy to the World" which the choir had been practising earlier. Had it perfect, so he told me!'

'And so he brought him along, drove him up to Shandon,
I suppose.' The Reverend Mother took only seconds to decide
that was the only way that Father O'Flynn's Shakespearean
company could have ensured that Enda would arrive, punctually, night after night. 'How did he manage it?' she asked
aloud. 'In my experience, Enda got bored very quickly.
Something he liked doing one day, he would refuse to do the
next day. Sister Philomena was at her wits' end with him.
How on earth did Mr Flewett do it?'

Father O'Flynn, to her secret amusement, was somewhat
taken aback. Of course, his teaching experience was with
mature and ambitious boys and well-behaved young ladies –
both groups intent on repaying parental expenditure on
education and attaining a good Leaving Certificate and, if
given the chance to act in a Shakespearean play, would have
turned up punctually to every practice and performance. His
Saturday and Sunday classes with stage-struck youngsters
were voluntary and so he would have little experience of
badly-behaved small boys.

'I'm not sure,' he confessed. 'Bribed him, perhaps. Yes, I
think he joked about it costing him a lot in sweets. Anyway,
he turned up with him, clean face and hair combed every night
of the week. I suppose that the little fellow enjoyed it. He
always got a great clap at the end. I let them come on one by
one so that everyone gets a chance of a clap.'

'Yes,' said the Reverend Mother sadly, 'I suppose that Enda
would do anything for sweets. Is the precentor, Mr Flewett,
a part of your group?'

For the first time in their conversation Father O'Flynn's
steady gaze faltered. He ceased to look across at her but stirred
the threadbare carpet with the toe of his boot. 'Well, no,' he
said after a minute. 'I have mostly children, you know, young
people, I should say. They wouldn't like to hear themselves
referred to as children. A few adults, well, we have a mix,
lots of different people, different reasons for joining. No, he's
not part of the group. It was just that he came along once with

the violin teacher, a Mr Hearn who teaches at St Vincent's Girls School and who was there to help one of his pupils who was playing the violin for us – very good, she was, too.'

The Reverend Mother said nothing. The man knew his own business. She thought of Gus Healy, the laboratory technician, crippled from childhood polio, who was a yearly success, playing the part of the crippled Richard III. All Cork went to see him and even stood in the laneway outside The Loft to hear him roar the words: 'My kingdom for a horse!' And then there had been that intelligent young man working as a labourer on the docks, whose terrible stammer had prevented him getting a job in the bank, despite the five honours he had attained in his Leaving Certificate examination. Father O'Flynn, with lots of patience, taught him to say: 'I will play Hamlet' without stammering once and he had gone on to play small parts until he did, indeed, manage to play Hamlet. Had gone to England, then, thought the Reverend Mother, with a sigh. A fresh start where no one would know his nickname of Stuttering Stanley. No, Father O'Flynn did have adults as well as children in his Shakespeare group. There had to be another reason.

'A bit of a responsibility, sometimes, all of those young people,' said Father O'Flynn breaking in on her thoughts. 'I like to involve the parents as much as I can. Of course, if they can sew or handle a hammer then they are doubly welcome, but there's a job for everyone who comes along.'

The Reverend Mother nodded. She approved of this way of getting the community involved. 'Mr Hearn,' she said aloud. 'Is he the son of the late archdeacon? If so, I met him at the cathedral yesterday. He and his brother, the rector of Midleton, were praying for their father's soul. A tall, thin man – would he be the son?'

'That's right,' said Father O'Flynn. His voice had a note of surprise in it. 'I'm very glad to hear that, very glad, indeed.'

'But a little surprised,' said the Reverend Mother.

'To tell you the truth, I'm astonished,' said Father O'Flynn with the directness which she had come to associate with him. 'Most surprised indeed, and very, very pleased. It just goes to show. God softens the heart when death comes to the doorway. The last time that I met the young man he swore that he could never, ever forgive his father.'

The Reverend Mother mused upon that statement for a moment. The young Mr Hearn had looked to be a reserved and self-contained man. 'What was the trouble between them?' she asked. The bishop had intimated something, but his words had been few.

'Well, they're all very rich, that crowd, you know,' began Father O'Flynn, his Shandon Street accent strengthening as he settled into a storyteller pose. 'God knows, envy is a sin, but *bejaysus*, I could do with just a small slice of the money that they get, Reverend Mother. All those rich Protestants, with no children, leaving money to their church, and, of course, they've all got endowments, own lots of land. Given to them by Oliver Cromwell and his like. You'd be astonished, Reverend Mother, if I told you how much that archdeacon was worth, according to his son.'

The Reverend Mother smiled. 'Don't tempt me into the sin of envy,' she said.

'You'd be like myself; it would be gone in a flash; you'd be spending it the minute you laid hold of it, but you see they have a different set-up in the Church of Ireland. They call themselves priests, but, of course, they are married men, and this archdeacon, Hearn, had a wife – dead now, poor thing, but also two sons. Well, like all wealthy men he thought a lot about his money, and he wanted it to benefit his boys. But, of course, he wanted them to get a finger into the honey pot for themselves too and like a good father he was willing to do his bit to pull a few strings for them. Got his eldest son into a nice, cosy little niche as curate to the Rector of Midleton who was eighty years old if he were a day and of course, the young man obeyed his father in everything, made himself popular in the parish and his father had the ear of the bishop, Dr Thompson, and made sure that he heard everything about all of the great things that young Mr Hearn was doing in the parish and so when the old man dropped dead of a heart attack or whatever old men die of; well, of course, the curate was made rector. But when it came to the younger son, the arch-deacon didn't have such success, because this one was cast from a different mould, and he rebelled. Didn't want to be a curate or a deacon or anything else, wanted to be a violinist and play in an orchestra. Very good at the music, he is, too. And I suppose that if his wealthy father had put a bit of money into him, sent him off to London, or to Paris, or somewhere like that, young Owen might have done well for himself, but staying here in Cork, well, God help us, Reverend Mother, we're a most distressful city and no one is financing frills like an orchestra.'

'And so, Owen Hearn had to turn to teaching,' said the Reverend Mother. 'And lucky to get a job,' she added briskly.

'You haven't heard the whole of the story yet,' said Father O'Flynn, raising an admonitory hand. 'So, a couple of weeks ago, Owen gets a note from his father, asking him to come and see him. Well, it's coming up to Christmas time, and all that, so off goes the young man, with a little hope in his heart. Goes into his father's splendid house – only seen it from the outside myself, of course, but I guess it's very splendid – taken into the drawing room, stands there, below the picture of his dead mother, in front of the blazing fire – now remember the fire, Reverend Mother – and his father comes in with a small steel box in his hand. Well, he doesn't greet his son, just a nod, but he puts the box on the table, takes out his bunch of keys, turns the lock, and takes out two rolls of parchment. And then he speaks.

'"Owen," he says. "I've had a bit of luck on the American stock market and so I've decided to remake my will. Well, I had my solicitor and his clerk here yesterday. Gave him a few extra grey hairs, but I made him draw up two wills. Here they are." And then he takes out a scroll, reads it carefully, rolls it up again, places it opposite to his right hand. And then he unrolls the second scroll, reads it carefully and places it opposite to his left hand. "And now, Owen," he says, "you have a decision to make. This scroll here, by my right hand, divides all that I own, all that I will die possessed of, between my two sons, Adam and Owen. And the other scroll, the one by my left hand, leaves all to my eldest son, Adam. Now the choice is yours, Owen, will you do what I say, give up this nonsense and become a churchman like your father, your brother, your grandfather, and many of your uncles, or will you persist in your folly. There are no second choices," he says to the lad. "I have promised my solicitor that one of these documents will be burned before twelve noon!"'

'I suppose that there can be only one ending to your story,' said the Reverend Mother.

'Yes, of course, Shakespeare himself would have written that one ending. It's the proper dramatic one, isn't it? Owen makes a little speech – about free will, and about a man doing what he wants to do, with his own life. The father puts the scroll by his left hand back into the box, locks it securely, takes up the scroll by his right hand, unrolls it, reads it through, very slowly and carefully, I would order him to do it aloud if I were directing this play. The audience holds its breath! And then the archdeacon strides forward, stands upon the expensive Axminster rug and without a glance at the portrait of his dead wife, he throws the scroll into the fire, stands, poker in hand, until nothing but ashes remain, looks at his son, wishes him a good day and leaves the room.'

The Reverend Mother thought about the story. There was one false note, she decided. According to Bishop Thompson, the archdeacon had persuaded the younger son, Owen, to come to the cathedral on Christmas Day and to attend the service celebrated by his father in the side chapel. There was something that didn't ring quite true about that invitation and about the obedient response of a son who, weeks earlier, had stood steadily by and watched his father destroy a will which would have given him half of a considerable fortune.

'What an extraordinary story,' she said aloud, inwardly deciding to relate it to Patrick, and Father O'Flynn looked at her with an amused smile.

'Now, let's get down to work,' he said briskly. 'Eileen says that you want to organize some sort of funeral for the poor child.'

'I'm worried that no one might turn up,' she explained. 'There's a bit of a local prejudice against the mother. No, not a bit. There's quite a lot,' she contradicted herself. 'I never can see why. I'm sure that plenty of people have relationships that were not blessed by the church.'

'She's been open and honest about it, from what I have heard. And that was the problem. We're great hypocrites here in Cork city,' said Father O'Flynn dispassionately. 'I think, myself, that it's something to do with having a great gift of the gab. You've noticed, I'm sure, Reverend Mother, that whenever you ask a Cork person to explain anything to you, you get a heap of lies. They can't resist making up a story to make matters a bit more dramatic, a bit more interesting. And so, it stands to reason that Cork people despise a woman or a man who can't be bothered cloaking their behaviour with a good piece of fiction. We're a city of Shakespeares, and there's nothing you can do about that.'

The Reverend Mother had to smile at that. A man after her own heart, she thought. Did what he could with what he could change and was compassionate towards the failings which were beyond him to change.

'The funeral,' she said firmly.

'No problem,' he said promptly. 'I can provide twelve pall bearers from Ophelia's funeral. We've just done *Hamlet*, so the costumes are handy at the top of the box.'

The Reverend Mother's eyes widened. 'Costumes!' she breathed.

'Just old curtains – from the Imperial Hotel, if you please – but lovely silk velvet. Nice, refined shade of purple. You'll like them, Reverend Mother.' He got to his feet decisively. The action of a man who never finds enough minutes in the day. 'Get Eileen to spread the word,' he advised. 'And to get hold of a photographer from the *Cork Examiner*. After all, the little fellow was one of our players and so it's only right and normal that we attend the funeral. I'll come along myself, too. I can leave the motorbike here in your yard. You've a nice handy lock on that gate of yours. Sensible woman. Any time that I'm in the South Parish, I'll call on your hospitality for my beloved old Indian bike. Thanks for the *cuppatay*! And the cake! Must go. I've a rehearsal in fifteen minutes.'

And with that the legendary Father O'Flynn was on his feet, shot off down the corridor, shouted a 'God bless you for feeding the hungry; charitable woman that you are!' through the door to Sister Bernadette and then was off, leaving the

Reverend Mother invigorated and slightly shamed by the breadth of vision that would spend time in organizing an almost state funeral for the small son of a local pariah of the slums.

She got to her feet as soon as she heard the front door slam and went straight to her desk. Yes, she would involve Eileen, and Eileen, she knew, would enjoy organizing the publicity and helping with the funeral. Half the parish would turn up once the word got around that the *Cork Examiner* was to be on the scene. They would have to wait, of course, until Dr Scher had released the body, but then poor Mrs O'Sullivan would have a funeral for her darling which might help to soften the anguish for an hour or so.

She wrote the note to Eileen, took it to the kitchen to find a young lay sister who would enjoy stretching her legs with a steep climb up Barrack Street after all the unaccustomed heavy food. Then when she had done that she went back to her fire and began to think about her neighbours in the wonderfully ornate cathedral. The murderer of the archdeacon could not have been a passing stranger, nor even an acquaintance, she guessed. No, it had to be someone who was familiar with the ways of the cathedral, knew how the archdeacon would pour wine from the cruet or jug into the silver chalice, and how he would then drink it down in one gulp. It had, also, to be someone who knew Enda, knew how easily he swarmed all over the roof of the magnificent building, finding footholds amongst the carved stone, knew that he could be bribed with sweets – that pathetic packet of Rolos still haunted her!

The Reverend Mother got up and walked restlessly around the room. She had been in an alien environment on that Christmas morning, and everything about it was clear and sharp in her mind. The statues, the stained-glass windows, the red marble of the font, the elaborate mosaic on the floor and the magnificent rose window above the west door, a window whose bottom pane of glass had been broken.

By accident, or in preparation for a greater crime?

Who should have been responsible for ordering its repair and ensuring that rain did not enter?

The faces of the men associated with the cathedral passed through her mind: the bishop, Dr Thompson; the dean, Dr

Babington; the Reverend Canon Wilson; the young deacon, Mr Robert Webster; and the sexton, Tom Hayes. And then, of course, there was the precentor, master of the choir and of the music for the services, Mr Flewett – the bachelor with the hospitable sisters who cooked his Christmas dinner.

Why, she wondered, did Father O'Flynn prevaricate when asked whether he wanted to have that musically gifted man and choirmaster join his Shakespearean company?

And what was the significance of the story he told about young Mr Hearn and his breach with his father, the now deceased archdeacon?

SIX

Inspector Patrick Cashman kept deep within himself the secret that he hated Christmas. Had always done so. During his childhood, his mother was always depressed over Christmas, always bewailing the absence of her husband, the father of her small son, always lamenting that she couldn't buy Patrick proper toys for presents. When he was young, he used to try praying that Santa Claus would find their house, but they had no proper chimney, so he had to be reconciled with no visit. He remembered the year when every boy in Barrack Street seemed to have received a present of a horn and the noise drove him so mad that he pretended he was ill and went off to bed pulling the blanket over his ears. He had conscientiously spent Christmas with his mother in the trim little house which he had bought for her with his first few years' savings. They had exchanged presents, eaten well, and he had endured many visits from neighbours and from old friends from Barrack Street, all congratulating his mother on having such a good son with a steady wage. He had, he faced the fact, lost his few school friends once he had gone to Dublin to train for the new police force and since arriving back to his native city, he had made no new ones.

Except perhaps Joe. Joe was his sergeant and a nice fellow. Once Patrick heard the cheerful voice asking the elderly constable in the office opposite the front door how his Christmas was, he straightened up, fixed a smile on his face, and tried to look like a man who had come reluctantly back to work after a jolly family Christmas.

'Hello, Joe,' he said cheerfully as the sergeant pushed the door open after a perfunctory knock.

'God, I'm glad to be back at work,' said Joe, sliding out the chair opposite to Patrick and sinking down onto it with an exaggerated sigh of relief. 'Don't mind Christmas Day, but it all goes on too long. Sick to death of all the eating and drinking and being polite to all the visitors. My father and mother seem to know everyone in the city of Cork, and I could swear that they have all been through our doors during the past few days. And, of course, the death of the archdeacon was a boon to them. My mother showed me off like a prize specimen. "Of course, Joe knows all about it, but he's not allowed to say a word!" Never felt such a fool in all my life!'

'I hope you went to church on Christmas Day,' said Patrick, brightening up at the prospect of getting down to work again. Joe was a member of the Church of Ireland, not a very enthusiastic member, and of course, unlike Roman Catholics, he had no moral obligation, no threat of hell fires if he did not attend church every Sunday, but Patrick hoped that Joe's mother would have insisted – after all the church of St Nicholas was only next door to Newenham Terrace where his parents' house was situated – and he was not disappointed.

'You don't know my mother if you think that I'd get away with missing the service on Christmas Day,' said Joe. 'Not that I wanted to duck out of it this year, for once. Hung around a bit afterwards, looking at all the decorations, even climbed up the pulpit steps to admire how the ladies of the parish had managed to fasten all those very tasteful bunches of holly and ivy to the canopy.'

'Well done,' said Patrick enthusiastically. He guessed what was coming next.

'Don't spoil my story!' Joe gave a grin. 'Well, by the time that I had climbed down, the rector, nice old man, had finished with everyone and was standing at the bottom of the steps, wondering what on earth the pair of legs were doing on top of the balusters. As soon as he saw me, he said, "Oh, it's young Joe, the tennis champion of Newenham Terrace!" He came and sat upon the steps to join me, and we had a good chat. I talked about how he used to climb on a ladder down to the area in front of the basement of the rectory and get out our lost tennis balls when we were children. And he remembered how myself and my brothers used to be sent around by Mum to give him a Christmas present to thank him for being so nice to us all through the summer. Luckily, I had thought of that before I came out and I had snatched a small bottle of cognac from the sideboard and stuck a bit of Christmas wrapping paper over it and so I produced it. Poor old fellow, he was so moved by that, and he invited me into the rectory to try it out. And so,' finished Joe, with a grin, 'we had a nice long gossip about the late Archdeacon Hearn. Nice old man, our rector, you'd like him. Dresses like a picture from one of Trollope's books, just like Mr Harding, the precentor in *The Warden*, you know.'

'Well done,' said Patrick enthusiastically. He had no idea who Trollope was and was certain that he had not read any of his books. Trollope was not on the Leaving Certificate syllabus – he was sure of that, and he never read anything that had not been on the syllabus. Never had the time.

Joe and he made a good team, he thought. Joe was a bit slapdash while he, himself, was meticulously careful. But Joe was good at getting people to talk in a relaxed fashion, and the fact that he was a Protestant, and a member of a respectable middle-class family, meant that he would have an insight into these people to an extent that would be denied to Patrick, the boy from the slums.

'I suppose that your rector knew them all; would do, of course,' he said. 'Small world, the Protestants – I mean the Church of Ireland!' he added.

'You know,' said Joe thoughtfully, 'you call it the Church of Ireland when you want to be polite, but no one in the city uses that name, do they? In fact, when we were young it used to be the *Proddies* against the *Cat-licks*, do you remember that?'

Patrick nodded. He didn't want to talk about the time when he was young. He remembered it as infrequently as he could, and never with any pleasure. 'What did he say about the archdeacon?' he asked.

'Didn't like him,' said Joe promptly. 'Didn't say so, of course. Wouldn't want to speak ill of the dead, but I definitely got the impression that he didn't like the man. I asked him, casual-like, when he had last seen the archdeacon and he told me an interesting little story. Told me that the sexton from the cathedral, Tom Hayes – and remind me to tell you something about Tom Hayes in a minute – well, he told me that Tom

Hayes had come to him last week asking for a job, said that he worked in the cathedral as a grave digger, bell ringer and boiler stoker and all sorts of odd jobs and that he had always given satisfaction, but then, one morning, a couple of days before, he reported to the archdeacon that a pane of glass from the rose window, the big circular window over the door of the cathedral, had been cracked during the night. And the archdeacon got very angry and accused Tom of breaking it when he had gone up onto the roof to repair a slate. He told Tom that he was going to dock a shilling from his wages until the repair was paid for. Well, my nice little rector guessed that the man wouldn't have been paid much as the archdeacon was notoriously mean – well, he didn't quite say that, but he implied it – and so Tom Hayes came looking for a job.'

Patrick made a few careful notes and then looked back at Joe. 'And I was to remind you about Tom Hayes . . .'

'Well, you know I was on call on St Stephen's night – you did Christmas night and I did St Stephen's – there was the usual trouble in the pubs, but one of the fellows that I let go with a warning was Tom Hayes. I did the usual, gave him a talking to – asked him why he got so drunk, and he looked me in the eye and said that he was celebrating. I didn't ask him why, told him he should be ashamed of himself, let him off with the usual talking to, and advice to drink moderately, but afterwards I found that it stuck in my mind. There was something about the way that he said it, and the defiant look on his face. I didn't ask him any more questions, didn't want him to incriminate himself. He was still quite drunk, of course, and you know the old saying: "when the drop is inside, the sense is outside". But when my nice little old rector told me that story, I thought about Tom Hayes celebrating. It wouldn't have been the death of the child. I saw the tears pouring down his face when he carried the little fellow into us. It must have been the death of the archdeacon.'

Patrick mulled over the story for a few minutes. 'Did he have Mrs O'Sullivan, the mother of the little boy, Enda, did he have her with him?' he asked.

'Not then. I looked down through the names afterwards in case I missed her in the crowd. But I hadn't. The world and his wife were there that night, so she might just have slipped away when we arrived.' Joe grinned. 'St Stephen's Night is a great night for the Beamish and for Murphy's Stout, of course,' he added.

Patrick did not smile back. Already he had taken out a new card from his boxful and had written Tom Hayes on the top of it. From his notebook, he copied out the details about the sexton from St Fin Barre's Cathedral. Age, occupation, place of residence, a digest of the preliminary evidence taken in the cathedral on Christmas Day and then added the new inform-ation from Joe about the search for a new job and the drunken celebration on St Stephen's Night.

The telephone shrilled into action as he wrote, but he nodded towards Joe and continued writing. Finish each job, if possible, before you start another was a motto of his and he tried to keep to it whenever possible.

As soon as he had replaced the card, he looked up enquir-ingly at Joe. 'Short and sweet,' he said, with a glance at the phone.

'Just Dr Scher. He's on his way over,' said Joe. And then, after a moment, 'I'll leave you in peace and get on with the paperwork. I'll tell the constable to put all phone calls through to me for the next fifteen minutes if you like. You'd probably want to have a bit of time to think before Dr Scher arrives.'

The perfect assistant, thought Patrick, as Joe closed the door carefully behind him. He took four more cards from his box. That should be enough to be going on with.

A small number of suspects, so far, but a horrendous crime. The small, crumpled figure with the dirty face, the raggedly torn clothes, stained with vomit and the bare feet would, he thought, haunt him to the end of his days unless the killer was arrested and handed over to the law. No other child should be in danger from a man who could commit such a crime. With renewed energy he went back to his cards and sometime later touched the bell to summon Joe.

'I thought that we could have a look at what we have got already from Dr Scher before he arrives,' said Patrick, noting that Joe had read his mind and was bearing a file marked: December 25, St Fin Barre's Cathedral.

'Probably nothing much to tell us; he was virtually certain that it was cyanide,' said Joe. 'And also, that the stuff was mixed with wine in the case of the archdeacon and put into the runny centre of the Rolo sweet in the case of the little boy. Perhaps,' he said a little diffidently, 'we could establish a profile for the murderer – I got that idea from one of my mother's favourite authors, Agatha Christie. The idea is that you don't think about who could have done it until you come up with a sort of sketch for the murderer. Call him or her X – that's the first thing to do.'

Patrick was sceptical, but ideas should always be encouraged and so he took a sheet of paper and wrote a large X at the top. And then neatly he printed the numerals one to ten down the side of the page. He looked at Joe expectantly.

'Number one: X knows that the server at the altar drinks the wine before anyone else in the congregation,' said Joe and Patrick wrote it down.

'Number two: X knows that the boy Enda is good at climbing,' he added.

Suddenly something struck him, and Patrick pushed the piece of paper aside. 'Joe,' he said, 'did you notice any glass on the floor?'

'There was none,' said Joe. 'I did look.' He clicked his tongue with annoyance. 'At least I did have a look around when they were carrying the body away. Dr Scher has the clothes. I should have looked in them. But would he have pocketed the pieces? Wouldn't be in character, would it?'

'Unless X told him to do so – but why should he do that?' said Patrick. 'We know that the glass had been cracked before, but it wouldn't have had that big hole – a hole large enough to fit the boy's body. What we are considering now is whether the large hole was made by a stone thrown from outside – in which case there should have been glass on the floor inside – or whether the panes were removed by the boy once he had climbed up. It was not just cracked when we saw it. There was a definite hole. X could have told him to do that. I suppose that is possible, but would Enda have remembered to do that? He was only seven years old, after all.'

'More likely to smash them or perhaps stack them,' said

Joe. 'He'd be a streetwise kid and he would know that it
wouldn't be too safe for him to be climbing with broken glass
in his pocket. I'll send someone up there to have a look.
Anyway, let's go back to X. What about a number three? X
knows that Rolo sweets are a favourite with little Enda. After
all, he had to give him an incentive, a good bribe, to do the
deed. For instance, I hate coconut and my younger brother
doesn't like peppermint. Why a Rolo?'

Patrick considered this. When he was a child, anything with
sugar in it would have pleased him. It was so rare to be given
a sweet that he couldn't remember any preferences. Still,
perhaps Joe was right. Little Enda had a reputation for stealing
from shops and stallholders. There had even been complaints
about him at the police station – that was unusual because
shopkeepers usually dealt with that sort of thing themselves
by a quick slap or a complaint to the child's parents. Perhaps
the choice of a Rolo was significant. He made a note on
his card.

'So, we are saying that X knows quite a lot about the little
boy,' said Patrick. He made another note on his card and added
another line to the profile of Mr X. 'When do we think that
the poison was added to the chalice?' he asked.

'I can help you there,' said Joe. 'My friend, the rector, told
me that he usually makes sure that everything is ready the
night before, but especially when preparing for Christmas
morning. He said in his good-natured way that the servers
were only little boys and that in the excitement of Christmas
present-opening, that he couldn't expect them to come in a
minute before it was necessary, so he always told them to
make sure that everything was ready the night before.'

'So X would know that everything was ready. I must have
a word with someone to check on who would have known
that. It may have been the archdeacon himself, but Canon
Wilson seemed an efficient sort of man so he or the dean may
be in charge of these matters.' Patrick took his notebook from
his pocket and wrote himself a reminder.

'X knows all about Enda, about his ability to climb, the
fact that a packet of Rolo sweets would tempt him. Patrick,'
said Joe urgently, 'I just don't know why I didn't think of this

earlier – there was all the fuss about the mother and how upset she would be. Surely she would have missed the boy when he didn't come home on Christmas Eve night. Wouldn't she have gone looking for him? We must be wrong about the poison being put in the night before. It must have been done in the morning. X must have arranged with the boy to turn up in the morning.'

Patrick bit his lip. 'I don't like it,' he said after a minute. This, he thought, was a time when his own background as a slum child was of more use to a case than Joe's background of living in a middle-class house, with clocks and probably alarm clocks and having a father who was earning a good salary and who left the house every morning at a particular time. 'Think for yourself, Joe. The woman lives in a basement, no clocks, no watches. These people rely on the church bell to tell them when to go to Mass. They wouldn't have any way of knowing the time, otherwise. X couldn't have relied on a seven-year-old not to sleep in, not to tell his mother about how he was going to play a trick on the archdeacon and give all the details about putting powder in the chalice. As for missing him, well, I'd guess that she came home drunk and tumbled into bed.'

'Might have just told him to turn up early, but I get your point,' said Joe affably. 'So, it was done the night before, on Christmas Eve, once everything was got ready and all the clergy had gone home, and after the cathedral was locked up by the sexton. The custom on Christmas Day in the cathedral was that the archdeacon performs the service for the elderly and for the mothers who want to get back and put a turkey in the oven as soon as possible and the bishop himself does the big, long Christmas service with the choir and then the children visiting the crib and, of course, getting a gift presented to them from under the Christmas tree. Shame it was all spoilt for them this year,' said Joe in a light-hearted fashion.

Patrick thought that the children who went to the Protestant service at St Fin Barre's Cathedral were probably from such well-off families that they would hardly miss some cheap toy presented by the bishop at the Sunday service. Life, he thought, was very unequal. Enda O'Sullivan was willing to risk life and limb by climbing up onto the cathedral roof, inserting his small body through a broken pane of glass, climbing down into a dimly lit church, and putting powder into the chalice on the high altar. And all for a packet of cheap Rolos. And then to die from cyanide poisoning as soon as the sweet taste of chocolate met his lips.

There would be no mercy for a man who could commit such a deed, swore Patrick to himself. He got up from his desk and went to the window. 'Here comes Dr Scher,' he said. 'Go and meet him, Joe, or else Tommy will keep him for five minutes while he passes on all the news from the city.' He waited until Joe had gone before surreptitiously blotting his eyes with a well-laundered handkerchief and blowing his nose. By the time Joe was back with Dr Scher, Patrick was sitting at his desk, studying his card index.

'Morning, Patrick! Happy New Year and all that guff,' said Dr Scher. He placed a large cardboard box on the desk. 'Keep an eye on that,' he warned. 'There's a king's ransom in that box and the dean was not at all pleased that I removed them. Very, very rare that old Irish silver. This stuff dates to the 1700s and they only take it out to use on Christmas Day and on Easter Sunday. So the bishop told me. I doubt the man knows the true value of that chalice and cruet, but he knows enough to make a fuss about it. Very proud of it and so he should be. I'd give a lot to have it, myself.'

Patrick eyed the box taking up a large portion of his desk. Too large to go in the safe. He made up his mind that personally he would deliver it back to the dean or better still, the bishop himself, as soon as possible. The police barracks had lots of unsavoury characters in and out of the building during the day and Dr Scher was a great talker.

'Never mind the silver,' he said, 'tell us about the poison.'

'Cyanide,' said Dr Scher briefly. 'Enough to kill a battalion, or more likely a bunch of wasps' nests. If I were in charge of the country, I'd never allow that stuff to be sold in a pharmacy. So easy to pretend that you just want to kill a few flying insects when really you want to bump off your rich grandmother or your boring husband, or wife for that matter.'

Joe was the one who asked the question that Patrick had had at the back of his mind for the last week. 'It's a quick death, isn't it?' he asked tentatively.

Dr Scher tightened his lips in a grimace.

'Isn't it?' persisted Joe.

'It's quick,' said Dr Scher. Then he added reluctantly, 'The agony is soon over, but, make no mistake about it, even tiny amounts of less than a tenth of a gram can leave victims to die in agony – it's a quick but agonizing death.'

Patrick scribbled a note – unnecessary as the words were seared into his brain – but it served to make a space, a moment for recovery.

'How was the cyanide administered, Dr Scher?' he said in a business-like manner.

'The powder was in a small, cellophane packet. I found it in the boy's pocket. Traces of cyanide still in it. He poured it into the cruet, the little jug full of wine, you know, and it would have dissolved instantly in the wine. And then, during the service, the wine was poured from the jug into the chalice and the archdeacon drank it.'

'And the Rolo?' Joe asked. He still had a shocked look on his face, but he had recovered. Enda wasn't the first slum child to be found dead during the last couple of years.

'Made a hole with a needle, or something like that. Quite carefully done. I found that he had poisoned another two of the sweets – probably in case one was dropped. Careful man, our murderer,' he added. 'It would have been a slow job, but he did it well. Poured it through a little glass funnel or some-thing like that. Took his time over it; let it settle into the sweets.'

'Didn't know too much about children like Enda O'Sullivan if he thought that he wouldn't pick up a sweet from the floor and put it straight into his mouth,' said Patrick. He took out the card with the name of Tom Hayes on its first line and made a note. Would the man have made provision for the first sweet to be dropped and have provided a second sweet and even a third sweet? On the other hand, if he decided to move in permanently with Mrs O'Sullivan, Enda could have been a nuisance, perhaps actively hostile, but also, possibly, a cause of him losing a respectable job if he failed to keep him under control.

'Something odd about the autopsy on the archdeacon,' said Dr Scher, looking from Patrick's face to his notes. 'You'll be interested in this, Patrick. Middle-aged man, in good shape, good weight, heart, lungs, liver et cetera, et cetera. Everything in good shape, but something interesting about the stomach. Well, this was a nine o'clock service and the Church of Ireland doesn't have the Roman Catholic obsession with fasting – stupid notion, delicate old ladies, and young ladies; men doing hard physical work, but to be told by their church to go out in the cold and the damp and the fog on a winter morning without a bite in their stomach. But that's not the way with the Church of Ireland, so see if you can answer this puzzle. Why had the man nothing in his stomach except the almost digested remains of a heavy meal the night before?'

'Well, that is interesting,' said Patrick, resolutely turning his mind from the pathetic image of the ill-fed, small boy with his Rolo packet. 'What do you think of that, Joe? Could he have been fasting before communion? Joe is a Protestant, a member of the Church of Ireland,' he corrected himself quickly as he delivered the explanation to Dr Scher.

Joe grinned. 'Never heard of it. I don't think a respectable parson would dream of doing such a thing. He would have been thrown out on his ear if he adopted such papist practices.'

'Perhaps he had an upset stomach,' suggested Patrick.

'Perhaps,' said Dr Scher. 'No sign of it, though. I'd have said that he was a man of remarkable good health. I had a look at the stomach lining when I checked the contents. No traces of an ulcer or anything else like that. A man who suffers from indigestion usually shows it on the stomach lining. I'd wager my professional certificates on your archdeacon being in good health.'

'Got up late,' said Joe suddenly. 'That would be it. Out at a Christmas Eve party the night before and slept in. Did it myself. Had to be hauled out of bed by my mother sending that overgrown puppy of ours to drag me out of bed. The archdeacon woke up, looked at the clock and decided to rush off to the cathedral, get his service over and done with, and then come back and have one of those big breakfasts. That will have been it.'

Patrick mused over that but made no comment. Joe was probably right, but he would check or get Joe to check. Talk to the housekeeper, check whether there might have been an unexpected visitor, a report of something amiss at the cathedral. He could also check at what time the archdeacon arrived at the cathedral and whether he had spoken with anyone or expressed any disquiet. Aloud, he said, 'Anything else that we should know, Dr Scher?'

'That's about it,' said the doctor. 'Bad business. Funerals can take place any time you want, now. I'll officially sign over the bodies to you.'

'I think I'll go and have a word with the bishop, Dr Thompson,' said Patrick slowly. He looked at the clock. 'Where would he be at half past nine on a Monday morning, Joe?'

'In his palace, I'd say,' said Joe. 'Want me to ring and make an appointment for you?'

'No, I'll do that myself,' said Patrick.

'Well, what a shame,' said Joe, getting to his feet. 'I'd love to have said to one of the girls in the telephone exchange, "Get me the palace, my good girl," but that's the boss's privilege, I suppose. Want to come into my room, Dr Scher, and I'll type up the report, let you sign it before you go, and I'll give you a good cup of coffee with a dash of Midleton whiskey in it so that we don't quite forget Christmas!'

Patrick waited until the door closed behind the two of them, animatedly discussing different brands of whiskey. Then he picked up the phone. 'Give me the bishop's palace, please,' he said and then with a touch of guilt reminded himself, while he waited for the number, to wish the woman a happy new year as soon as she put him through.

SEVEN

'Come with me, Joe,' said Patrick. 'We'll drop into the archdeacon's house and have a quick look around and then you can take the Ford back to the barracks, and I'll see the bishop on my own.' It would, he thought, be more discreet to see the bishop without a witness. There was more chance of getting him to open up about the other clergy if he did not feel there was a witness present, silently noting his words. 'We'll park on the street, just outside the archdeacon's place. It's next door to the bishop's palace.'

'I know it. Big house. Funny to think of one man living alone in that place,' said Joe. 'My mother would give her eye teeth for a place like that. She's always complaining that our house is bursting at the seams.'

Patrick did not comment, but he reflected that Joe's mother already possessed a well-built, three-storey house with an attic to accommodate her servants. Ten families from Barrack Street could have been housed within the walls of Joe's family home.

The door was opened instantly when they arrived. It was obvious that they were anxiously expected. Behind the aproned and capped housemaid who opened the door, there was another one polishing the silver on the hall table, a second polishing the elaborately carved banister rail and a third was dusting the tops of the many pictures that lined both walls of the hallway. Behind them hovered a well-dressed woman holding herself very straight, but whose face was lined with anxiety. She came forward instantly.

'Mrs Connelly? I'm Inspector Cashman and this is Sergeant Duggan.' Patrick tried to shake hands, but she ignored his gesture and said quietly. 'Come in, Inspector. And you, Sergeant. We'll go into the front parlour.'

Quite a lady, thought Patrick. Very well-spoken, too. She'd probably earn a bit of money for herself and would have free board and lodging and a few maids to order about. Would a job like this suit his mother, he wondered? Recently it had occurred to him that his mother might be lonely. He had insisted upon her giving up her job of scrubbing out offices, but perhaps she missed the other women, the gossip and banter. He thought about this as he followed Mrs Connelly into a small, back parlour where a cosy fire was already burning brightly, and the window overlooked a trim garden.

She didn't offer tea or refreshments of any kind. Just waited for them to sit down and then placed herself upon an upright chair at the end of a small table, her knees neatly concealed behind one of the folded oval flaps.

'Just a few questions, Mrs Connelly, we won't keep you long. You've been employed as housekeeper in this house for . . .?'

'Ten years, Inspector. Ever since Dr Hearn, the archdeacon, moved into this house.'

This was an unexpected bonus. If anyone knew the archdeacon, she must.

'So, you knew his sons?'

'Yes, Inspector, and his wife, poor lady. A very nice woman and a great mother.'

She didn't say anything about the archdeacon being a good father, but perhaps that would come.

'You must have missed the sons when they moved out of the house,' he remarked.

She bowed her head but added no comment or gave no response to his supposition. Hard to get gossip out of this lady, guessed Patrick, but he didn't want to allow any awkward silence and he quickly followed up with another question.

'What time did the archdeacon come back into the house after the Christmas Eve ceremony?'

She did not hesitate to answer this; had already thought of it, perhaps.

'Just nine o'clock, Inspector. I had a cup of tea and some hot mince pies ready, but he said he wasn't hungry, just tired, and so he went off to bed.'

'Were you surprised at that?'

She looked slightly taken aback at the question. Not a curious woman, perhaps.

'It was for the archbishop to decide,' she said quietly. 'I like to be prepared, but they didn't go to waste. The girls enjoyed them. They're young enough to be excited about Christmas,' she said in an indulgent fashion, adding reflectingly, 'and I must say that they were lovely mince pies. Mrs McCarthy is a great cook. And, of course, he had eaten a good dinner before he went over to the cathedral.'

Patrick made a few notes, though he knew that Joe would write down everything in his accomplished shorthand. Nevertheless, making a note was a useful strategy, often. It made a pause in the conversation and served to indicate to the witness that every answer was of importance. The housekeeper had given him a good opening.

'I suppose that he ate a good breakfast next morning, on Christmas Day, before going out in the cold.'

She did not hesitate. 'Yes, sir, finished up everything.'

Patrick was taken aback. Dr Scher had said the man had had no breakfast and Dr Scher, in his experience, and by repute, was meticulous in his examination of dead bodies, had been doing the job when Patrick was a young schoolboy. He would not have made a mistake like that. And then he thought of the solution. One of those bright young sparks, demurely polishing and sweeping out the door of the parlour, had probably finished off the lot before returning the empty plates to the kitchen. They were, he thought, of an age when they were still growing and could eat an astonishing amount of food if they got the chance.

'Which of the girls waited upon the archdeacon at breakfast time?' he asked.

'Oh, I did that myself, Inspector. I always . . . always used to wait on the archdeacon at breakfast. It was a useful time for him to give me any instructions or to let me know what he was going to be doing during the day and when he wanted meals served – and, of course, if there were any visitors coming to the house, or any tradesmen to be summoned. His mind worked like that. It suited both of us. If there was nothing to be said, he just read his paper, but sometimes something that

he was reading reminded him that he wanted me to buy
something or do something. It worked very well for both of
us, Inspector.'

'So, you were in the room all the time with him?' Patrick
was feeling puzzled. Dr Scher had been so certain.

'No, not all the time, Inspector. I would go in and out. It
would annoy him to have me standing over him while he ate.
So, I would put down his pancake – he always had a pancake,
never porridge, never liked porridge, just a nice pancake with
some honey – and then I would go off to the kitchen, and
when I thought he'd finished it, I would bring in his bacon
and eggs, and some black pudding. He was very particular
about his black pudding, so I liked to keep an eye on the cook
while she was frying. You see, he always liked black pudding
done medium firm, not hard, but not soft, so I kept an eye
and occasionally, I would have to ask her to do it again.'

Some people, thought Patrick, have an easy life, everyone
bowing and scraping and making sure that their black pudding
is perfect. 'And when you brought in the bacon and eggs and
black pudding, Mrs Connelly . . .?'

'I would just wait for a moment or two while he tasted
everything and then when he seemed to be enjoying his fry,
I would slip back to the kitchen and make sure that the coffee
pot was warm, and that the bread was ready to be toasted.
And then I would go in, collect his plate and then come back
with the coffee and the toast.' Mrs Connelly sat back with the
air of one who has done her job to perfection.

'And he ate the bacon, egg, black pudding, ate up everything?' asked Patrick, being careful to allow no shadow of
doubt to come into his voice.

'That's right, Inspector, and the toast. Sometimes he left
something behind, but this time he didn't. He was in good
form, too. Had stocked the anthracite stove, himself. It was
blazing away when I came in. I wondered whether to turn it
down, but he was reading his paper and I didn't want to disturb
him. I heard him go upstairs when I went back to the kitchen
and after about ten minutes he came down and I heard the
door slam as he went across to the church. And that was
the last I ever saw or heard him, Inspector.'

She had said the last words in a meditative way, thought
Patrick, but there was no sorrow in her voice. He might have
paid well, or at least adequately, but his long-dead wife had
been the one who evoked affection.

'Did any of the staff attend the service in the cathedral?'
he asked.

'No, Inspector,' she replied with a slight air of surprise. 'We
all go to the South Chapel.'

Of course, he thought. His wits were wandering. The
Protestants in the city were mainly well off. They had jobs in
the banks, or the offices on the South Mall, but not cooking
and cleaning and serving the gentry. That was left to the other
community. He rose to his feet.

'Now, Mrs Connolly, the sergeant and I need to make an
inventory of what is in the dead man's bedroom, so perhaps
you could show us upstairs.' He was rather proud of the word
'inventory', it sounded so much better than revealing that they
were going to sort through all the victim's possessions,
including his underwear and socks. The housekeeper, anyway,
showed no surprise, but was on her feet, and had gone to open
the door for them before he had finished speaking.

They followed her silently to the first landing and waited
while she selected a key from the formidable bunch that she
took from her pocket. Patrick already had in his own pocket
a bunch of keys, taken from the dead man's pocket, given to
him by Dr Scher and he was not too pleased to see that
someone could have had access already to the room.

'I will keep the key for the moment,' he said quietly but
firmly and held out his hand for her bunch. His nails were
strong and quickly he detached the key and slid it into the
lock. Well-oiled, he noticed. Probably like everything else in
this well-run household.

'Good view,' said Joe when the housekeeper had gone
back downstairs. The archdeacon could have gazed out at
every inch of the cathedral spires and its roof from his
window. He turned back. 'What did you make of the breakfast
story?' he asked in a low voice.

'Hmm,' said Patrick. The housekeeper hadn't looked like
the sort of woman who listened at doors, but one never knew.

It was interesting though. Either the housekeeper was quite wrong, or making up a story, or Dr Scher was incorrect in his report. Of the three options the last was the most unlikely; he had perfect trust in Dr Scher's professional excellence and clear-minded reports. He would have to think about it, but not now.

'You check the wardrobe, Joe. I'll start with the desk.' He took from his pocket the bunch of keys belonging to the dead man and inserted the smallest key into the lock.

A tidy man, the late archdeacon; everything orderly, and allocated to its own drawer; bills and household expenses on one side and affairs to do with the cathedral on the other side. It looked as though the care of that splendid building was on the shoulders of its archdeacon, rather than the responsibility of the bishop. Top drawer for plans, second drawer mostly bills for repairing the roof, and the third drawer concerned the outside walls, the washing and repairing and the care of the stained-glass windows. The bottom and largest drawer was of the most interest as it contained a file on each of the clergy connected to the cathedral. Without hesitation Patrick put each one into his attaché case. No one, but possibly Joe, need know that he had these files and he promised himself that, if necessary, he would sit up all night in order to digest the contents and would return them discreetly, at a convenient time. He glanced through them quickly, interested more in the archdeacon's rather uncharitable notes on each person, rather than in the details of their job descriptions and their academic qualifications. One file was noticeably thicker than the others and he paused over that one.

'Joe,' he said in a low voice, 'come over here, will you. I want you to look through something.'

It was a photograph album, not a big one, just about the size of a substantial notebook. On the cover was written: Choir Outing, Summer 1928. Patrick kept his face as dead pan as he could while Joe leafed through the pages and then went back through it again.

'Ballycotton,' said Joe after a few minutes. 'I recognize that sign MEN ONLY and of course the two islands with the lighthouse on one of them. We used to go there when I was a kid.'

Patrick held out his hand and Joe placed the photograph album in it and watched, without comment, as Patrick replaced it within his attaché case. He then relocked the desk.

'Time to make our farewells, I think,' he said. He surveyed the room carefully and then said, 'Joe, what was the name of that table the housekeeper sat at downstairs in the parlour?'

'Blessed if I know,' said Joe with a surprised look. 'Why do you want to know?'

'I just thought that was the sort of table that my mother would like,' said Patrick. 'I thought I might buy it for her.'

'I bet she would like it. I know, now. It's a Pembroke table. We had one like that in our dining room when I was young, but the flap came off it when myself and a couple of brothers turned the table upside down when we were pretending it was a ship in a battle and the flap was the sail. When it was mended, my mother took it into her own room to keep it away from us little savages.' Joe grinned happily at the memory and Patrick thought that it wasn't just money that had made Joe's childhood so happy, it was the fun of a big family of boys. Mentally, he made a resolution that if he ever got married, he would try to have a big family and then, hastily before Joe could suspect his thoughts, he changed the subject back to what was on his mind. 'Just occurred to me, Joe, why did he take the choirboys to Ballycotton. Why not to Youghal?' And then, when he saw Joe looking at him with a puzzled air, he said, 'No train to Ballycotton, Joe. And yet one of those photographs showed them all climbing into a railway carriage.'

Joe looked a little surprised and then nodded. 'I get your point,' he said slowly. 'They probably got off the train at Midleton station and then got a bus to Ballycotton. Whereas if they had stayed on that train, they could have gone straight to Youghal, crossed the road and there's a three-mile-long beach in front of you, but just a beach, women, girls, babies – the lot, great beach, but all wide open to the road as well as to the sea.'

'And no "Men's Swimming Pool",' supplemented Patrick.

'True,' said Joe, thoughtfully. 'Though I do know people who swear by Ballycotton, love the little village, the pier, the fishing boats, and wouldn't be seen dead in Youghal, with the crowds. Still, well, yes, I do get your point. Now, do you want to keep the car and I'll walk home, or do you want me to take it back and cheer Tommy's heart. He likes to chase the kids away from it. Gives him a purpose in life.'

'You take it. I'll walk back,' said Patrick. 'The walk will do me good. Now for the palace!'

EIGHT

The bishop's palace was more of a very large house than a real storybook palace, but it was a splendid building. Patrick had just walked through the gates when the bishop emerged from a well-mown path in the grounds and came crunching across the well-swept gravel to welcome him and to usher him inside, telling him that the building was Georgian and pointing out that it had been built 150 years previously. With his mind full of questions, Patrick had to stand politely silent and listen to a lecture about what a beautiful house it was. Words like 'Georgian', 'moulded limestone cornices' and 'shouldered architrave' poured into his ears and though he appreciated the bishop's kindness in enlightening his ignorance, he couldn't help clearing his throat and taking a step forward once the reverend gentleman began to explain to him the difference between a pilaster and an ordinary column.

'I won't keep you long, my lord,' he said, once they were seated in the bishop's study and the bishop had shut the door against the sound of someone playing the piano at the top of the stairs, thumping on the keys, and a chorus of girls' voices singing 'West End Blues'.

'My daughters,' said the elderly man. 'I can hardly hear myself think some days!' He said the words with a proud smile and Patrick rather liked him for being so fond of his family.

'I'm sorry to disturb you during the Christmas period,' he said. 'First of all, I wanted to tell you that Dr Scher has now released the bodies and so you may make arrangements for the funeral and burial of the archdeacon. Or would you like me to get in touch with the reverend gentleman's sons. I understand that his wife is dead.'

'Leave it to me, my dear fellow, leave it to me. Let me write it down. I have,' said bishop sadly, 'the most terrible of memories.' He took from a small stand beside the telephone a leatherbound book decorated with a sketched picture of an elephant with alert ears and below it, printed in large capital letters: BE LIKE THE ELEPHANT. DON'T FORGET! He made a note and then put the open page just beside the telephone.

'That's a good idea,' said Patrick with a smile and a nod towards the notebook. He was beginning to feel at home with this friendly bishop. 'I could do with something like that.'

'Well, don't betray me to my daughter who so kindly did this for me, but I'm afraid it has been known that I write something down in this book and then forget it after all. But you're young! You don't need anything like this. Now tell me what I can do for you.'

The straightforward, friendly tone of this took Patrick aback. 'My lord,' he said hesitating slightly, but feeling increasingly sure that he would receive a frank answer to his question. 'My lord,' he repeated, 'I would not wish to put you in a difficult position, and I hope that you can feel assured that everything you say to me is in confidence, but my experience is that no one is deliberately killed unless there is something to dislike about him or her. My difficulty is always that no one wants to speak ill of the dead and that means it's hard for an outsider like myself to get information that I need. So, let me put to you a question. Can you imagine that anyone might have a reason to wish that the archdeacon was no longer here on this earth?'

'That's a good question,' said the bishop with an approving nod. 'And I'm afraid that the only honest answer to that is the one word "yes". Now you are going to ask me another question or several questions and I'm not so sure that I will be able to answer them as frankly and as quickly as I did your first.'

That's all very well, thought Patrick, but it is the law of the land that you assist the police and the fact that someone is a friend, a parishioner or a fellow clergyman doesn't absolve you. He did not utter those words aloud; he had a native caution, an inner voice that always warned him to go slowly, to say nothing that would offend, unless it were strictly necessary.

'I'm sure,' he said energetically, 'that your lordship and I agree that a person who would murder a man and a very small boy in a way which the police doctor tells me would cause terrible agony before death released them – that a person like that must be stopped from doing another such murder. The trouble I find, my lord, is that when someone has got away with a crime, they are quite likely to commit the same crime again. That is why I put my heart and soul into getting the criminal into court to face their sentence and be put safely behind bars.' He stopped and waited. No apologies, no appeals, he thought severely. I must solve this crime and solve it before any other life is lost. The bishop was looking taken aback and slightly guilty, so he decided to pursue with his little sermon.

'It might make it easier for your lordship,' he said, 'if I explain that it appears likely that whoever planned this crime had an intimate knowledge of your cathedral and of the procedure for the drinking of the wine. They would also have to have known the child, Enda O'Sullivan; would have known his ability to scale heights, and his intense fondness for sweets.'

'Every child is fond of sweets,' said the bishop. He said the words in the abstracted fashion of someone who is trying to come to some conclusion.

'Not every child is so fond of sweets that they would climb onto the roof of a building about a hundred feet high and would slip into a dark church and pour some powder into the chalice.' Patrick hesitated for a moment and then continued energetically, 'My lord, I had a childhood where I can remember every individual sweet that I had through the years. Yes, I loved sweets, craved them in my dreams, but no, I would not have had the courage, the daring, the disregard of consequences, to do what Enda did. Whosoever did this deed knew this child well, knew that, perhaps, unlike me, he feared neither God nor man.' He stopped there and felt a rush of pride in himself. He had not known that he could talk so fluently and that so many words had come almost effortlessly to his lips.

The bishop looked at him for a moment and then bowed his head. 'Ask your questions,' he said.

'Who would benefit from the archdeacon's death?' asked Patrick, now grimly determined to pursue the path which he had cleared for himself.

'I believe that the archdeacon left his considerable fortune and his house and all else that he possessed to his eldest son, the Rector of Midleton,' said the bishop. 'Sadly,' he added, 'his younger son was cut out from the will when he refused to become a clergyman and to the best of my knowledge that will, made hastily and made in anger, was never altered.'

These words came quite easily and without hesitation and the bishop, thought Patrick, probably told himself that this information could be easily found from a lawyer. Quickly he asked his next question.

'Who in your church would benefit? I'd guess . . .' said Patrick, thinking of the opulent surroundings in the house which he had just visited. The bishop's palace, of course, was even more splendid. Nevertheless, most people in Cork would have admired the archdeacon's house almost as much. 'I'd guess,' he repeated, 'that the position of archdeacon might be coveted by many. It's the next step below bishop, isn't it?'

The bishop did not answer for a moment and then he heaved a sigh. 'There is no firm answer to your question,' he said. 'Sometimes surprising decisions are made, and the obvious candidate overlooked in order to appoint someone else. But I suppose the dean and the canon, even perhaps the deacon, would all be considered. All three would certainly be considered if they were to put themselves forward, though possibly the dean and the canon might be considered a little old for a new position.'

'Not the man who manages the choir, Mr Flewett?'

'I doubt the precentor would be interested. His life's work is the choir, and the organ is hugely important to him. We have a wonderful organ, set in a pit. It was renovated in—'

'But he, the precentor, would have known Enda O'Sullivan very well, wouldn't he?' Patrick tried to make his interruption as gentle as it could be, but he was alert and suspicious at the sudden change of subject from murder to the renovation of an organ. The bishop, he thought, was uncomfortable with discussing Mr Flewett. He knew that tone of voice, the false enthusiasm for a matter nothing to do with the murder.

There was a moment's silence after his remark. Patrick was determined not to break it and after a minute the bishop said, 'Yes, he would have known Enda O'Sullivan. The boy hung around the cathedral. I've seen him, and indeed heard him sing, on many occasions. I think that our sexton, Tom Hayes, knew the child.'

Patrick made no comment on this. He could find plenty of people to talk about Tom Hayes and his relationship with Enda's mother, but Tom Hayes was not a matter of interest for the moment.

'How did the archdeacon get on with Mr Flewett?' he asked. He was uncomfortable using the word 'precentor', having never heard it before this case. What exactly was a precentor? He made a mental note to look it up in his dictionary.

'They clashed over a few matters which would seem of little importance to you, Inspector, but you see the Church of Ireland is to a certain extent a broad church and it incorporates two groups whose ideas on how services should be conducted differ somewhat. I would deem that the precentor, Mr Flewett, was on the High Church side and the archdeacon was an enthusiast for the Low Church beliefs and practices.'

'And so, they clashed frequently?' Patrick made a note in rapid shorthand and inwardly resolved to ask the Reverend Mother to explain the matter to him more clearly. It seemed a lot of nonsense, but experience had taught him that fights over religion were important and often ended in bloodshed. He went back to something more comprehensible.

'In the case of hierarchy here in the cathedral, you would be the . . . the . . .?'

'The boss man,' said the bishop with a friendly smile. 'That was what you wanted to ask, wasn't it?'

Patrick returned the smile and felt more at ease. 'I was wondering how the rest of them went?' he asked.

'The hierarchy could be deemed to be bishop, archdeacon, dean, rural dean, canon, deacon,' said the bishop concisely.

'But the rural dean wasn't present during the Christmas ceremonies, is that right?'

'No, he is based in Fermoy. He would be needed in his own parish on Christmas morning,' said the bishop.

'So, the dean, the canon, the precentor and the deacon would be the four people who would have the most contact with the archdeacon and all four were present on Christmas Eve when the wine was got ready for the two services on Christmas morning.' Patrick had recently acquired the habit of prefixing questions with the monosyllable 'so' and found it a most useful little word for triggering nuggets of information.

'That is correct.' The bishop had the look of someone who knew that a more difficult question was coming up.

Patrick knew he would have to be careful. 'Which of the four would you say was most intimate with the archdeacon? My lord,' he added quickly.

The bishop smiled at that but did not speak for a few minutes. 'Of course, we are all brothers in Christ,' he said cautiously.

Patrick did not respond, not even by a nod of the head. He had met people like the bishop before, fluent talkers. They were often the most difficult to extract hard evidence from. He waited, pencil in hand, and kept his eyes fixed on his lordship.

After a few moments, the bishop gave in.

'Of course, Inspector, a man can choose his friends, but not his family.'

Patrick nodded agreement. 'And you are saying that would apply to "brothers in Christ", wouldn't it?' he ventured and was rewarded by a quick smile. He needed, he thought, to rephrase his question.

'Which of the other four, the dean, the canon, the precentor, or the deacon, would the late archdeacon have had the most in common with?' he asked, wondering whether he should follow the name of the dead man with the customary 'May God have mercy on his soul' but then decided against it. In the case of a Protestant clergyman, it might be taken as an insult to imply that he had committed sins. After all, they didn't go to confession or anything like that.

He had to be very careful and very polite. Nevertheless, he was not going to let this bishop get away with not answering a straight question and so he waited, pencil in hand.

The bishop seemed to hear the resolution in his voice and so he bowed his head. 'To tell the truth, Inspector, the late archdeacon was a most meticulous hard worker for the church. He adored this cathedral, was fanatical about his care of it, but his relationships with others who perhaps did not share his fanaticism, were, I must admit, not good. The canon is, like myself, an elderly man who wanted a peaceful life, serving God and his fellow men, of course, but in a relaxed fashion. There were, I have to admit,' he repeated, 'frequent clashes between the two men.'

'Over anything in particular?' queried Patrick.

'Golf, I think,' said the bishop vaguely.

That didn't sound too promising, but Patrick, nevertheless, made a note. 'And the dean?' he asked.

'Golf, again, I think.' The bishop was getting impatient. 'Really, Inspector, I cannot give you any more information. I noted, with regret, that the archdeacon did not seem very friendly, very brotherly, if you like, with the rest of our brotherhood. The deacon, of course, was a young man, and Canon Jack Wilson, although not so young, was a bachelor, also, so these two seemed to be very friendly, talked a lot about golf,' added the bishop in a hopeful manner. 'And the dean, of course, being a newly married man with a big family, tended to go home immediately after services.'

'And Mr Flewett, the precentor, what were his relations with the archdeacon like?' asked Patrick, stubbornly determined to get something out of this interview.

The bishop's face changed. There was quite a silence and then he said, 'They were not at all friendly. They seldom spoke unless it were essential. I grieved very much over that.'

'What was the cause of the trouble?'

'I cannot say,' said the bishop.

Patrick braced himself. 'It is the duty of every citizen to give full co-operation to the police and to answer every question put to them.'

'But I haven't refused. I have answered by telling you that

I cannot say. There is an authority higher than the law of the land and that is the law of God. I think if you talk to your own priests, they will tell you that,' said the bishop firmly and then rose to his feet. 'And now, I am afraid that God calls me to other duties.'

Patrick got to his feet. The bishop had been cautious, but he had, to a certain degree, got what he wanted. He made his farewells in a manner that left the door open for a further visit, complimented his lordship on the accomplished piano playing and singing from the top of the stairs and left with a feeling of relief. He would talk matters over with someone who understood these religious scruples.

The Reverend Mother was strangely quiet when Patrick arrived. She had not replied to his tentative knock on the door. He knocked again, but still no reply. Sister Bernadette, with a pile of clean laundry in her arms, stopped at the sight of him standing in the corridor.

'I could have sworn that she was in her room,' she said. 'Perhaps she has gone to use the telephone.' Sister Bernadette placed the laundry on a convenient table, gave a perfunctory knock on the door, louder than his own, and then turned the knob of the handle.

'Oh, it's just Inspector Cashman, Reverend Mother,' she said, and held the door open for him.

Patrick entered rather reluctantly, but it was obvious that the Reverend Mother was not busy. True, there was a pile of documents on the table, but she was neither writing, nor reading, but was sitting, half-turned away from her desk and looking towards the window. Her face was even paler than usual, and the heavy eyelids drooped, almost hiding her eyes.

Sister Bernadette's voice roused her, though, and she stacked the pieces of paper neatly and smiled at him.

'You're welcome, Patrick. I was thinking about you. Do you need refreshments?'

Patrick shook his head hastily. He knew that tone of voice. 'I've just been to the bishop's palace to see Dr Thompson,' he told Sister Bernadette.

'Do you hear that, Sister Bernadette. He's been to the palace, so he despises our simple offerings.'

The Reverend Mother, Patrick realized, was making a decided effort to shake off whatever lethargy had afflicted her this morning. The pen in the pen tray, he noticed, had been dipped in ink, but the ink had long dried upon it. She had started to work and then some thought had come to her.

'I didn't get a bite to eat, there. Didn't even offer me a cup of tea. Not like here at all, but it's just as well. I had too many mince pies last night. Joe brought me a dozen that his mother baked especially for me and without thinking I ate the whole lot of them!' he told Sister Bernadette. 'But I did hear the bishop's daughters playing jazz and singing some jazz also,' he added, sensing that the Reverend Mother needed a moment to tidy her desk and make ready for the visitor. She always did that. It was one of the ways that she had to show that you were welcome and that you would have her whole attention. 'No,' he answered Sister Bernadette, he didn't know how many daughters the bishop had, but it sounded like about four. 'And,' he added, still with half an eye on the Reverend Mother who was now locking a drawer of her desk, 'he has a very splendid house indeed. Lots and lots of bedrooms, I'd say. Huge house, as big as a convent! In fact, it's called a palace,' he finished.

'Well, I never! Seems strange to have a bishop with daughters and them playing jazz in the bishop's palace!' Sister Bernadette went off happily to spread the news about the Protestant bishop's daughters to the butcher, baker and all who might appear at her back door throughout a busy day.

Patrick was left with the Reverend Mother. 'Are you all right?' He asked the question, uneasily aware that he sounded rather childlike and incompetent.

She gave him a smile, nevertheless. 'It's good to see you,' she said, somewhat surprisingly. He had expected her to deny briskly that anything was wrong. 'I was thinking of my shortcomings,' she added to his shocked surprise. Nevertheless, he pulled himself together quickly.

'I didn't know that you had any,' he said with a smile. 'You should hear what everyone says about you,' he added.

She shook her head at him. 'Ah, Patrick, I fail so often. I failed with that little boy – and such a little boy. I, we, here at the school, taught him nothing if we did not teach him that a crime should not be committed, even for a packet of chocolate sweets.'

Unbidden, he pulled out a chair and sat near to her. 'Reverend Mother, I believe that Enda didn't know what he was doing. He didn't know that he was sent to kill a man. It would have been a joke, a trick to be played upon the arch-deacon, that's what he would have been told, and if he were like most people, he wouldn't like the archdeacon much. The man was not popular. Only the bishop has a good word to say about him, and he mostly dwelt on how hardworking he was. And how he was so obliging at deputising for the bishop at those meetings that they have in Dublin. The bishop doesn't like meetings. Not good at them, he told me, but the arch-deacon very kindly took a lot of that unpleasant part of his duties from him and allowed him to meander along just chatting to members of his flock, I suppose. He told me that he didn't know how he was going to manage without the arch-deacon as the man had taken so much off his shoulders.'

The Reverend Mother had recovered her composure. She looked interested in this as she sat beside him. 'So, who will take over from the position of the archdeacon?' she asked.

'I'm not sure,' said Patrick. 'In fact, the bishop is not sure. He's a bit vague about most things. He knew about the arch-deacon's will, though. In fact, he is quite upset about that. Apparently, everything the man possessed goes to his eldest son, the Rector of Midleton, and nothing whatsoever to his youngest son, the music teacher, Mr Owen Hearn. And,' he went on, pleased to see that the Reverend Mother was inter-ested in the archdeacon's family, 'apparently, the younger son is a gifted musician, from what I have heard. He wanted to go to London, or Paris, or Leipzig to train or to play in an orchestra, not sure which, but his father threw him out when he refused to go into holy orders. Everybody seems to know about this will, otherwise I'd suspect Mr Owen Hearn of killing him to get money to go abroad. Though, I haven't ruled him out. Perhaps he did it in a fit of anger against his

father. It would have been easy for him to get little Enda to
do the job for him if he did plan to kill his father. He knew
him well. I know that as he was the one who introduced
Enda to Father O'Flynn because of his wonderful voice.
You've heard about that and about him flying on a wire while
singing a song, have you?'

The Reverend Mother nodded. Eileen told her, thought
Patrick. Eileen told everyone everything, he thought. He would
have to be very careful never to tell her anything that should
remain confidential.

'The archdeacon was apparently a rich man,' he said
hurriedly. 'He married a wife who would eventually inherit a
country house and estate. And another estate from an elderly
aunt. I'd have thought that he would want his younger son to
become a squire, or something like that, but no. Dr Scher
tells me that the Rector of Midleton has a five-year-old boy
who was the apple of his grandfather's eye, and the country
estate is for him.'

The Reverend Mother nodded. 'I see,' she said, but he
guessed that she had known all that before. 'So, the Rector
of Midleton profits from the death of his father,' she said. 'Are
you suspicious of him?'

'Well, no,' said Patrick reluctantly. 'For one thing, he was
supposed to be on very good terms with his father and his
father was very good to him, bought him a very nice house
in Midleton, just at the end of the town, where the river
widens, a beautiful and very big house according to Joe who
has seen it on his way to Youghal.'

'And, in addition, I suppose that he has an alibi,' said the
Reverend Mother, and when he looked surprised, she added,
'Christmas Eve would be a busy time for all the clergy, whether
our own church or the Anglican Church of Ireland.'

'That's right,' said Patrick, sparing a moment of admir-
ation for his former teacher's sharp mind. 'You're quite
right, Reverend Mother. They have a big, long service on
Christmas Eve in Midleton parish church. Apparently, every
child of the parish gets a chance to do a reading, sing a hymn
or recite some verses and after that they all have a present,
wrapped up and "Don't open until Christmas morning!"

written on it. And when that was all over, the rector, the archdeacon's son, had a party in the rectory for his male
parishioners. They didn't get home until near midnight, some
of the men, or so I heard from Joe. I'll check, of course, but
I'd say he's in the clear. In any case,' he added, 'he'd really
have no way of getting to know Enda and knowing that the
lad could climb like a monkey and would sell his . . . I mean
would do anything for sweets. No, I'd say he's right out of
the picture,' concluded Patrick, a depressed expression
on his face.

'And who inherits the position of archdeacon? Is it up to
the bishop? It would be in our church, though I'm sure that
there is some official process to be gone through, but, in
reality, it would be the bishop who would decide on who was
to be the next archdeacon. Apparently, salary levels in the
Church of Ireland,' said the Reverend Mother with an air of
keen interest, 'are poor for the lower positions, but excellent
for those on the upper rungs of the ladder. I cannot for the life
of me think how I came to possess that piece of information,
but I do believe it to be true,' she added.

Patrick smiled. He enjoyed talking to the Reverend Mother
when she was in one of her confiding moods. It made him
feel pleased with himself and with the status that he had
attained by being a police inspector. The hard work had been
worth it. He relished that thought almost every day of his life
and almost wished that there were more examinations to sit,
more hurdles to overcome.

'Well, there's Dean Babington, he would be next on the
list.' Patrick took his notebook from his pocket. 'Aged fifty-
five, married with five sons, who are aged between twenty
years old and seven years old.' He put down the notebook
onto his knee, keeping his finger on the page. 'I put a query
about the sons when I made out a card for him,' he said. 'I've
told you about my card system, Reverend Mother, haven't
I? Well, it did occur to me that if he had a son about Enda's
age it might help him in making friends with the little boy if
he came across him hanging around the grounds and perhaps
helping Tom Hayes, the sexton, with cutting the grass or
picking up the leaves.'

The Reverend Mother said nothing for a minute. Patrick could see that she was mulling over the idea in her mind.

'What sort of man is the dean?' she asked.

Patrick thought about it for a moment. He was always careful not to criticize any member of the religious orders in front of her, but perhaps it didn't matter if they were Protestants.

'A bit starchy, hard to talk to,' he said. 'I liked the bishop better.' He thought for another moment. 'I suppose, really, Dean Babington wouldn't be the sort of man who would be friendly with Enda, though he might have caught him climbing on top of the roof one day, I suppose. Probably wouldn't think of him as being like one of his own sons, either, I suppose,' he said and was pleased to see that the Reverend Mother gave an emphatic nod at his observation. 'And then, of course, there is the precentor. The bishop didn't seem to think that the precentor, Mr Flewett, would be interested in the position of archdeacon. He thought he might prefer to stay as choirmaster and organ player. What do you think, Reverend Mother?'

Her reply came instantly. 'The bishop is an elderly man, and I would suspect an easy-going man. May never have been particularly ambitious himself. He may well be the sort of person that is blessed with an abundance of the goods of life, and you know the old proverb, Patrick. "To them that hath, more shall be given!" He may not accurately judge those more worldly than himself. The fact that Mr Flewett is a good choirmaster, and a good musician does not, in my mind, rule him out from having secret ambitions. A man can always play the organ when he chooses, but that position of archdeacon of Cork could be a plum job in the Church of Ireland. And, of course, my dear Patrick, we must bear in mind that these men are not like the priests and canons and bishops in our own church. These are married men with wives and families, with sons for whom they are ambitious, and with a way of life in the community that demands wealth and status.'

Patrick wondered whether he could possibly open his mind to the Reverend Mother about the precentor, Mr Flewett. Men who liked little boys would not be new to her. Only a few months ago she had brought a case to his notice and the man was now languishing in prison. At the time, he had been slightly shocked and very embarrassed to hear the forthright way in which the Reverend Mother had spelled out her reasons for suspecting this man who hung around the school. She, to his shame, had known far more about the subject than he had ever learned when qualifying as a policeman. People tended to shy away from the subject, but the Reverend Mother had said to him that she feared that reticence and false modesty allowed men like that to exist and to commit their crimes. He had never forgotten that and had impressed it upon Joe, much to the embarrassment of both.

However, he thought he would say nothing now. She looked tired and he didn't want to burden her with his worries. He sought for another subject with which to end the interview.

'I wonder could you solve the puzzle of the archdeacon's missing breakfast,' he said with a slight smile.

She brightened immediately. 'That sounds most intriguing – rather like an Agatha Christie detective story. Have you heard of her? She writes about crimes which her detective, a former member of the Belgium police, solves with the greatest of ease, just by using the little grey cells in his very large brain. I shall have to lend you one. My cousin buys them for me, and I stick a plain black wrapper over it before putting it into my bookcase just so that they match the other books on my shelves, you must understand.'

Patrick smiled in answer to the joke. He was glad to think that she had some amusements in her life. 'Well, the puzzle about the secret of the missing breakfast is that Dr Scher says that the man had no breakfast. Nothing to eat since the night before, nothing until he drank the poisoned wine from the chalice. And I've never known Dr Scher to be wrong about anything. But the archdeacon's housekeeper swore that the archdeacon ate an excellent breakfast, pancake with honey and then eggs, rashers, black pudding, followed by slices of toast and washed down with a pot of coffee. So, Reverend Mother, which one of them is right? It can't be both.'

The Reverend Mother pondered over this. 'Did the housekeeper serve the breakfast herself?'

'Yes, she did, just she.'

'She saw him eat?'

Patrick cast his mind back. 'I suppose she might have, but perhaps not. She did tell us that she didn't stay in the room, said she came in and out with the dishes, just as she always does. She gave him time to finish one plateful before bringing in the next plateful, I suppose.'

The Reverend Mother looked across at him. 'Tell me, Patrick, was there a fire in the dining room? Would you know that?'

'Yes, in fact, I would, even without checking my notes. It caught my attention because she said something about the fact that he had put some more anthracite on his stove and, of course, that made me think of Dr Scher's anthracite stove.'

The Reverend Mother sat back in her chair. 'Well, that's it,' she said with a triumphant smile. 'I think I might have solved your problem for you, Patrick. The man didn't feel like eating, perhaps he had an upset stomach or perhaps he just thought he'd get the Christmas Day service over and then have a snack, have a whiskey and a mince pie, perhaps. But, of course, he didn't want to offend the kitchen after they had gone to the trouble of cooking this elaborate breakfast, so once the housekeeper left the room, he just opened the top of the stove, emptied in his plate, and then put some more anthracite on top so as to cover it up. Don't tell Sister Bernadette, but elderly people sometimes do that sort of thing.'

Patrick got to his feet with a broad smile on his face. He would have liked to have stayed longer but the Reverend Mother looked very tired and there were black shadows under her eyes. 'I'm most grateful to you,' he said earnestly. 'You are so clever, and you know so much about so many people that you can work out why they do things.' He stopped for a moment and his face became more serious. 'You've heard that Dr Scher has released the bodies. Poor little Enda! And poor Mrs O'Sullivan. My mother was saying that the other night. She said Enda is at rest, but his mother will never get over this.'

'I hope that she can be comforted, poor woman,' said the

Reverend Mother. 'Eileen is organizing a funeral,' she added. 'I think that she will make an excellent job of it. She will be in touch with you, I'm sure. She will be anxious to make sure that it will meet with your approval.'

'It's very good of her,' he said soberly. 'Eileen has a kind heart.' He hesitated for a minute, and then he said, 'It's not just that she is so clever, and I know she is clever, but she doesn't ever want to forget Barrack Street and the people there. I think that is good, don't you, Reverend Mother? I don't think she will ever change, do you?'

And then, without waiting for an answer, he slipped through the door, closed it softly after him and went as quickly as he could to the front door. He didn't want to be delayed by Sister Bernadette offering him slices of Christmas cake to take home for his supper. He had a job to do. A very small child from the Barrack Street area had been cruelly and brutally murdered and he was going to make sure that the man would never have an opportunity to commit a crime like that again.

NINE

Eileen was in a buoyant mood when she arrived at the university on the first day of opening after Christmas. She had dropped into the office of the *Cork Examiner* before coming on to the university and had had a most satisfactory conversation with one of the editors. The murder at the Church of Ireland cathedral had already been covered in full detail, but he was interested in the story of the little boy and of the elaborate plan to console his grieving mother with a funeral worthy for her little angel.

'Yes, write it all up. Sort of thing that you do well,' he said with a nod of approval. 'I think that if you make a good job of it that I can give you two slots. One about the murder on the day before – something about the police – more about the boy, of course, but just mentioning the plan for the funeral. Father O'Flynn and his players are always news. And a photographer to cover the event itself. And a piece of heart-rending writing describing the funeral from you, of course. Cloaks, did you say?'

'Made from old purple *velvet* curtains from the Imperial Hotel,' said Eileen, putting a strong emphasis on 'velvet' – a word that she loved. 'Father O'Flynn got to hear that they were having new curtains in the Imperial Hotel, and he jumped on his Indian motorbike, went straight down to the manager and had them delivered to The Loft the day after they were taken down. Well, you know what he's like – he had a group of workers turning them into cloaks and medieval headgear within a week. It's a great story, isn't it?' she added innocently, and he grinned at her.

'Don't be practising it on me. You know I have a heart of stone. You write it. We'll keep you a couple of slots,' he promised, and she went off with a smile on her face. Her scholarship paid for fees and books with something left over for food and fuel for her bike, but the *Cork Examiner* payments for articles meant that her mother could reduce the number of hours spent scrubbing out pubs. And have a few treats to make her life more interesting.

She was still smiling when she left the Aula Maxima with a couple of law books tucked under her arm and walked across the Quad to treat herself to a cup of coffee before settling down to a few hours of study. As soon as she opened the door to the students' restaurant, she could see that her lecture had not been the only one cancelled as the place was full. Every table appeared to be full and there was a rule against consuming drinks and food while standing up. 'No Loitering!' The somewhat ridiculous notice by the door admonished her and she slunk to one side of the room and hoped to avoid the gaze of the manager. She stood for a while, hoping that some group would finish up quickly before she was thrown out for loitering and then noticed that there was a spare chair available on a table where a pair of young priests were playing chess.

'You don't mind if I sit here, do you, Father?' she said to the one who was sitting back in his chair looking around, while his opponent bent over the chessboard. 'I won't interrupt you. I won't say a word. I'm just waiting for a seat.'

'You're welcome to sit down, but I'm not your father, nor anyone else's either,' he said with a radiant smile at her. 'And we always have room for a pretty girl at our table, don't we, Tom?'

'I resign,' said Tom, dramatically tipping his king over and then bowed to Eileen in a theatrical fashion. 'Welcome to our table. Did you have a good Christmas? You're studying law, aren't you? We've noticed you, haven't we, Bob? We always have our eyes open for the prettiest girls.'

His superior would not like the sound of that, thought Eileen taking the empty chair and then someone switched on the overhead lights, and she saw the edging of grey shirts beneath the familiar 'dog' collars. 'Oh, you're . . . Protestants, Church of Ireland clergymen, are you?' she said, swallowing the word 'just'. 'I was wondering . . .'

They didn't ask what she was wondering about, and she felt a little embarrassed. 'I'm Eileen MacSwiney,' she said hastily. 'I'm doing first year law.'

'I know,' said the one called Bob. 'I've seen you around. We're both doing post-grad work in philosophy and law. At least we do a bit of law, sometimes. I've seen you coming out of one of the lecture rooms. Must take more of an interest in law, mustn't we, Tom?'

The ordinary student flirtations seemed odd when coming from clergymen wearing dog collars, but then Eileen forgot her embarrassment. 'I know you,' she said to Bob. 'I've seen your face on the *Cork Examiner*. It was a group photograph. You're from the P . . . Church of Ireland cathedral, aren't you? It was an old photograph, but they dug it up out of some drawer or other after all the fuss about the murder. You're all lined up in front of the steps going down to your organ. Weird to have an organ underground, but there you are. I suppose different churches; different customs.'

'Taken the time that there was an appeal for funds for repairing the organ. I remember that photo. The precentor, Mr Flewett, that's our organ player, got us all lined up for a photo. I suppose that they dug it up because of our murder. Oh, must you go, Tom? What a shame. Still . . . duty calls!'

Eileen was very taken aback. Tom had been blatantly told to clear off and had quickly taken himself away and she was left alone with this man, dressed so like a priest that she felt embarrassed. It was so obvious that he fancied her! She was well used to university students, and their flirtatious ways, but the dog collar made the situation decidedly odd.

'Do you play chess?' he asked.

'No,' she said firmly. His name had come back to her. Bob Webster, captain of the Cork University Chess Team. The photo of the team had been up in the entrance porch to the Aula Max. She did play a little chess, but not to his standard. 'Just know the moves,' she added, afraid that he might have seen her play with one of the lads from her law class.

'Give you a queen for odds,' he said instantly and before she could object, he had put the board between them and removed his own queen. Eileen bit her lip, but she seldom refused a challenge, so cautiously she moved her pawn to king four. Anyway, it seemed more respectable to be playing chess than to be parrying his efforts to flirt with her. I owe it to Patrick to get to know something about the blokes in the cathedral, she told herself. He'll be a bit out of his depth with these posh-spoken Protestants. I'll see if I can get a bit of information out of this fellow once he beats me.

A clever chess player, she thought. He was trying to panic her by moving fast – barely a second's thought before he pushed out his pawns, and then shot his bishop into a threatening position. It was tempting to emulate him but deliberately she slowed down to a snail's pace. He was trying to push her into reckless, panic-driven moves. And she was determined not to allow him. He would beat her, despite the generous odds, but that should not mean that he was able to lure her into an indiscretion. She could see what he was doing. Developing his pawns so that he could replace his missing queen. She ignored the lures and concentrated on getting her king castled into safety and then on developing a solid defence of her back rows.

'Doing anything nice on New Year's Evening,' he asked, casually shoving out another pawn to add to the formidable slanting line which he had built up.

'No,' she said curtly. The talking could come later. She would be finished once he managed to get a supported pawn into her half of the board. A plan began to evolve in her mind. Yes, she could play slowly and cautiously, taking a long time over every move and making no move to attack. Throwing all her efforts into the defence might be the safest thing to do, but Eileen seldom went for the safe option. A plan began to evolve in her mind. After all a queen was very substantial odds. Surely even an inexperienced player like herself could manage to win if she had a queen, the most valuable piece on the board, and he had none. But wouldn't her advantage be even greater if the number of pieces were reduced? Quickly she swooped down with her bishop and seized his knight. He shrugged his shoulders, took her bishop with a pawn. Still nine points in advance, she thought. A bishop and a knight were worth the same, so she had not altered the odds.

Now she began to get a bit excited. Bit by bit she had manoeuvred her pieces to set up a situation where she could do apparently meaningless swaps of equally valued pieces. The rooks she left in position so that they could guard her vulnerable back row and stop him queening one of his wretched little pawns. And her valuable queen stood solidly in position beside her king.

She leaned across and this time she sacrificed a knight to break up his solid, slanting line of pawns. He shrugged as he accepted another apparently meaningless swap.

'You're tired of life,' he said. 'That must be it. It couldn't be that you are tired of me, could it?'

She didn't reply. Against all the rules she had left most of her pawns untouched, just two small slots for the bishops to slide out to join the active, leaping knights. The other six pawns and the two rooks had stayed in their original positions, guarding the eight squares where one of his pawns could be transformed into a queen.

Quite a crowd had begun to gather. A few broad grins from the chess players as they looked at her chaotic development. Eileen didn't care what they thought. She had him rattled. She looked across at the smooth, cleanly shaven face and the well-groomed head of blond hair and wondered whether he had guessed her strategy. Probably, she thought. But could he, at this stage of the game, do anything about it? That was the question. She was playing a waiting game, now idly moving her queen to the second row, and then just as idly moving it back beside her king again.

He was thinking hard, deciding to go for the kill. Taking out his rooks, positioning them, one behind the other, directed at her king.

There was a slight stir in the audience. He had slowed down, now thinking out each move and she could guess what he intended. His rooks and his pawns would set up an attack. And, incautiously, he had now brought his king into play also. Interesting fellow, she thought, examining the smooth, expressionless face opposite to her own. She moved the queen into the bishop's space and looked challengingly at him. It was dreadfully bad play – even someone as inexperienced as she knew that. One should never make a meaningless move, but she was playing a game of wits rather than chess. Now she fiercely wished to avoid defeat at his hands. Once again, she performed the meaningless movement with her queen.

Suddenly he laughed aloud. Threw back his head and displayed a magnificent set of teeth.

'Oh, come on! I give up! Offer you a draw, what about that?'

'Play on,' said Eileen, sitting very still, very upright, and not lifting her eyes from the board. Suddenly she had an idea. Yes. Now her queen and her rooks could mount a fatal attack.

'Well,' he said five minutes later as he toppled his king and reached across to shake her by the hand. 'I underestimated you seriously. You must join the chess club. Cork could be the first university to field a woman player in the annual inter-universities event.'

'I'll think about it,' said Eileen getting to her feet, but she wondered where she could find the time. She didn't like to turn him down though and smiled in a friendly fashion as he rose to his feet, leaving the chessboard to another pair and walked with her through the restaurant and across the quad to the porter's office.

'I leave my bike here. The porter keeps an eye on it for me,' she said in a casual fashion as she undid the padlock. When she looked up, she would see an expression of horror on his face, she guessed, but she was wrong. He was smiling at her in quite an attractive fashion.

'I have a couple of tickets for the New Year dance in the Rushbrooke Tennis Club tonight. Like to go?'

'Goodness,' she said. 'Are you allowed? I'm a Catholic, you know. At least a sort of one,' she amended rather guiltily.

'Oh, the bishop is very broad-minded,' he assured her. 'And you are a fellow student.'

'I don't possess a ballgown,' she said bluntly.

'Doesn't matter,' he said. 'Who cares? Wear what you like! These leather boots are quite attractive. Quite informal, just a hop. Jazz evening, really.'

Eileen thought about it. It would be a great opportunity to probe into the background of all those quite alien people in the cathedral. Patrick had looked very drawn and anxious when she had seen him last. He could do with a bit of help from her brains. 'O.K.' she said casually. 'I'm very keen on jazz. Not so keen on tennis clubs, but I'll survive it. What time does it start?'

'Eight o'clock,' he said. 'May I call for you?'

'God! Don't do that!' she exclaimed. 'What would the neighbours say? I'd never live it down. See you at eight. Don't wait outside in case it's cold and wet. I'll find you if you are somewhere near the lobby. Thanks for the game.'

Patrick wasn't busy, thought Joe, meeting Eileen in the entrance to the police station. He'd check and be back in seconds, he assured her, and he was as good as his word.

'How is he?' she asked as they went down the corridor together.

Joe took a quick look around, pursed his lips and then said in a low voice, 'Worried!'

'Tell me something new,' said Eileen in exasperated tones. 'Even when I was seven years old, I used to think that he looked worried. Used to see him walking up Barrack Street with a big bag of books on his back and a really worried look on his face. I used to be sorry for him. The other boys seemed to have more fun, thumping each other, throwing stones at policemen, "waxing a gazza" and all that sort of thing.'

'What on earth is waxing a gazza?' asked Joe with a broad grin. He didn't wait for an answer but tapped on the door and threw it open so that Eileen could enter.

'God, that's an ignorant langer you have there, Patrick,' she said. 'Doesn't know what waxing a gazza means. Don't suppose that he has ever climbed a gas pole in his life, what do you think?'

Patrick was looking worried, she thought. He essayed a smile at her comment, but it was a reluctant effort and he had dark shadows under his eyes, and she could tell from the appearance of his hair that he had been running his fingers through it. It was as she had thought. This job wasn't suiting him. She had seen him calm a riot down on the docks and had been impressed by the way that he had shown himself to be relaxed and authoritative. But this business with the Protestant cathedral was proving a bit outside his usual competence. Eagerly she leaned forward.

'Guess who I've been playing chess with down at the university,' she said. 'With a Protestant clergyman! Would you believe it?'

'Who won?' Patrick had a weary sound to his voice and his expression was of someone trying to be polite.

'Never mind that. Wait till you hear. It was one of guys from the cathedral. He's the deacon there. A fellow called Bob Webster. He's a deacon, whatever that is.'

'Bottom of the list in order of status,' said Patrick, fingering through a box of cards that sat prominently on his desk. 'It goes bishop, archdeacon – though he's dead – then the dean who is a Dr Babington, a very old man, and then it's the precentor, Mr Flewett, he's the choirmaster and the organ player. And then comes the canon, Mr Wilson, another elderly man and then the deacon, the man that you met. He's a mister also. Mr Webster.'

'Well, he's pretty sure to be a Dr Webster by this time next month. He's already had a first honours for his thesis and he just needs to be formally passed and conferred with his doctorate next month,' said Eileen, feeling proud of herself that she was being such a help to him. She leaned across the desk, widened her eyes and said emphatically, 'And I'll tell you something, Patrick. If I'm any judge of men, and you can take it that I've had plenty of experience in that direction – well, that fellow would end up being the pope if he wasn't a Protestant. I've been listening to him talk and I've watched the way that he plays chess, and that fellow is as ambitious as Mark Anthony in *Julius Caesar*.'

He said nothing to this, so she went on. He was pretty stubborn, and she had to convince him that she knew what she was talking about. 'Listen to me, Patrick,' she said earnestly. 'I've sat for over an hour, as close to that man as I am to you, and I can tell you that Mr, or Dr Webster is mad for domination and power. I can tell by the way that he handles his chess pieces,' she ended. She wasn't too sure about the significance of her last statement, but she thought that it sounded rather good and should impress Patrick. She leaned back, saying as impressively as she could, 'Look at your own notes, Patrick, you've got it all written down there. The archdeacon gets murdered and who will be the next archdeacon? Well, not the dean; he's as old as the hills. I've seen him doddering around, toddling up and down Bishop Street for his daily exercise. Not Canon Wilson. I met him once and I thought he was a bit senile. Not Mr Flewett, the Precentor, I'd guess. That's a man who lives for music. I've seen him up at The Loft when they were doing *The Tempest*. Father O'Flynn introduced him. You should hear him talk about the wonderful organ in the cathedral and how he gets boys to sing A flat and then to sing A double flat – something like that, anyway. That man loves his job. I'd say that if you offered him a new job, he'd turn it down. Not an ambitious type either. A sort of ladylike fellow, very, very Church of Ireland, if you know what I mean. But Bob Webster, now he's a different kettle of fish. You can take my word for it. I've played chess with him and I know the man. Mad ambitious, I'd put him down as. The sort of fellow that doesn't like to be beaten for anything. Anyway,' she finished, conscious of a disappointing lack of appreciation from Patrick, 'anyway, I'm going to the New Year Jazz dance in Rushbrooke Tennis Club with him, and I'll be able to tell you more about him afterwards.'

'Well, it's very kind of you, Eileen,' said Patrick in what she recognized as his most starchy manner. 'Now, if you'll excuse me, I'd better get on with my work.'

He made a pretence of studying his cards and then got to his feet and went over to the bookcase and took down an ancient and slightly mildewed volume bounded in an unpleasant shade of dirty green and placed it in front of him. While she sat wondering what to say to convince him that she could be of use, he pulled out the desk drawer with a jerk, tore up a couple of pieces of fawn-coloured paper and then deliberately opened the volume with a rather obviously feigned expression of interest, only raising his head when there was a knock on the door and Joe stuck his head in.

'Sorry, Patrick,' he said. 'The superintendent would like to have a word with you when you have a minute. He's had the archbishop of Dublin on the phone about the murder.'

Patrick, Eileen noticed, got instantly to his feet. Deliberately she took her lipstick from her handbag and went over to the small mirror which hung beside the bookcase. Carefully and slowly, she outlined her lips and watched him in the mirror as, indecisively, he fiddled with a few pens, selected one, went towards the door and said over his shoulder, 'You'll be able to see yourself out, Eileen, will you? I may be some time.'

'Sure, Patrick,' she said casually. 'Don't you worry about me. I know my way around this barracks.'

As soon as they both had gone, she went across to the wastepaper basket and took out the torn-up pieces of fawn-coloured paper. As she had feared, they were tickets. Two tickets for a New Year Evening dance in the Rushbrooke Tennis Club. She looked at them with a grimace. Why on earth had Patrick bought tickets to a dance at that incredibly snobbish place? She could not escape the conviction that he had intended to ask her and might have done so if she had not mentioned Bob Webster's invitation. Did she really think that she would have enjoyed it? And then she saw the price and could feel herself flush with embarrassment as she dropped the ripped tickets back into the basket.

Quietly she stole out of the room and closed the door with the smallest of clicks.

TEN

S lightly guiltily, on the evening before the funeral of little
Enda, the Reverend Mother prayed for a fine day. She
had been to so many funerals and most of them seemed
to have had additional sadness poured upon them from the
heavens. When she got up at her usual early hour she went
straight to the window. Not raining, thank God, but a thick,
heavy mist. Nothing unusual about that, but she prayed that
it might be lifted before the funeral for the little boy, and she
continued that prayer while she washed and dressed and
allowed it to stay in her mind during the morning mass in the
convent chapel.

But, to no avail. The fog was still as heavy and thick as
ever when she emerged from the chapel. Not a light grey mist
such as could be seen by the sea, but a Cork city fog: dark
yellow, smelling of the river, of the local gasworks and satur-
ated with flecks of pollution. The Reverend Mother grimly
went through the morning's work while using every spare
second to bombard heaven with her prayers, but the fog, if
anything, grew thicker as the day progressed. By the time
that the South Chapel bell sounded the hour of two, she had
begun to despair. She leafed through her well-worn copy of
the thoughts of her patron saint, Thomas Aquinas, but the
page that she opened said blandly, '*Quidquid recipitur ad
modum recipientis recipitur*', and she shut it again with a
moment of irritation. So very like a man to shift the blame
onto the shoulders of the recipient! Misunderstandings,
she told herself firmly, would not occur if everyone took the
trouble to speak clearly and with a view to conveying meaning
rather than to obscuring meaning. Perhaps, she thought, it
might be a good conversation point at the next meeting called
by their own bishop, ostensibly to hear the views of the clergy
within his jurisdiction.

She took her well-worn umbrella from its place on her study

wall and set off on the short walk to the church. All very well for Aquinas to preach that whatever is received is in accordance with the nature of the recipient. The learned saint didn't live in Cork, but in the sun-drenched south of Italy. She wondered how cheerful he would be if his plans were ruined by a fog like that.

The church was virtually empty, confirming her worst fears. Two people only. Mrs O'Sullivan, weeping in the front seat, and the sexton, Tom Hayes, discreetly huddled into the corner of the seat by the door. She wondered whether to go up to the front seat and to kneel beside Mrs O'Sullivan, but then she decided that this would only embarrass the woman and so went to her usual seat towards the end of the church.

The coffin was still open. A beautiful little coffin lined with white velvet. Without hesitation the Reverend Mother had spent the money handed to her by the bishop, Dr Thompson, contributed by his parishioners, to purchase this for the funeral and to make sure that it was delivered in plenty of time to the undertaker. She salved her conscience, which had told her that the money was meant for Mrs O'Sullivan, by telling herself that the relatively small sum would not be enough to make any difference to the woman's material circumstances and would probably be spent drowning her sorrows in the nearest public house. The alcohol would do her nothing but harm, but the memory of her little angel in his beautiful coffin might help to soften her grief. And a good funeral, of course.

But would the boys and girls from Shandon come down onto the flat of the city in this thick fog? Right through the mass, as the priest's words echoed in the unusually empty church, the Reverend Mother, to her shame, said few prayers, but worried intensely about what was to come afterwards.

But she need not have done so. No sooner had the tiny congregation risen to their feet for the recital of the last gospel, than a sound of a motorbike driven at high speed came through the door behind her. And then a loud backfire and various noises that she associated with the decrepit vans used by small businesses and shops.

The door behind her swung open, letting in a strong smell of mingled city fog and pungent exhaust fumes. A moment later, Father O'Flynn inserted himself into the pew beside her as she stood for the last gospel.

'Sorry,' he said into her ear. 'One of these days when everything goes wrong. Van wouldn't start, terrible fog, accident on North Gate bridge. I've told the boys and girls what to do. Don't worry; we'll put on a good show.'

The Reverend Mother nodded very slightly. She was conscious that, although she had placed herself in the back row, she had been quite conspicuous in this remarkably empty church. The priest seemed to be directing most of his words down to herself which had rather embarrassed her but now Father O'Flynn had joined her, and both made the *Deo Gratias* response in loud, clear tones.

And then the miracle began. The church doors behind them were opened wide, flung open and then there was a noise of feet, a very disciplined and deliberate tramping on the stone tiles. Father O'Flynn beckoned to the leaders, three large well-grown boys, wearing Farranferris School blazers and the four of them slipped up the side aisle. But the Reverend Mother's eyes were on the centre aisle. Sixteen boys and girls, all wearing, over their school blazers, purple velvet cloaks; quite short cloaks, but the beauty of the velvet was enhanced by the small lighted bowl that each held before them. Nightlights, not candles, hoped the Reverend Mother looking at the velvet cloaks, but for once worries slipped from her mind and she blessed Father O'Flynn as she saw how reverently he and the three scholars lifted the tiny coffin to their shoulders. The priest on the altar hastily whispered to the solitary altar boy and then he walked behind the four bearers swinging the single chain thurible and broadcasting the sweet smell of incense through the almost empty church, while the boys and girls, lining the middle aisle, sang a two-part arrangement of '*Nunc dimittis servum tuum, Domine*' as the small coffin, followed by the weeping mother, went down the aisle.

The fog was still thick and heavy when the Reverend Mother slipped out of the back door after all, including the celebrating priest, had left the church. By the time that she emerged, the coffin bearers had halted in the centre of the church yard and Eileen was efficiently stage-managing everything, with one *Cork Examiner* photographer standing near to the gate and another recklessly perched upon the wall. Mrs O'Sullivan had stopped crying and was standing behind the small, closed coffin, dry-eyed and bewildered, as she looked at the guard of honour of those cloaked and gowned singers paying homage to her little son.

'That was lovely, most moving,' said the Reverend Mother to Father O'Flynn. She spoke in her usual clear and carrying tones, but not one of the medieval mourners turned a head in her direction. Dressed in their purple velvet medieval bonnets and cloaks they formed a disciplined line behind the tiny coffin. And Mrs O'Sullivan humbly stood, silent and very still, tears running down her cheeks.

'Good youngsters, aren't they?' Father O'Flynn surveyed his troupe and then nodded with satisfaction. A few faces had appeared outside the railings around the church.

'Time for another hymn, give the crowd a time to gather, let the word spread, don't you think?' he said.

He was right. Children had now gathered outside on the pavement and a few more women with them. Father O'Flynn and his disciplined choir took no notice. He took a small triangle from his pocket, gave them a note and then in a full and melodious baritone began to sing, 'Holy, holy . . .' and the choir joined in singing in parts in a most accomplished way.

The Reverend Mother narrowed her eyes at the crowd beginning to gather and then slipped away, going unobtrusively toward a small side gate. She had recognized one of the onlookers. Mrs O'Connor was a gossip and a know-all, but she had a kind heart and a large brood of children. A word in her ear was sufficient. Mrs O'Connor took on the stage management. Quick whispers to a few other women and boldly they came through the small side gate and lined up behind the choir. To the Reverend Mother's satisfaction, Mrs O'Connor seized the weeping mother by the arm and then another woman, emboldened by that action, went to the other side and took the other arm and escorted her to a place

behind the small coffin. The *Cork Examiner* photographer
took another few photographs with a series of clicks as Mrs
O'Connor, overcome by the solemnity, mopped her eyes with
her shawl and her numerous progeny looked uncertainly at
each other and then very solemnly at the camera. The choir
finished their hymn. There was a moment's silence. One of
the altar boys slipped back into the church and the solemn
toning of the bell began. Seven strokes and then silence.

The undertaker's black car began to move and the choir,
with no direction from Father O'Flynn, began to sing '*Libera
nos, Domine . . .*'

What a good service the church did in laying a solid ground
of Latin for the children of this most religious country by this
memorization of Latin hymns and Latin prayers from an early
age, thought the Reverend Mother. For the children of those
possessing the means of sending their children to secondary
school, she amended in her thoughts. During all her years of
teaching only one pupil, Eileen, was sufficiently advanced to
be taught Latin. For the rest, she had to be content to teach
them to read and to write and enough elementary arithmetic
to enable them to get a job in a shop or a market stall. For a
moment, she envied Father O'Flynn and was even conscious
of a feeling of annoyance and even jealousy, she had to admit.

Yes, he had done wonders with getting these young people
to have confidence in themselves, teaching them to love
Shakespeare and to know enormous chunks of the plays off
by heart to a degree where they would probably never forget
the words and the iambic pentameter rhythms of the poetry
– but he started with the already literate and the slightly
privileged.

Nevertheless, there was a chance that she had become too
defeated, begun to have a '*cui bono*' attitude, to be more and
more reluctant to try something new, to allow that fatal thought
of 'what's the good?' to prevent trying something new.

Children's memories could be trained. She knew that. They
learned the words of popular songs from America and many
of those songs had words that were incomprehensible to slum
children on the island of Ireland. Little Enda had, after all,
with the incentive of flying high above the stage, learned to

sing 'Full fathom five, thy father lies' and she could be sure that, if he had lived, the word 'fathom' would have stayed in his memory.

I shall read the children the witches' chant from *Macbeth* on Monday and any child who can remember it on Friday afternoon shall have a sweet, she promised herself and looked speculatively at the sweet factory van from Shannon Street. Was there any chance that she might be able to negotiate a cut price from them?

'Do you think that my motorbike will be safe if I leave it here?' asked Father O'Flynn in her ear. 'I wouldn't like my beloved Indian to be stolen,' he added.

'No, I'm afraid that it would not be safe,' she said bluntly. 'Why don't you let the funeral go ahead and then walk back with me to the convent and leave it behind a locked gate. You can collect it after the burial. What about the man with the van?'

'He's got a few deliveries to make,' said Father O'Flynn. 'Don't worry about him. And don't worry about the funeral. All is well. More people turning up by the minute.'

He spoke the truth. The word had got around, and people were erupting from all the surrounding lanes. The usual funeral, but there was an undertone of anger. The Reverend Mother winced slightly as the words 'them Proddies killed him; poor little mite' could be heard swirling around.

'Oh dear,' she said. 'I hope that there won't be trouble tonight. I think I should telephone Inspector Cashman and warn him.'

'I'll get them singing again,' said Father O'Flynn, responding instantly to her worries. 'That'll distract them. You won't mind standing guard over the Indian for a few minutes, Reverend Mother? I'll send Johnny Twomey back to you. He's a good lad – you should have seen his Falstaff! – but he's no great singer. He'll walk back with you, and you can show him where to put the bike and tell him how to catch up with the funeral.'

Father O'Flynn was gone almost before he had finished speaking. With a few long strides he reached the top of the line of cloaked and bonneted mourners and a minute later

the young strong voices filled the air with the rather catchy
tune of 'Glory, glory . . .'

He was right. By the time that the boy named Johnny
Twomey had reached her, the Reverend Mother could hear
that high-pitched women's voices had joined in with the
familiar sounds of a hymn, well-practised by all who attended
weekly high mass.

She stayed where she was, though. That motorbike was
probably valuable and although Father O'Flynn seemed to
place perfect trust in his players, she couldn't be sure that the
boy might feel like taking an illicit ride on the machine if no
adult were present.

'Tell me what you think of Falstaff – I hear you played him
in one of Father O'Flynn's productions?' she asked when a
very plump and rather spotty youth arrived at her side.

'Well,' he said without a hint of shyness, 'Father O'Flynn
gave me a choice of which way to play him. We had a few
chats about it. Father O'Flynn said that he had seen someone
called Irving play him as a clown and that it had gone
down well with the audience, but that I could make up my
mind. We had quite a session looking through the speeches
and I thought I'd play him more like a bit of a swine, milking
Prince Hal for all that he could get out of him. Don't know
whether I was any good, or not,' he added modestly, walking
at her side down Cove Street.

'Well, Father O'Flynn told me that you were excellent,' she
said encouragingly. 'What else have you played?'

He was articulate and full of stories. She listened with
interest and realized that the Shakespearean club filled most
of the evenings and Saturdays for him and for his friends. 'A
great laugh!' was the way that he summed up Father O'Flynn
as he told how the priest would say the lines in a rich, sing-
song Cork accent and then change over into English. The
priest, she thought, had a magnetic quality, the streets were
ringing with the sound of voices singing. The tall derelict
Georgian terraced houses on Cove Street were spewing forth
crowds of people. Some spared a moment to give a puzzled
glance at the Reverend Mother walking along beside a boy
and the notorious Indian motorbike, but most were rushing to

join the funeral and to get their picture in the *Cork Examiner*.
Mrs O'Sullivan was going to have a funeral for her little angel
which would live in the annals of Cork history.

What was to become of her once the euphoria of the day
began to die away? Well, thought the Reverend Mother, I
must not forget about her, but she wondered how much she
could manage to achieve. She felt slightly humbled by the
achievements of Father O'Flynn. Perhaps, she thought, I
spread myself too thin. I have too many aims. I am too
available to all, too anxious to make a success of too many
different projects.

Once Johnny Twomey had selected a suitable spot for the
motorbike, and had rejected her offer of refreshments, returning to join his friends in the St Mary's of the Isle graveyard,
the Reverend Mother went indoors to phone Patrick and alert
him to the possibility of some bad feeling arising from the
death of a south-side child in the Protestant cathedral.

Patrick thanked her very politely, though he told her that
he already had a man patrolling the area, had, indeed, fore-
cast the possibility of bad feeling. He sounded depressed,
dispirited, she thought with a measure of surprise. Patrick
generally was at his ease with dealing with these sudden
upsurges of sectarian and political bad feelings. Nevertheless,
she had done her duty and so when he had put down the
phone, she summoned the lady in the telephone exchange
with a few quick jabs on the bar of the phone.

'Could you get me Bishop Thompson's telephone number,
please?' she asked and then braced herself. This would arouse
great interest in the telephone exchange. She could just
imagine the whispered conversations amongst the ladies there:
'Ye'll never guess who *she* wanted to speak to!'

'Lovely funeral for that little boy, Reverend Mother,' said
the telephone exchange voice politely, and despite her depression the Reverend Mother smiled to herself. How on earth did
a woman who was immured within the telephone exchange
from eight o'clock in the morning manage to find out what
was going on at the other side of the city? She murmured
something but Miss O'Shea was in full flood, had memorized
every detail from her callers.

'And Father O'Flynn down there with his players! And the *Cork Examiner*, so they do be telling me,' finished Miss O'Shea, in a lapse from her usual gentile mode of speaking into the more familiar language of her Gurranabraher youth.

'Yes, I'm just about to have a word with Dr Thompson about it,' hinted the Reverend Mother with an eye on the clock that ordained the wall of the corridor, placed there by order of her own bishop who, though he had reluctantly agreed to the installation of telephones in schools and convents under his care, had made it clear that bills would be scrutinized carefully for extravagance.

'I'm afraid that you're not going to be lucky, Reverend Mother,' said Miss O'Shea. 'I've just had Miss O'Donovan on the phone, and she was talking about seeing the Protestant bishop in the bank. He'd never be home yet. But I'll tell you what I'll do, I'll put you through to their canon, Canon Babington. I'll get his number for you in a jiffy,' said the helpful lady.

The canon, however, like the bishop, was out – had gone to visit a friend, apparently. The Reverend Mother quickly agreed to talk to Mrs Babington and allow Miss O'Shea to go on with her self-imposed job of passing the news around Cork. If the funeral were stale news, at least the Reverend Mother of St Mary's of the Isle, and the Protestant bishop being on telephone-calling terms would provide an interesting snippet of gossip.

Mrs Babington, thought the Reverend Mother, as she put down the phone after a brief message, had sounded rather young. But the man himself, from what she had seen on Christmas morning, had looked to be in his late sixties. And surely that had been the sound of a very young child calling 'Mummy' in the background. Intrigued, the Reverend Mother allowed a quarter of an hour to elapse to avoid stirring up Miss O'Shea's curiosity and spurring her to make connections, and then she phoned her cousin, Lucy.

She would, she told Lucy, now be available for family visits – whenever it suited her cousin and heard with satisfaction that Lucy would be with her at three o'clock in the afternoon.

ELEVEN

Father O'Flynn's motorbike had been removed from under Sister Bernadette's watchful eye before Lucy arrived, driven by her chauffeur. The Reverend Mother was sorry that she had not had the opportunity of thanking Father O'Flynn and complimenting him once more upon the good manners and talent of his pupils. In fact, she was quite sorry that she had not been able to thank the young people individually and express her appreciation of the giving up of precious free time and of the beauty of their singing. She sincerely hoped that their pictures in the paper would have been a slight recompense. Nevertheless, she could not neglect her community of nuns. The funeral of the child had been dealt with successfully and this time of the year, with all the Christmas celebrations, could be a source of depression for some of the nuns and she made sure to provide a happy atmosphere and a few treats to fill the gap between Christmas Day and the beginning of the new school term.

Lucy, of course, knew all about the funeral. 'Heard it on the radio,' she said as she kissed her cousin and wished her a happy new year. 'Yes, indeed, they even recorded the singing, and I must say that it sounded beautiful, most professional. According to the announcer, there was a dead silence when they sang the '*Nunc dimittis*' as the body was being lowered into the grave. Beautifully sung; poor little fellow!' said Lucy, dabbing her eyes with a lace-trimmed handkerchief.

The Reverend Mother thought about this. That must always be the most poignant moment for any mother, she had often felt. And Mrs O'Sullivan had only the one child. She hoped and prayed that the elaborate funeral, the velvet-cloaked mourners, and the beautiful singing had softened the edge of her anguish.

And she breathed another prayer that God had received the

unstained soul of the small boy who yet had not made his
Holy Communion and First Confession and so was deemed,
by Church and State, to be guiltless of any crime that he may
have been inveigled into committing.

His murderer, however, was guilty of the most horrendous
of crimes and deserved no mercy so she turned her attention
to that matter as soon as she had made all the usual enquiries
about her cousin's daughters and their increasing offspring.
She listened with interest to Lucy's recital of the number of
parties which she and Rupert had attended in the last few
weeks, exclaimed at familiar names, and noted that one had
been to the Cork Golf Club on Little Island.

'Tell me, Lucy, do you, or Rupert, ever come across any of
the Church of Ireland clergy?' she enquired, and was not
surprised to hear that the murdered man, the archdeacon, the
dean, Dr Babington, and Canon Wilson all played golf and
not surprised, either, to have to listen to another story about
how the archdeacon had cheated at golf and was generally
considered to be a most unpleasant man. The dean, Dr
Babington, was most popular, and Canon Wilson also,
according to Lucy who quoted her husband's view that both
were gentlemen and were rather ashamed of the bad manners
shown by the archdeacon.

'Mortified when that story about cheating got out,' said
Lucy with relish. 'People sidled away from the archdeacon,
didn't want to play with him and so the other two were
often forced to include him in a threesome and, according
to Rupert, you could see that they were embarrassed by him.
Rupert was telling me a funny story about how once Frank
Babington accepted a lift from the archdeacon and got so
sick of the way he was talking about their bishop, saying
how hopeless the bishop was at his job, that when the car
slowed to a stop at the Grand Parade junction Frank just
got out, slammed the door and walked the rest of the way
home. And the funny thing was that the archdeacon never
mentioned it, never asked him where he had got to, and
Frank Babington told everyone that he guessed the archdeacon just went on talking and never noticed that his
passenger had disappeared.'

'What about social events at the golf club?' asked the Reverend Mother. 'Did the archdeacon turn up?'

Lucy made a face. 'Unfortunately, yes,' she said. 'Of course, he is a widower and that made things difficult. No hesitation in asking other men's wives or partners to dance and so some poor man had to stand at the side just because he was too lazy, or too mean, to bring a partner. Monopolized Frank Babington's wife, his second wife, of course; very, very pretty girl, very dishy, and they have only been married for a couple of years.'

'Oddly enough, I've just spoken with her, left a message for the bishop. And I did think that her voice and manner – yes, I did think that she sounded rather young,' said the Reverend Mother with interest. 'And I thought that I heard a child in the background.'

'That's right,' said Lucy with a chuckle. 'They laugh about it at the golf club, Rupert tells me. The dean had four children, all boys, by his first wife, and now he seems to be starting all over again. I hear that she's pregnant for the second time. They call him "Go forth and multiply" – you know what men are like for silly jokes! Expensive for him! The first lot all went to school in England and that must have cost him a lot in boarding school fees as well as travel and the extras that children nowadays seem to need.'

'You surprise me,' said the Reverend Mother, thinking back to the white-haired figure that she had seen in the cathedral on Christmas morning. 'Isn't he a bit old?'

'He looks older than he is, I think,' said Lucy. 'Prematurely grey, I would think. Very vigorous on the golf course. I've watched Rupert play with him, and poor old Rupe was worn out because Frank, as soon as he picks his ball out from that little hole, just runs to the next tee, not just the usual gentlemanly stroll and chat that Rupert favours. He plays golf at high speed, and I've seen him down in Crosshaven, they have a house there, on top of the cliff, and I've seen him swimming with his older sons and yachting with them as well.'

The Reverend Mother considered Lucy's words. She had built up quite a picture of the man. In her mind, the rather distant figure of an elderly Dean Babington had turned into a man of vigour, an energetic golfer, swimmer and yachtsman, a good father for his first family, sent them to expensive boarding schools in England, had a yacht for their amusement, a house by the sea.

'Tell me, Lucy,' she said aloud, 'do they get very well paid, these Church of Ireland clergy? I'm surprised that he can afford all that – boarding school fees, yacht, house by the sea, golf club fees and I suppose all the trappings that go with that lifestyle,' she ended.

'I don't suppose that he can afford all of that out of his salary,' said Lucy. 'Rupert told me that Church of Ireland bishops get well paid and the archdeacons, but not anything below that. Canon Wilson is a bachelor, of course, and so he should be able to manage fine on what the church pays him. I seem to remember that Rupert said something once about Jack Wilson not being as well off as Frank Babington, but that he lived with his mother and so had more spare cash. But now that you mention it, Frank Babington would have had enormously more outgoings than Jack Wilson. Children are expensive, especially boys as it is so important for their futures to send them to the right sort of schools.' Lucy thought about it for a moment and then nodded. 'I remember now. Of course, his first wife was very well off. She was the Honourable something or other. Inherited quite an estate in England. Somebody told me that he's had the income, or is it the benefits, from the estate even after her death until the eldest boy reaches twenty-one, which I think is in a few months' time. But then everything will go to the lad and Frank Babington will be in a bit of a pickle with three of his boys from his first marriage still at school and the second oldest at university in Oxford. He'll have to cut his coat according to his cloth then, particularly as he seems about to embark upon a new set of boys,' finished Lucy.

'But he still plays golf and yachts, from what you say,' said the Reverend Mother. 'Lives like a titled gentleman, or a bishop,' she added, watching Lucy's face.

'Well, he'll probably be a bishop one of these days,' said Lucy. 'Dr Thompson is quite elderly, and someone told me that his heart is not too good. No, Frank Babington would be the obvious choice, now.'

'Especially now that the archdeacon is dead,' said the Reverend Mother with emphasis on the word 'now'.

'You nuns have such terribly suspicious minds,' said Lucy. 'I've noticed that. You invariably think the worst of everyone. Now don't deny it. I can see the way that brain of yours is working. You think that he killed the archdeacon first, to clear the way, and then he will kill the nice old bishop, a man that he likes and admires, just because he wants his job, isn't that it?'

The Reverend Mother sighed. There was, perhaps, truth in Lucy's accusation. Perhaps she did look for the worst in people. She had been over fifty years in the convent, but it had not been a sheltered life. Human misdemeanours, cruelty, criminality, corruption, and delinquency had been part of her daily life. Her earnest endeavour had been to salvage some children from this mire of evil. With some she had just about succeeded, with others she had failed and with a small proportion, like Eileen, and indeed Patrick, she felt that she may have helped to make a difference in their lives which were now successful and fulfilling. And, she reflected, thinking now of Patrick, from time to time she could still lend a helping hand. This murder of an archdeacon would be a difficult but most important case to solve. There was little doubt in her mind that his superiors in Dublin would be keeping a sharp eye upon the progress of a case so notorious that it had made front page headlines on every single one of the English Sunday papers, or so Sister Bernadette had heard from the man who delivered the daily *Cork Examiner*.

'Well,' she said mildly, 'I don't know why you are making such a fuss. A child, a boy from my own school has been murdered as well as a man, the archdeacon from the Church of Ireland cathedral. It seems to be only human nature to speculate on what happened. Particularly,' she added, 'as it appears most likely that someone connected to the cathedral committed the murder.'

'And, of course, they all had keys, did you know that?' asked Lucy, enthusiastically shelving her efforts to defend the Church of Ireland clergy. 'At our annual dinner at the golf club, that unpleasant archdeacon, Dr Hearn, kept rattling his keys while our newly elected president was making his speech. It was a shame, really, as he is a nice man, but has a bit of a stutter so it was an ordeal for him to make a speech in public. I was sitting next to Frank Babington and when the speech was over and everyone had clapped, he turned to me and said, "That was typical of Hearn! Did you hear him rattling his keys? I suppose it makes him feel big, makes him feel like he's the man in charge." But that shows you. I bet anyone who met him would feel like murdering him. What about the sexton? I wonder would he have the keys? Bound to, I suppose. He'd have to get the boiler going in these wet, freezing mornings. Was it he who found the little boy?'

'No,' said the Reverend Mother slowly. She decided against passing on to Lucy what Patrick had told her about the arch-deacon staging a ceremonial handing over of the keys to be locked in the safe in the bishop's palace. She was always most careful not to repeat anything told to her by Patrick and she knew that he relied upon her for that. 'Enda,' she said, 'was found after the archdeacon dropped dead, poisoned from what he drank from the chalice. The child was lying at the back of the church, just between the font and the broom cupboard. He had been poisoned with a sweet from a packet of Rolos. Two of the sweets were poisoned, but it only took one to kill him.' She stopped and looked out of the window for a moment. The prospect was dreary. A heavy, sullen mist, a few sodden, decaying leaves strewn over the lawn, dripping trees and a grey sky. The Reverend Mother straightened her spine and said firmly, 'The guilty person must be caught. Anyone who could do that to a small child is a person possessed by the Devil. God may forgive, but I'm afraid that I cannot. He must be caught and turned over to the state and should not be allowed to go free.'

'How is Patrick coping?' asked Lucy, and then nodded wisely without waiting for an answer. 'A bit out of his depth, is he? They're rather a starchy lot, these C of I crowd. Find it hard to let go of the feeling that they are the rulers of this island. I got a clever idea the other day about Patrick. I bet this hasn't ever occurred to you, but what would you think of Patrick marrying Eileen? She'd be incredibly good for him, brimming with confidence, that young lady. Rupert is extremely impressed by her. Usually he moans about his apprentices, goes on about how stupid they are, and how it is impossible to make a decent solicitor out of such poor material, but he's most impressed by Eileen. Works at twice the speed of anyone else that he has ever had, excellent manner with the clients, too, not like most of them, tongue-tied or too chatty.'

'That's good news,' said the Reverend Mother, resolutely turning her mind from the memory of the small body lying on the stone tiles beside the elaborately carved red marble font.

'Yes, quite a person, your former pupil, according to Rupert,' said Lucy. She had shot a quick glance at her cousin and the Reverend Mother was aware that her lethargy and depression had not gone unnoticed. Lucy, she guessed, was trying to cheer her up. She appreciated the effort and smiled with a show of interest as Lucy told her tale.

'Rupert had her in his office the other day when old Mrs Power came to see him, and he said that Eileen was excellent. Kept quiet for the first half of the interview,' said Lucy, 'but she looked so interested, nodding her head wisely when Mrs Power went on about how terrible these taxes were and then she came up with a notion of saving tax by putting money into repairing some of the workers' cottages, worked out the savings in a flash, and went on about enhancing the value of the property and asking about the stables, promising to look up to see if there was a grant for improving them. Mrs Power was delighted, and she asked Eileen whether she rode. Rupert said he was impressed at how open and honest Eileen was, and how she laughed a little about how much she had cried over *Black Beauty* when she was young, and how she had made up a new story about how she had rescued Black Beauty and stabled her behind the one room cabin belonging to herself and her mother. And Mrs Power laughed a lot at that little story and invited her out to Powerscourt

and the groom would teach her to ride. She explained to
Rupert that Sarah's jodhpurs should fit his girl and went off
in such a good mood. Rupert said that he didn't like to tell
Eileen that Sarah's jodhpurs were probably about thirty years
old and mouldy into the bargain since Sarah herself had
been married to an English army captain and had gone off
to India about thirty years ago, but that he was sure that
Eileen would cope, and she had done a valuable piece of
work for the firm as Mrs Power was old and cranky and just
the type to switch solicitors if something didn't suit her.
He's really impressed by Eileen and how hard she works
and what a quick brain she has,' finished Lucy.

'Would Patrick want a pony-riding wife?' enquired the
Reverend Mother, but she knew what Lucy meant. Nevertheless,
she thought, Patrick had to fight his own battles and find his
own way. Success, she thought, was the stepping-stone to
achievement. And so, she turned her mind from Eileen and
back to Patrick. This was a most important case for a young
inspector to solve, and it was important that he did solve it.
Only the other day, her chaplain had remarked that the superintendent was nearing his sixty-fifth birthday. Surely time for
him to resign. Patrick had made the transition from the position of sergeant to inspector in double quick time due to his
own hard work, but a superintendent was a different matter.
No hard work, no examinations would be the road to that
post. Patrick would have to be considered a suitable person,
acceptable to people of importance. Solving this case would
be quite a feather in his cap when it came to attracting notice
from his superiors in Dublin. The problem was that on the
face of it, there seemed little mystery as so few suspects
were involved. But which of them had a sufficiently strong
motive to engage in murder?

'It's a difficult thing to envisage murdering someone,
isn't it, Lucy?' she said in a light, conversational tone.

'You only think that because you are a holy nun,' said
Lucy promptly. 'I'm always thinking of murdering people.
Rupert gets a bit shocked at me, sometimes, when I say,
"I could murder that woman!" I suppose some of the time I
don't mean it, but other times I do. If anyone did anything

to one of my daughters or to my granddaughter, I'd stick a knife in them. That's if I were pretty sure that I would get away with it, of course.'

The Reverend Mother pondered over that. She had, herself, just said that the man who had murdered little Enda deserved death at the hands of the law, not an easy death, either, but by slow strangulation by a noose around the neck. She, despite her devotion to her religion, would therefore be capable of condemning someone to death. 'So,' she said slowly, 'We need someone who deems that their own needs and desires are of the utmost importance and that the only obstacle is the danger of being caught and hanged.'

'Someone who is selfish, self-centred, and who has confidence in their own cleverness,' said Lucy promptly and added, 'Goodness, I can think of such a lot of people that description would fit.'

'But in this case, we are not thinking of a whole "lot of people", we are thinking of a very small band of people. It must be someone who knew that the wine had been poured into the small jug, was standing there on the side table, someone who knew Enda, knew that he could easily climb to the roof of the cathedral, could fit through the broken glass of the fourth pane in the rose window depicting the creation of the world, and knew that he was enormously fond of sweets, even, I guess, to the extent of knowing that he could not resist a Rolo. Have you ever eaten a Rolo, Lucy?'

'Goodness, yes, I suppose I have. They have a skim of chocolate on the outside and something like a liquid toffee on the inside so that when you bite the liquid flows out into your mouth. Terribly sweet! My granddaughter adores them.' Lucy gave a slight shudder. 'I don't think that I could ever buy a packet for her again,' she said in a low voice.

'Would they be something that an adult would buy for themselves?' asked the Reverend Mother, ignoring Lucy's closing words.

'Probably too sweet,' said Lucy promptly. 'A bit messy too. No, I doubt that an adult would buy Rolos, except for a child.'

'So, among the people present in the cathedral on that

evening and on the following morning, we look for someone who, not only knew all about the communion wine and where it had been placed, knew enough to give directions to Enda, but someone who has close contact, not just with Enda, but with children in general. Someone who knew that a packet of Rolos was an irresistible attraction and that it was certain one, at least, would be immediately consumed. The bishop,' she added, 'has a grandchild the same size as Enda. He told me that.'

'And the dean, Dr Babington, has a small boy of his own and older ones, of course, though I can't see him murdering a child. He's such a nice man. As is the bishop . . .' Lucy shrugged her shoulders, shook her head decisively and added, 'No, I can't see either doing such a deed. It wouldn't be in either of them.'

'Mr Flewett, the precentor, is not married, I understand,' said the Reverend Mother steadily. 'But,' she added in a neutral tone of voice, 'he meets choirboys every day of his working life and so would probably know their taste in sweets.' Her mind went to Father O'Flynn, and she wondered whether she could induce him to confide in her about Mr Flewett. Lucy, she thought, didn't know much about the choirmaster. She did not appear to show much interest at the mention of his name.

'And the canon,' said Lucy, speaking rather reluctantly.

The Reverend Mother said nothing. She shot a quick glance at her cousin. 'Mr Jack Wilson,' she said encouragingly.

'Yes, Jack, that's right,' said Lucy, still with that reluctant note in her voice. 'A nice man,' she said then and grimaced slightly.

'He would be well advised to tell all relevant facts to the police,' said the Reverend Mother in a slightly detached tone of voice. 'You need not, however, be afraid that anything you say to me in confidence would be told to a third party. I think that you are worried, Lucy, aren't you?'

'It's just that I wouldn't want Rupert's name mentioned,' explained Lucy. 'It's a legal thing, not one of his cases, and this is not something that I heard from him, but at the same time . . . It was Joan Arkins who told me that Rupert was involved, gave advice. Of course, you know what Rupe is like! He's always completely silent about anything to do with a client. But Joan Arkins, well, you remember what a gossip she is. Still the same as she was when we were in school.'

The Reverend Mother gave an encouraging nod. She did remember Joan Arkins, but she did not want to interrupt Lucy's flow of talk. She could understand Rupert's reserve about private legal matters, but she felt that if a gossip like Joan Arkins, if she remembered the schoolfriend correctly, possessed this piece of information it could do no possible harm for Lucy to impart it to her cousin. And she, the Reverend Mother, would have no compunction about imparting this piece of gossip to Patrick. After all, she thought, it was important for him to have all the facts as early as possible in the investigation so that he could not be thrown off course in the final stages.

'You see,' said Lucy, 'apparently there is a magazine published by the Church of Ireland, it's probably quite a dull affair, but they make an effort to brighten it up at Christmas time and so they write around to all the parishes asking for funny short stories with a Christmas theme and last Christmas Jack Wilson wrote a story called "Reverend Scrooge" and it was, apparently, a funny story about this Reverend Scrooge going around and buying the cheapest of everything, and even returning an ivory waistcoat after wearing it under a dinner jacket for a whole evening at a diocesan dinner, but telling the shop that it was the wrong size.'

'And had the archdeacon done such a thing?'

'Probably. It was just the sort of thing that he boasted of to his golfing friends,' said Lucy energetically. 'But, worst of all, there was an anecdote about this "Reverend Scrooge" seeing the corner of a pound note sticking out of the collection box and he extracted it with tweezers and popped it into his own pocket. Well, the archdeacon immediately hit upon Jack as he had been the only one present when that happened, though the archdeacon, apparently, changed the story to one where he had used the tweezers to push the pound note securely into the box. But, anyway, he sued Jack, said he had brought him into disrepute. You see, the trouble was although the story was published under the name of "Santa's Little Helper", whoever put the magazine together brightened up the page by putting a big clear photograph of the Cork cathedral as one of the prettiest of the Church of Ireland cathedrals. Well, you can imagine the fuss. No one would believe such things of the nice old bishop, but everyone believed it of Archdeacon Hearn and about a month ago, a parishioner showed him an advance copy of the magazine with the story in it.'

'I gather he didn't just laugh it off,' said the Reverend Mother.

'No, indeed, he went straight to his lawyer – not Rupert, of course, one of their own – and he filed a case for defamation against Canon Jack Wilson but said that he would settle out of court for a thousand pounds.'

The Reverend Mother's eyes widened. 'A thousand pounds,' she said with interest and a small amount of envy. 'I wonder would someone like to write a libellous statement about me,' she remarked. 'I would so like to be bribed by an offer of a thousand pounds.'

'Don't joke. It's terribly serious for poor Jack Wilson,' said Lucy reprovingly. 'He's a youngish man, will want to get married at some stage, and really the Church of Ireland, despite all their wealth and their property, pay the clergy at the bottom of the ladder very poorly indeed. He'd probably have to borrow that one thousand pounds from the bank, if they'd lend it to him, and if not from some moneylender who would extract a pound of flesh from the poor fellow by charging huge interest rates.'

The Reverend Mother turned the matter over in her mind. 'This is an interesting case,' she remarked. 'I haven't spoken about it to Patrick, but I would imagine, because the communion wine was poisoned, that he will be concentrating on those closely associated with the cathedral. So that leaves us with the sexton, Mr Tom Hayes; the deacon, Mr Bob Webster; the canon, Mr Jack Wilson; the precentor, Mr Arthur Flewett; the dean, Dr Frank Babington, the man with the large family and two wives; and, of course, the bishop himself, Dr Thompson – and I must say that I find the idea of Dr Thompson planning, executing, and squaring it with his conscience to murder one of his cathedral staff to be most unlikely,' she added.

'Ah, but,' said Lucy, 'you are forgetting his family. He has a pack of lively young daughters to whom, according to Jack Wilson, the bishop is absolutely devoted. They are the apple of his eye.'

'"For thus saith the Lord of Hosts; After the glory hath he sent me unto the nations which spoiled you: for he that toucheth you, toucheth the apple of his eye",' quoted the Reverend Mother and added helpfully, 'Zachariah, I believe.'

'Well, your friend Zachariah might have something there,' said Lucy. 'I don't know much about the girls. Went to school in Dublin, I believe. I could probably find out, though. These boarding schools have long holidays, plenty of time to get up to mischief. I still don't believe it, though. Would the bishop poison the little boy, even if he brought himself to poison the archdeacon?'

'I don't believe it either,' said the Reverend Mother. 'Not really, but during my long life here in the south side of Cork I have seen almost unbelievable incidences of man's inhumanity to man. I have reluctantly concluded that, just as when a new lion becomes head of a pack, he will kill off the existing cubs, so do human beings in this city of ours regard the children of the poor to be *sui generis*.'

'I wish you'd stop saying things in Latin,' said Lucy, helping herself to some more cake. 'It's such an insufferable piece of showing-off!'

'It's just that it often seems to sum things up neatly,' said the Reverend Mother apologetically. 'It's a very neat and concise language. I've often noticed when translating a page of Livy how the English version stretches to almost double the Latin text. But just to accommodate you, I will rephrase and say that the rich and well-off of this city regard the children of the poor as of a different species to their own children. The murder of a slum child might cause a pang but would not arouse the same feelings of outrage as would the murder of a clean, appealing, sweet-smelling offspring of their own class.'

'I've got another idea. Now, how about one of the bishop's

daughters taking her father's keys – I'm sure that he is a fairly
absent-minded old man, so a daughter could snatch his keys
– thinking about poisoning the archdeacon herself and then
see Enda climbing all over the roof and hand the job over to
him. What would you think of that for an idea?' said Lucy
enthusiastically.

The Reverend Mother did not answer. She had heard a
ring on the doorbell and now there were raised voices in the
corridor outside. Sister Bernadette talking, and then exclaiming
in tones of delight and then dropping her voice again. As she
listened, she frowned slightly. She knew that voice, slightly
girlish in tone, trace of an English accent, but with an Irish
lilt.

And then there was a knock at the door. She went to it
immediately, curious about that voice. Where and when had
she heard that accent before?

'It's Mrs Babington, Reverend Mother, and she's brought
such lovely clothes, clothes for little boys, you'll be delighted
with them.' Sister Bernadette's voice was enthusiastic, but
she had an apologetic expression on her face. Normally she
was always protective towards the Reverend Mother's
enjoyment of her cousin's visit, had even been known to tell
a 'white lie' to the bishop's secretary to deflect him from
interrupting. Now she was beaming with excitement as she
ushered in the visitor.

'Here you are. Shall we bring them in. They're all in such
good condition. Nanny dug them out of the cupboard, they
smelled of moth balls, but they've been hanging on the
line all day and nothing now, not a whiff! Bring them in,
Jenkins!'

An extremely young voice and a young face above a heavily
pregnant body. The second wife of Dr Babington, dean of St
Fin Barre's Cathedral, must certainly come as a surprise to
those acquainted with the elderly-looking man with pale grey
hair and a lined face. She greeted Lucy, smiled confidently at
the Reverend Mother, and signalled to her chauffeur who was
carrying an enormous trunk. 'Put it on that chair, Jenkins,
and open it up,' she said, and the tone of her voice was that
of an excited schoolgirl. 'There you are,' she said. 'They're

all in perfect condition. Nanny says that those boys grew so quickly that they never wore anything out.'

The Babington family nanny was quite right. Tweed knickerbockers and jackets, elaborate shirts, immaculately white sailor suits with caps to match, woollen socks and well-polished shoes. There were enough clothes to furnish a shop window and every single item could have been brand new. The Reverend Mother looked at them with surprise and then glanced at the woman. Yes, she was definitely pregnant and there was already a young child in the house. It was Lucy, however, who gave voice to her thoughts.

'Wouldn't you keep them for your own little boy, or boys, Mrs Babington?'

'Oh, no. My boys aren't going to have any old clothes. I've got it all planned,' she said in a confidential manner to the Reverend Mother. 'I was thinking that I'd like to have five boys and I'll dress them all in those new corduroy pants, just like little Americans, just to the knees, you know, and a lovely chestnut brown colour with yellow blouses. They'll look so smart, won't they? I love children dressed alike, don't you?' And then, without waiting for an answer she swept on. 'I thought I would bring them to you because I heard about your little boy and the terrible clothes he was wearing, all torn and dirty and . . .' She shuddered a little and then bestowed another bright smile upon the Reverend Mother and then on Lucy, beckoned to the chauffeur and rapidly left the room.

'Where would you like me to put the trunk, Madam?' enquired the chauffeur.

'I'll look after it, Reverend Mother,' snapped Sister Bernadette. 'Come with me.' And then as the chauffeur shouldered his burden and she closed the door behind them, her voice rose up irately. 'You don't call our Reverend Mother "Madam", my man. Didn't I tell you what to call her?' Her tone was what everyone in the kitchen would have recognized as signalling that she had reached the limit of her patience and there was no reply from the chauffeur.

Lucy giggled. 'Dear Sister Bernadette. I'm so glad that she approved of me. Tells me that I take your mind off your worries! Now, you know if Mrs Babington is planning a long line of little boys, that must be a bit of a worry for the dean. I wonder when the bishop is going to retire. It's a good job that . . .' Then Lucy stopped.

'Go on,' said the Reverend Mother. 'What were you going to say? Or shall I say it for you? The death of the archdeacon has put this charming young lady's husband on a higher rung of the ladder and might ensure him a salary sufficient to bring up a second family of boys. That was what was in your mind, Lucy, wasn't it?'

'Five more boys!' said Lucy. 'And the fees at Marlborough are sky high! She'll want them to go there, of course, when they've grown out of the stage of running around in chestnut brown corduroy pants and yellow blouses. But that's not to say . . .' She paused.

The Reverend Mother said nothing. The murder of the archdeacon was one thing; the murder of the pathetic small child was another. And yet, she herself had quoted the Latin tag about *sui generis*. 'Clytemnestra murders Agamemnon because of her love for her daughter, Iphigeneia,' she said. 'And, here in Cork, there was a tragic case of the pregnant woman who stuck a knife into an old man who was trying to turn her out of the basement when she wanted to give birth.'

'How awful!' said Lucy with a shudder. 'What happened to her?'

'She died in childbirth,' said the Reverend Mother briefly. 'She had been tramping the streets looking for some-where to go and then having found a place, I suppose a surge of maternal feeling overcame her and she used her knife to ensure a place for her baby. Would the court have sentenced her to death, or would they have taken into account the overwhelming emotions of maternity? I don't know the answer to that, but I have seen some surprising deeds done by mothers for the sake of their children.'

'Would a salary big enough to pay fees for five boys at Marlborough be enough to trigger the maternal instincts?' wondered Lucy and then visibly pushed the matter aside. 'No, that's nonsense, of course. Now, tell me, did you hear from Cousin Brenda about Florence winning a scholarship? She filled every blank spot of her Christmas card to me all about it. Talk about the maternal instinct. Brenda just worships that girl.'

It was, thought the Reverend Mother, time to forget the two deaths in St Fin Barre's Cathedral and concentrate on family matters. She still had to enquire about Lucy's children and her precious grandchild. She would, however, keep in her mind the matter of a murderer who could kill a small boy by poisoning a Rolo sweet. That person deserved no mercy.

TWELVE

Eileen was most impressed to find a shiny and expensive-looking car waiting at the gate of the Rushbrooke railway station. It didn't need the two-stroke beep of a horn to alert her. She immediately recognized him, despite the absence of the dog collar. That glossy black hair, very good-looking, most polite, also, she thought as he swung his long legs out of the car door and went around to open the passenger door to her. She cast a quick glance at the group of girls who had travelled down from Cork with her but did not attempt to negotiate a lift to the tennis club for them. I'm on business, she told herself to assuage her guilty conscience as they waved at her and looked around to see whether any other lift might be forthcoming.

'No dog collar, tonight. What will the bishop say?' she remarked as he wove a way through all the train passengers, most of them making their way uphill towards the tennis club.

'Oh, the bishop is blind as a bat and semi-senile,' he said, touching his horn to emit a series of bleeps. 'Don't suppose for a moment that he would notice anything unless you hit him over the head with it,' he added once a way had been cleared for his expensive car.

She was a little repelled by the contemptuous tone. The Proddy Bishop, as he was known in Shandon Street, was generally considered to be a nice old man. However, she bit back a sharp rejoinder. She was here for a purpose, and she was looking forward to giving Patrick the benefit of her investigations into a man who should be one of his suspects.

'Time they had a younger man,' she prompted, but allowed a light note to enter her voice. No point in letting him think that I am laying it on too thick, she said to herself.

'What a very perspicuous young lady you are,' he said.

'I am reasonably intelligent,' she said making no effort to

sound modest. 'Aren't you lucky that I consented to come out with you tonight.'

He glanced across at her. 'Will you have to confess to your priest that you spent New Year's night with a Protestant cleric?' He smiled at her, but there was a note of innuendo in his voice which annoyed her.

'In the first place, I never go to confession,' she said. 'And, in the second place, I fully intend spending the night, as usual, in my mother's house. I may, however, spend the evening with a fellow law student, that's if he behaves himself.'

'Touché!' he said with a smile. And to give him his due, she thought, he handled that well.

'Goodness, what a crowd,' she said, looking through the window. 'I hope we get in.'

'Don't worry about that,' he said carelessly. 'I'm a member and we are allowed in through the back door. The plebs queue at the front door until all us members are inside. Now tell me all about you. What are you hoping to do when you leave university? Before you get married, of course. I'm sure there is a long line of gentlemen waiting for you to give them some encouragement.'

The evening, she thought, was getting off to a bad start. She had enjoyed playing chess with him. He had treated her like an equal, then, had criticized her moves, shown her better ones, had talked of strategy and of tactics, shown her how to take her time, cultivate the patience to look ahead and to go, meticulously, through the many possible outcomes to a move. These stale compliments bored her.

'Oh, I'm hoping to be a judge,' she said in an off-hand manner. She thought of saying, 'I think I'll practise on that murder in your cathedral. I've already got the suspects lined up in my mind and as soon as I decide on one, then I'll subject the evidence against him to a forensic analysis', but then she rejected the idea. It might make him cautious about talking and she wanted to pump him for information about possible suspects from the cathedral clerics. 'Look,' she said, 'there's a parking place over there, quite near to the door, too. Quick, before someone else grabs it.'

He backed the car into the space with an adroitness that

impressed her, despite herself. The sort of man who likes to do everything well, she said to herself and gave a nod of satisfaction. It all fitted with what she had said to Patrick. This was a man who might literally murder to get his foot on the ladder. About mid-twenties, no, perhaps thirty, she decided as she turned to look at his profile. His face was quite young, but there were a few tell-tale grey hairs above his well-shaped ears, and he had a very assured manner which was unlike most of the post-graduate students that she knew.

'What brought you back to university at your advanced age?' she queried as he switched off the engine.

That took him slightly aback, she was pleased to see as she peered into the mirror and touched up the outline of her very scarlet lipstick.

'Ambition, I suppose,' she added.

He recovered himself. 'That's right,' he said. 'If I'm thinking of climbing the tree, then I need a doctorate. Of course, normally I would take some time out and go back to Trinity, but . . .'

'I see,' said Eileen. To her satisfaction, he cast a slightly puzzled look at her. Wondering whether she had guessed the real reason, guessed that he hoped for promotion.

'You're hoping to become an archdeacon, I suppose, so that you want to stay on the spot and keep your name up in lights,' she said. She tossed this surmise into his lap before getting out of the car. It would be overdoing matters to look into his face while she said those words, but she was sure that there had been a moment of hesitation as he got out of the car.

'The oldest tennis club in the whole of Ireland; quite exclusive,' he said, once she had slammed her door closed and he had come around with his keys to lock it.

'Yeah, well, it looks old, OK. Let's hope the roof doesn't collapse with the sound of that band,' she said, determined not to be impressed. A snob, she thought disdainfully. Trying to impress her. Had anyone ever correlated the incidence of snobbery among murderers? Did an envy of those above you lead, in some cases, to murder? An interesting point, she thought and determined to share her thought with Patrick. It was time that he had a bit of intellectual conversation.

'So, every archdeacon must hold a doctorate, is that right?' She kept her voice light and waved to a girl that she knew, so as to give him a chance to think about that.

'Most of them do,' he said, but there was a false note in the lightness of his voice.

'What about the canon, Canon Wilson, is that right?' Eileen cast her mind back to the neatly written cards in Patrick's box.

'Oh, he's got a doctorate all right – in geography. I ask you, geography! Imagine getting a doctorate in geography. Memorized all the countries in the world, I suppose! That's about his limit, I would say. As for original thought . . .'

'Don't be so scornful,' she said. 'Not everyone can be a chess genius.'

That struck the right note and his face lightened.

'That's true! Not all can be as clever as thee and me!' he said and gave her a squeeze.

She moved away. A bit early in the night to start this sort of thing! She took two steps back and waved enthusiastically at a reporter from the *Cork Examiner*. 'Excuse me, for a moment,' she said. 'I must just say hello and Happy New Year to Tommy. He's a sweetheart. Always drops me a hint when I'm in danger of putting a foot into the sensibilities of the management.'

Then, quite deliberately, she left him, deposited a kiss on the cheek of the young reporter, shook hands with his sister and then in his ear whispered, 'Rescue me if I send you a signal. A bit frisky, that fellow. Starting early in the evening, too.'

'Well, if you will go out with a Protestant cleric,' he said, returning her kiss enthusiastically.

'I'm working,' she hissed at him. 'Wait till you see the story that I uncover.'

'Oh, work!' he said. 'I must say that is rather a dishy dress that you are wearing for work.'

'Don't you flirt, too,' she retorted and strolled back to Bob Webster.

'Who's Tommy?' he asked.

'Just a reporter on the *Cork Examiner*. Don't tell me that you didn't know that I wrote for the *Cork Examiner*,' she said lightly and added, 'Surely my wonderful prose has stayed in your memory.'

'Never read the rag, myself. I read the *Irish Times* and that wastes enough time,' he said. 'I suppose if I have to read a newspaper, I might as well read a well-written one.'

Eileen felt an angry colour heating her cheekbones. No point in quarrelling with the fellow. Her good sense told her that. She had accepted his invitation to get to know him better and he had to be encouraged to talk in an unguarded fashion, otherwise she would have wasted an evening.

'Goodness,' she said lightly. 'I've never thought about *reading* a newspaper. I just write for them to get enough money to pay for my books. Otherwise, I just use newspapers to light the fire. If I want to read, I read a book. Mostly in French,' she added. 'Now that I'm just studying law, I don't want to forget my languages.'

He was slightly taken aback at that, she saw with satisfaction and thought that she would go on in this strain.

'I don't know about you,' she said pensively, 'but I am extremely ambitious. I want to be somebody in the world, and I want to make lots of money, and I want to be able to buy my mother the sort of house that she would love to live in.'

'You'll have to marry a rich man,' he said lightly.

'You're trying deliberately to annoy me,' she said, copying his tone. 'I want to be the one who has made a fortune and I want to become a top lawyer, even a judge, perhaps. I want to have the bank manager bowing obsequiously when he meets me walking down the South Mall. What about you? I suppose that you want to be a Church of Ireland bishop – Bishop of Cork, I suppose you would call it. And you want to have bank managers bowing to you. Perhaps they do already,' she finished with a note of query in her voice.

'No chance!' he said, and now he sounded relaxed and amused. 'When I see a bank manager, I duck down a side street.'

'Living beyond your means,' said Eileen sympathetically.

'Well, I don't have that trouble. My bank sits on the shelf above the fire where my mother cooks. It's a very small bank. Just an empty jar of pickles. Whenever I have anything left at the end of the week, I put it in there. Otherwise, I draw money from the bursar at the university as he keeps my scholarship money, pays my fees, and doles out money for books and food. One of the scholarship boys a year or so ago got into terrible debt by spending his scholarship money on drink and high living so they set up this arrangement. It would never do for scholarship lads or lassies to be out drinking with taxpayer's money, or so the bursar told me. But I suppose that you get a nice salary for your duties as deacon,' she added.

'You're joking,' he said angrily. 'I was lucky enough to have a legacy from an old aunt who died, conveniently on my twenty-first birthday, but without that I would probably be going around in rags and begging at street corners.'

'And have to give up your subscription to the Rushbrooke Tennis Club,' she inserted slyly, and he laughed.

'Come and meet a friend of mine, my tennis partner, John Fielding,' he said and took her arm, steering her skilfully through the throng who were waiting for the band to finish tuning their instruments.

'Eileen, this is John,' he said tapping the glossy shoulder of a man in a splendid dinner jacket and satin waistcoat. 'John is a great friend to have, Eileen, he will get you a wonderful potion if you drink too much tonight; you should see the back rooms of his pharmacy.'

Eileen shook hands. In with a lot of rich people, this young deacon from the Church of Ireland cathedral, she thought. She knew the Fielding pharmacy, of course. An old business and a very profitable one. If the Church of Ireland paid their young clergymen so badly it would be hard for Bob Webster to keep up with wealthy merchants.

And then an idea came to her. A memory. Yes, of course, a pharmacy. She looked at the young man speculatively. Needed to see him by himself and to get rid of her escort for five minutes or so, was her thought. She fanned herself vigorously.

'Goodness, I'm thirsty,' she said and looked hopefully at the young clergyman. 'Just some orange juice,' she said to him with an appealing look.

To give him his due, his manners were excellent. 'You're sure you wouldn't prefer a glass of white wine?' he asked, and when she refused, he took an order from John Fielding and went off. With satisfaction she saw that the queue at the bar was lengthening by the minute. She turned to John Fielding.

'I remember your name,' she said. 'You see I work part-time in the *Cork Examiner* office, just around the corner from your pharmacy. I remember, quite a few years ago, we had a wasps' nest, right outside the window of the men's lavatory. The place was full of wasps and there were all these men begging to be allowed to use the ladies' and then someone got a bright idea and sent one of the messenger boys around the corner to your pharmacy. Do you remember the boy coming in for something to kill wasps? He came back with a jar of stuff and all sorts of instructions about how careful they had to be. In the end, Mr Crosbie's secretary allowed one of the men to go into the ladies' lavatory and pour the stuff down a hosepipe and into the nest. He had to close the window quickly as the wasps started to swarm up towards him. Don't know what the stuff was, but I remember that it was supposed to be terribly dangerous,' finished Eileen, looking innocently at him.

'Must have been cyanide,' he said promptly. 'I don't remember your wasps' nest but every summer we get someone with a wasps' nest. My father always insists on dealing with them and reads them a long lecture about how dangerous the stuff is. He even insists on them returning the empty bottle by charging them a shilling deposit on the bottle, just to make sure that they don't leave it lying around the house and have some child drink it.'

'Your father sounds a most careful man,' said Eileen, hoping that her broad smile would be taken as an appreciation of his father. Inwardly she hugged herself. It had been a good story with a nice amount of detail, she thought. A direct question might have aroused suspicion. She would be able to pass this piece of information onto Patrick and give him valuable help in solving the murder of this important man, a Church of Ireland archdeacon.

It would, she thought, be quite a step up for a lowly

deacon, Mr Bob Webster, to inherit the position of archdeacon. He was taking a considerable time over fetching the drinks, she thought after a while. She and John Fielding were beginning to run out of small talk once she had told him about her experiences at university and he had confessed that he hated pharmacy and was bored by all those medicines and would much prefer to pay an assistant to do the tedious work while he chatted a little to customers and checked the books.

'Who's that girl that Bob is talking to?' she interrupted him. It had been lucky that she was not particularly thirsty, she thought, as he had not moved from the same position for the last five minutes. It seemed a very intense sort of discussion. Their heads were close. At one stage, she saw them embrace and then Bob handed the girl his large and snowy white hand-kerchief. What was going on? Not very good manners from someone who fancied himself a gentleman; she didn't care too much for Bob, but he had invited her to the tennis club dance, so it was a bit much to desert her for another girl.

'Who is she, anyway?' she asked with a shrug of her shoulders.

'Oh, that's Jacinta, she's a member of the tennis club, the bishop's daughter, you know,' he added.

Well, there were two bishops in the city of Cork, but only one of them could legitimately have a daughter. Just as she had come to that conclusion, John Fielding looked at her rather tentatively and said, 'He must be polite to the bishop's daughter, you know. Poor old Bob, clever fellow, don't know why he went in for this parson business. I believe it was an aunt of his who sort of pushed him into it. Promised to supply him with enough money to let him lead the life of a gentleman if he took holy orders, but then died without a will and her money all went to her sister in England.'

'How very annoying for him!' said Eileen sarcastically, and just stopped herself from asking how much money was necessary to lead the life of a gentleman. 'Well, I'm not going to hang around for ever,' she said firmly. 'There are some people I know over there from the university, so I think I'll go and join them.'

'Don't do that,' he said. He raised a hand and jerked his head in the direction of Bob Webster. The girl, Jacinta, turned, surveyed them both, waved in the direction of John Fielding and then turned with an obvious question to Bob. Eileen was tempted to go, but curiosity got the better of her and so she waited while the girl made her way through the crowd towards them.

'Bob wants you,' she said with a jerk of her hand towards John. And then, as though regretting her abruptness, she kissed him on the cheek and said, 'Hmm, lovely to see you, Johnny, darling.' Once he had gone, though, she turned in a business-like manner to Eileen. 'Let's go into the ladies and repair our lipstick,' she proposed and without waiting for an answer, seized Eileen by the arm and steered her through the crowd to a small door at the back of the hall.

'The "ladies" is in the opposite direction,' pointed out Eileen. She didn't resist, though. It might be interesting to chat to the bishop's daughter. A little more information for poor old Patrick who was probably sitting alone, pondering over the case, and reading his notes.

'That's just for the crowd here for the dance,' said Jacinta. 'We'll go to the club members' rest room.'

Rest room! What a silly name, thought Eileen; she couldn't stand these polite euphemisms, but she said nothing. Her curiosity was aroused. What was Jacinta, the bishop's daughter, going to say to her? *Hands off Bob! He's mine!* Perhaps that was going to be it. With a feeling of amusement, she allowed herself to be led through a hallway, up a flight of stairs and into the 'Ladies' Restroom'. There was a key on the inside of the door and as soon as Eileen had stepped onto the glossy black-and-white tiles, Jacinta locked the door and then pock-eted the key. Eileen raised an eyebrow but said nothing. What was Jacinta up to?

'I usually carry a gun,' she said mildly, but Jacinta ignored this.

'Just want to be private,' she said briefly. And then, after a moment's silence when she seemed to be turning over words in her head, she appeared to have come to a decision.

'Bob's been telling me all about you,' she said.

'All,' said Eileen. 'Goodness me, even I don't know all about myself.'

Jacinta ignored that. 'I mean that he told me that you live in a slum,' she went on hurriedly. 'I don't mind, you know, it's not that. It's just that you might be able to help me and . . . and, well, don't be offended but I'm not one to be mean when I am obliged to someone.'

'Are you offering me money,' said Eileen. 'Well, that's interesting. Yes, coming from a slum, I'm always short of money. What do I have to do? Give up seeing Bob? How much are you offering?'

'No, not that, silly. Who cares about Bob! I wouldn't have to pay you if I wanted him, but as a matter of fact, that's not what I'm talking to you about. It's just that living in a slum, Bob says that you would probably know a woman who would be able to help me.'

'Help you? Help you in what way?' Was the girl looking for a servant? wondered Eileen. And then suddenly she knew that was not the issue. She said nothing more, however. Just took out her lipstick and began to touch up the bright red outline with great care, and then filled it in with a lighter shade. She had seen an Arts student do that a few weeks ago and had saved up for a second lipstick. The effect, she thought, was excellent and she smiled at herself in the mirror.

'You needn't find it all so funny,' said Jacinta angrily. 'I wouldn't laugh at you if you were in trouble.'

Eileen turned around. 'I don't know what you are talking about,' she said. 'Do you want to tell me, or would you prefer to go on insulting me and trying to pick a fight with me.'

And then, as she saw tears come into the girl's eyes, she said, more gently, 'Come on, what's the matter?'

'I need a woman, someone who knows what to do. I've tried everything that I know, but nothing has worked. I need someone who knows what to do,' Jacinta repeated. She opened her handbag and touched up her own lipstick. In the mirror both pairs of eyes met.

Eileen was beginning to guess, but she said nothing. Why did I come to this silly dance and get mixed up with these people? she thought as she clicked her handbag shut and then washed her hands with meticulous care.

'I have to go. I want to meet a friend,' she said as she towelled them dry. The key was in the girl's pocket, but if it came to a fight, she would be the tougher of the two. Then she saw tears in the large blue eyes and felt a little ashamed.

'Are you pregnant?' she asked briskly.

Jacinta nodded and then shrugged her shoulders. 'I think I might be,' she said. 'I've missed two periods, three probably, and I keep getting sick in the morning. I remember my sister, my eldest sister, she was like that a few years ago. Of course, she was married so everyone was delighted for her.'

Eileen scanned her mind for snippets of talk about missed periods. 'It could still happen,' she said trying to sound cheerful and wishing that she had never come to this wretched place. And then something occurred to her. 'Is it Bob Webster's child?' she asked. 'Well, he'll just have to marry you and then you can pretend that the baby came early. There might be a bit of gossip, but you don't care. Why should you?'

'It's not Bob Webster's child,' said Jacinta, mopping her eyes. 'And he won't marry me, not unless I get rid of the . . . of the, well, you know. He would then, he said, but he doesn't want to have another man's bastard sitting at his table. That's what he said.'

'He's a bit of a bastard himself,' said Eileen cheerfully. 'But what about the real father?' And then a doubt came to her mind. Some people used to say that Protestants had no morals. Perhaps this girl might sleep with every man who asked her. 'You do know who the real father is, don't you?' she finished on a dubious note and once again looked at the locked door.

'Yes, of course I do! Do you think I sleep with a different man every night of the week!' snapped Jacinta.

Eileen ignored that. 'So, who is it?' she asked. And then when she got no reply, she changed the question. 'Why don't you marry him?' she asked.

'Because I can't! Do you think that I'm stupid? Don't you think that I could work that one out for myself?'

Eileen thought this might be the moment to grab the girl's wrists, hold them tightly with one of her own hands and use the other to extract the key, but then she saw tears rolling down Jacinta's cheeks. They were making tracks through the expensive make-up and it was only now that she realized how pale the girl was under that layer of Max Factor.

'Why can't you?' she asked patiently.

'Because he's dead, stupid.'

Eileen resisted the temptation to say: *You're the dead stupid one.* She took a deep breath and then it flashed into her mind. A recent death! Someone who would have seen this Jacinta on almost every day of his life.

'Not the archdeacon!' she exclaimed, and then remembered the carefully penned article that she had written for the *Cork Examiner.* 'But he was a married man. He had two sons.'

'His wife is dead,' said Jacinta sullenly. 'In any case, I never thought about marrying him. He told me that no one gets pregnant the first time that they do it. I thought that might be true because my sister, the married one, didn't get pregnant for more than a year after she got married. And . . . and, well, he'd been doing things to me for years and I didn't, well, I didn't think it was going to go so far this time.'

Eileen stared at her in speechless dismay.

'Have you told your father?' she asked eventually.

'Don't be stupid!'

'Or any of your sisters?'

'They'd just blab. I'd be in a worse mess. Anyway, if I could just get rid of it, I'll be all right. Bob will marry me. It would be a good marriage for him, and he thinks now that the archdeacon is dead the Archbishop of Armagh would be very likely to appoint the bishop's new son-in-law. If only I wasn't so stupid as to tell him that I thought I was pregnant. You see he wanted to have a summer wedding, he had it all planned out, so I had to tell him that we should be married as soon as possible and that we'd have to think up some excuse.'

'When did you tell Bob? When did you ask him to marry you?' asked Eileen.

'On Christmas Eve. I was due a period three days before

and I'm always very punctual. So, when nothing happened, I thought I definitely was pregnant. I had to tell him that I thought I might be pregnant, and he turned me down. But I tried again tonight, and he suggested asking you for the name of a woman. He said you'd know of someone. He said that in the slums they were always getting rid of babies.'

'Well,' said Eileen after a few moments of reflection, 'I can do nothing for you. I don't know anyone like that and from what I heard these methods are dangerous. I must go now.' Reaching over, she quickly extracted the key from the girl's pocket and went out, dropping the key on the floor as she shut the door firmly.

She had no fear of being followed and now she had no further interest in the dance. She went straight to the cloakroom in the front hallway.

'Could I have my coat please. I'm going home,' she said.

'Certainly, Madam, shall I call a taxi?'

'No, thank you,' said Eileen. 'I'm getting the train back to Cork. It's a short walk.'

The woman looked uneasy. 'It would be better to get a taxi. I'll just send for the manager. Lily,' she called to a girl carrying a tray of empty glasses.

Eileen bit her lip with annoyance and then had an idea. 'Lily, could you get Sergeant Joe Duggan?' she said. 'He's a friend,' she explained to the woman. A policeman always sounded reliable. Joe could walk her to the gate and then slip back inside to his girlfriend. But even if Joe could not be found, she was determined not to go back and pretend to that Deacon Bob Webster that nothing had happened. How dare he think that she would be party to that grubby little plan to kill an unborn baby.

THIRTEEN

'Happy New Year, Patrick,' said Joe as he popped his head around his superior's door on the second day of January. 'Have a good weekend?' he queried and then wished that he had not as he saw the bleak look on Patrick's face. What had his superior done with the tickets that he had bought at his request, wondered Joe? There were more girls in the world than Eileen. Expensive tickets, too. Surely, he could have found someone to go with him. Good-looking fellow, with a great job in a city full of unemployment.

'Yes, thank you.' Patrick made an obvious effort to sound sociable. 'And you? Did you go to the Rushbrooke Tennis Club dance? Was it good?'

'Dreadfully crowded. Don't suppose anyone enjoyed it much,' said Joe. That was a lie, of course. He had enjoyed himself immensely with his latest girlfriend and Eileen had certainly looked as though she were having a good time with that young Church of Ireland cleric before some sort of bust-up. At least he had talked her into coming back inside and teamed her up with some of her university pals and she had certainly seemed to enjoy the rest of the evening, having fun with the university crowd. More her own kind than that snobbish cleric, he had thought at the time. The train had been full, both on the journey down to Cobh, and the journey back to Cork when everyone sang the latest songs and snuggled into each other, exclaiming about the cold.

'Well, back to work,' he said. Then added, 'This really should be an easy murder to solve, shouldn't it?'

That worked. Patrick straightened up and pulled his card box towards him. 'So, for prime suspects, we just have the sexton, Tom Hayes, and we have the Church of Ireland clergy: the dean, Dr Frank Babington; the precentor, Mr Arthur Flewett; the canon, Dr Jack Wilson; the deacon, Mr Bob Webster.'

'And the bishop, Dr Matheus Thompson,' said Joe. 'I've been wondering whether we are doing the right thing in excluding the bishop just because he seems to be such a nice old man, someone who wouldn't hurt a fly.'

'You're right, of course, Joe,' said Patrick, feeling slightly annoyed with himself. He did have a card for the bishop, but he hadn't read out his name, had mentally blotted him out from the list of suspects. 'Yes, you're right. We shouldn't rule anyone out at this stage. He fits the profile in some ways. He was there in the cathedral the night before; he knew the whole procedure. But did he have a motive? What could make a man like the bishop commit a murder? Could the archdeacon know of a guilty secret? Something disreputable which the bishop had kept quiet?'

Joe puckered his lips. 'To be honest, I can't see it, myself. Everyone from our congregation and including all the hundreds of my mother's friends in the city, loves our bishop. Can't see him doing anything that would give grounds for blackmail. He's a bit old for having a secret love affair.'

'Not as old as he looks,' said Patrick, examining the card. 'Sixty-five years of age. When do they retire?'

'Not until seventy-five,' said Joe promptly, and laughed as Patrick raised an eyebrow. 'No need to look impressed. I don't carry all those pieces of information in my head; the old vicar at St Nicholas told me that he was too old to climb down to his basement area after tennis balls now as he was seventy-four and he had just another year to go before retirement.'

'So, Dr Thompson has another ten years to go before retiring. Mind you, he has some young daughters, doesn't he? Some still at school, I think that he said. Could the archdeacon have been blackmailing him for any reason? Any gossip about a mistress, or anything like that?'

Joe shook his head. 'Not that I've heard. In any case, he's a widower so I suppose that it would be his own business. There might be a bit of gossip, but it wouldn't make a man commit murder just to keep a relationship secret. To be honest, I can't see him, can you?'

Patrick did not answer, but meticulously inscribed a

question mark before the words 'female relationship'. It still seemed very odd to him to think of a bishop with a wife and a family and an illicit relationship seemed to make the whole matter stranger. After all, the man's daughters might be terribly upset if they thought that their father was insulting the memory of their mother. The bishop, he thought, had seemed very fond and most proud of his daughters.

'Odd, isn't it?' he said aloud. 'Five clergymen at the cathedral and two of them are widowers. The third, the choirmaster, has never been married and the fourth is quite young, so I suppose that there is time for him yet.' His lips tightened as he thought of Eileen going to the tennis club dance with that young clergyman. He glanced back at his cards. 'Mr Bob Webster, aged twenty-six, deacon and university student,' he read aloud and then, after a brief struggle with himself, he put forward Eileen's theory. 'I suppose that if he were the ambitious type, he might get rid of the archdeacon just to inherit his job,' he said tentatively and looked across at Joe to see how he was taking it.

'Doesn't seem too likely to me,' said Joe promptly. 'After all, the other three men are senior to him. Even if they didn't fit the picture for the new archdeacon, I can't see the Archbishop of Armagh appointing someone junior to all of them and, what's more, from the same diocese. I'd say that would be a recipe for disaster. Not at all the way the Church of Ireland would go about things. I can imagine my mother and all her morning coffee friends gossiping about it.'

'I think you are right,' said Patrick, making a quick note. 'Fourth in line of succession' he wrote under the name of Mr Bob Webster.

'Mind you,' said Joe, 'if you were looking for a chancer, a man who would seize the opportunity to do himself a bit of good in the world, well, he'd be my choice out of the lot of them.'

He had an odd expression on his face, thought Patrick, almost as though he were wondering whether to speak or not. Deliberately, he occupied himself with his cards, translating dates of birth into actual ages. When it came to leaving a lucrative position open to inheritance, why then a man's age might be of importance. So, it was the Archbishop of Armagh, in the north of the country, who would be the one to fill the position. No pope, of course, in the Church of Ireland.

'Would the bishop himself have anything to do with filling the job of archdeacon?' he asked when a long enough space had elapsed to make it unlikely Joe was going to say anymore. Something about Eileen was on Joe's mind, guessed Patrick. After all, she had been at the tennis club dance with twenty-six-year-old Bob Webster. Perhaps Joe had been going to say something about Eileen and then decided not. He waited for an answer to his question while his sergeant made a visible effort to turn his mind to a different matter.

'I'd say that he would definitely be consulted,' said Joe after a short interval. 'After all, he would have to work quite closely with the archdeacon who would be his second in command. They're all very sociable in the Church of Ireland clergy, or so my mother tells me. She said that the vicar at St Nicholas had a great cook and that they bought the best as he was always having dinner parties.'

'So, the archdeacon would be in and out of the bishop's house,' said Patrick. 'Well, from what I've seen of his lord-ship,' he said with a quick glance at his cards in order to check dates of birth, 'yes,' he continued, 'I would reckon that sixty-four-year-old Bishop Thompson would have more in common with the dean, Dr Frank Babington aged fifty-five.'

'And the archdeacon was aged—' began Joe when he was interrupted by the ring of the phone. The internal one, noted Patrick, and waited with some impatience as Tommy's voice boomed down the line. Tommy had been the duty constable at the barracks since before Patrick was born. He dated back to the time of English rule, had been in the barracks for over thirty years, was immensely proud of being a Protestant and esteemed himself to be second in the line of importance, after the superintendent himself. Joe thought that both were a waste of space, but Patrick was cautious enough to keep his own opinion to himself. At least he had managed to convey to Tommy that he could give messages to Sergeant Duggan and didn't have to reserve them for Inspector Cashman himself. Now he tried to busy himself with his cards while Joe exchanged New Year goodwill compliments with Tommy and then listened to what he had to say. 'Just a moment, Tommy, I'll have a word with the inspector,' he said. Then, covering the receiver with the palm of his hand, he murmured in a low voice to Patrick, 'It's Mr Owen Hearn, the younger son of the late archdeacon. Would like to have a private word with you, what do you think? Shall I go and bring him in here?'

Patrick nodded, heard Joe tell Tommy that he would be down in a few minutes and waited until the receiver was replaced before saying, 'What does the fellow mean by private? This is a police station, not his solicitor's office.'

Joe shrugged. 'Well, I've plenty to be getting on with, but it's up to you.'

Patrick thought for a minute. The request for a private interview might well be an invention of Tommy's. The superintendent had once or twice expressed his opinion to Patrick that he might get more out of people if he didn't have Joe sitting in the background making notes. 'You can always write up notes afterwards – nobody has ever questioned my notes,' the superintendent had said with his usual air of knowing far more about policing business than Patrick. Patrick had carried out his usual procedure of listening politely, leaving a couple of days where he appeared to be carrying out the superintendent's advice and then had slipped back into having Joe sitting in on interviews. The superintendent could not last for ever. To give him his due he had recommended Patrick for promotion to the rank of inspector and when he went, Patrick would be the obvious choice for superintendent. When that day arrived then he, in his turn, would promote Joe to the rank of inspector. By that time, Joe would know everything that Patrick knew, or so he planned.

'Bring him in and then go and sit down in your usual place over there. That's the way that we do things here,' said Patrick. It angered him to think that Tommy might have been put up to that little manoeuvre by the superintendent who must know by now that his advice hadn't been accepted. Originally, he had asked the interviewed person whether they minded Joe sitting in, but now he thought it just put it into people's heads that they might have a right to object. Joe was the soul of discretion and had never interrupted an interview or called attention to himself in any way.

Patrick looked through his notebook. So far, he had not made a card out for Mr Owen Hearn, younger son of the late archdeacon, but he did have a few details. Lived in a boarding house in Dominic Street, just off Shandon Street, so not a very salubrious area for the son of an archdeacon, Patrick had thought at the time, though it probably was convenient for his places of work. Taught music and singing to the boys in Farranferris, and violin playing to the girls in St Vincent's School. A bit of a hand-to-mouth existence, probably. Both schools were well supplied with nuns and priests who gave their services free of charge and cost only their board and lodging and this Mr Owen Hearn would probably be employed for only a few hours a week in both schools. Patrick had inserted a tiny 'tick' of approbation at the end of his notes, and he clearly remembered thinking that the man came across as honest and straightforward. His father's death did not benefit him in any way; in fact, it had probably closed the door to any hopes that he might have had that this quite rich man would have funded a period abroad to enable the younger of his two sons to become established in the profession that he had chosen. But why had Mr Owen Hearn come seeking another interview with the police? Mechanically, Patrick tidied an already tidy desk, and selected a newly sharpened indelible pencil. Since this was indoors, he could just as easily have used a pen, and the inkwell was filled carefully by Tommy every morning, but somehow Patrick preferred the pencil. The business of dipping the pen into the ink had a tendency, he often found, of interrupting a flow of talk, and a pause in the conversation meant a held pen resulting often in an untidy blot which would have to be meticulously scratched out with a sharp knife if his notes needed to be presented in court.

'Come in, Mr Hearn,' he said, rising to his feet and endeavouring to make his voice sound friendly and welcoming. He shook hands across the table, wondered fleetingly whether he should ask the man how things were going in the world of music, but decided that he didn't know enough about the subject and so, like most Cork people, fell back upon the weather. 'Terrible day, isn't it? Do sit down, Mr Hearn.'

And now, he knew by experience, was the time to wait. Eileen had taught him that. When he had first started, he used to want to fill the silence with nervous remarks about the price of butter or the state of the land or the flooding on the quays, but Eileen had told him that she had found, when interviewing people for the *Cork Examiner*, that it was always best to give people time and to make sure that you didn't distract them. And so, he waited, musing over what he knew about the father of the man sitting opposite to him. Luckily the silence did not stretch too long. Mr Owen Hearn had a decisive look about him and after a quick look around the room, he focussed his gaze upon Patrick.

'Sorry to interrupt you, Inspector. There are just a few things on my mind, and I thought that they might be of use to you. Obviously, my father's murder is quite a puzzle. I've heard it discussed all over the city. There were a couple of women on the tram yesterday were chattering away, saying that . . . well, I seem to remember that the phrase was "sure, he didn't have an enemy in the world; poor soul!".'

Patrick smiled a little, more at the exactly accurate mimicry of a north-side accent, than at the words themselves. He said nothing, however. Just waited.

'But . . . I'm afraid, Inspector, that was not quite true. My father did have enemies. They may have had nothing to do with this complicated and elaborate murder, but there were people who disliked him and perhaps even hated him.' The man stopped and then resumed. 'And I would have to include myself, I'm afraid. There were times when I hated him and mostly, I'm afraid, almost from the time of my mother's death, I have disliked him.'

Patrick waited. Joe was in the background, his pencil would be moving over the page of the notebook, neatly labelled 'Cathedral Murder'. There was no need for Patrick to fill a moment or to add emphasis to the statement, by making any notes himself. He said nothing. There was no need, either, for a word of encouragement as the man was a fluent talker and had come to the barracks with his mind made up to tell his story.

'I wonder whether you have looked at my father's bank account, Inspector. He was well-paid, of course. The Church of Ireland pay those in higher ranks most generously. Nevertheless, my father's bank account must come as a surprise to anyone who would have imagined that he was just dependent upon his stipend from the Church of Ireland. You see, Inspector, my father received a substantial legacy, and a house with grounds of a couple of acres, from one of my aunts, a single lady who, as the only remaining member of the family, after the carnage of the Great War, inherited all the wealth on her father's side of the family. By this time, my older brother had embarked upon a career in the church, and I must confess that I had hoped that "Seven Beeches" would be bestowed upon me as I had always loved my visits to my aunt's house and had spent lovely peaceful hours fishing from the small river that ran through the grounds.'

'But it didn't happen.' Patrick thought it was time to put in an encouraging word as the man seemed to have come to a standstill.

'No,' he replied rather slowly. 'No, it didn't happen. In fact, my father had other ideas for this place. He was friendly with a nurse, one of our parishioners, a woman who was herself a nurse and married to a male nurse with no children and so she continued to work. Both worked in the Victoria Hospital. You know the Victoria Hospital, Inspector?'

Patrick nodded. He said nothing, just waited attentively. The Victoria Hospital catered for Protestants. Joe would know all about this place as it was situated just across the road from where he lived. He need ask no questions to interrupt the flow of words from the archdeacon's second son and after a few seconds, the man resumed his story with a well-practised ease.

'Well, Inspector, whether he had this idea himself, or whether she put it into his mind, he decided to invest some of his legacy in turning the house into a nursing home for elderly people. Spent quite a bit on the ground floor, added a whole new annex to it, with a series of bedrooms, single and double bedrooms, with a bathroom attached to each room. The original drawing room was left more or less intact, piano and everything, just some extra chairs and little tables introduced. The dining room, also, was not altered too much, but the long dining table was moved to one side of the room and a selection of small tables were added for those who liked to keep their own company or just to dine with a couple of friends. No cost was spared on expensive linen tablecloths and table napkins with individual napkin rings, just to add a homely touch – and expensive cut glass vases for fresh flowers from the garden, of course. Cost quite a bit, as you can imagine, but it became hugely popular – a home from home for the wealthy whose physical health and wits were deserting them. Every room occupied and quite a long waiting list, or so I am told.'

Mr Owen Hearn sat back and looked across at Inspector Cashman, and Patrick looked back at him, and, after a few moments' silence, said, 'Why are you telling me about this, Mr Hearn?'

The man was in no way disconcerted by this. Indeed, he smiled broadly. 'Just be patient for a moment, Inspector. There is a point to my story. My father had, of course, a perfect right to invest his legacy in a lucrative business and I, of course, having rejected my father's planned career for me, had no right to expect anything from him. But bear with me while I explain all to you. You see, Inspector, when Ireland regained its freedom from Britain it left a lot of Anglo-Irish elderly ladies, British, I suppose, marooned here in Ireland. Their brothers, their male cousins, and sometimes fathers and uncles were killed in the Great War. And even in their heyday of girlhood, there was a dearth of young men available to escort them to dances, to play tennis with them, and, even more important, to propose marriage to them as most joined the army, or went to India, or recognized that the future in Ireland for those of English blood was poor. And then, as these women came into old age, they found they were left without many males in their own families as the brothers and cousins had, in huge numbers, been killed on the battlefields and those who had survived the war did not want to try to make a living in a country which had now declared itself to be the "Irish Free State" and had wanted no more to do with England. These women who had reached their thirtieth or fortieth year in the early days of King Edward, were now getting to be old women and there was no family to support them. You can see, Inspector, the brilliance of my father's idea. He would set up a home from home for these single and lonely, though wealthy, old women who were living alone and poorly cared for. They were to have companionship, medical attention as they sank into their dotage, and it was all to be not in the alien situation of a hospital, but in a setting which mimicked the houses of their youth.' As Patrick mulled over the words, the archdeacon's son added, 'But, of course, for a sum, for a substantial sum of money, paid out monthly from their banks, more in most cases than the remains of what had been left to them could possibly afford as shares in this country fell rapidly after independence and the value of land plummeted.' He stopped as though waiting for an expression of interest or perhaps for a query, but Patrick said nothing and so he continued.

'And there lay the crux of the matter. My father, the respectable archdeacon, of course, kept out of these matters and his front of the house lieutenant was the woman, the nurse and her husband, a timid sort of man who was completely under her thumb. Her name, this woman's name was Clodagh. An ugly name I've always thought, though an Irish scholar told me that it originated from the ancient Irish language and was associated with the name of a river. Well, I'm not sure whether that was correct or not, but this Clodagh was as hard as iron. If the regular payments from the bank ceased, then she started upon relatives and if the relative did not pay up quite quickly, then they found that an old, incapable, frequently incontinent, woman was delivered to their doorstep. Once that had happened a couple of times, well, you can imagine how the money would be found, even if a begging plate had to be sent around wealthy relatives in England.'

Patrick sat back and thought about this. It was a terrible

story and showed up the late archdeacon as a most unpleasant person, but did it have any relevance to the murder which he was endeavouring to solve? After all, both he and Joe were fairly certain that using Enda to climb into the church late at night and bribing him with a packet of Rolo sweets meant that the murderer was connected to the cathedral, had a knowledge of the boy's skill in climbing and of his love of sweets and it probably pointed to the fact that Enda had been fed sweets on previous occasions so that he knew the promise would be kept. Also, the murderer had to know where and how the communion wine was set out so that clear directions could be given to the boy. There was a question that he could put, though he was not sure whether it would be answered truthfully. He made a note on a new page to give him an excuse for removing his eyes from the man's face while he made his query.

'This is most interesting, Mr Hearn,' he said. 'Did you, personally, know any of these unfortunate elderly women?'

Now that he was looking straight into the face of the man, he could read the expression of a person who had been asked a welcome question. This story had a purpose.

'Yes, indeed, Inspector. I got the whole story from Canon Wilson, Canon Jack Wilson. His own aunt was one of the relatives who had been "tapped", if that is the right word, for a contribution to keep an elderly second or third cousin in the nursing home which had, indeed, been her home during the previous ten years of her life.'

'I see,' said Patrick. This was slightly unexpected. Was he being told these unpleasant facts about the late archdeacon to deflect suspicion from the disinherited son? 'And does Canon Wilson know that you were coming here to tell me about it?'

'Yes, certainly. We talked it over and thought that you should know. There is, as you probably know, a lot of coming and going between this country and the mother land. A pleasant sea journey from Liverpool to Cork. Many people come for the hunting at this time of the year. We have so many packs here in County Cork – the West Carbery Hounds and, of course, the Duhallow Hounds, both have been going for almost a hundred years. And St Stephen's Day is the big hunting day of the year, of course. A great crowd come across for St Stephen's Day.'

This was something new. But, of course, it was true. Patrick couldn't see the point of chasing an unfortunate fox over fields and through woodlands. He had wondered sometimes how the farmers put up with it, but there was no doubt that there were a lot of English accents around the best hotels in the city for the post-Christmas period. And, he supposed, men who liked killing foxes might find it easy to kill someone who had hounded and humiliated some unfortunate elderly relatives.

'Well, it's good of you to take the trouble to come and see us, sir,' he said. 'Is there anything else that you would like to mention?'

'No, that's about it.' The archdeacon's son was on his feet. And Patrick rose, also.

'Do you hunt yourself, sir?' he asked as he escorted him to the door.

'What! And me a musician! My hands are devoted to playing the violin, Inspector. I don't think that it would do them any good to be tugging on a horse's reins and crashing through thorns, not to mention the chance of a broken arm when jumping over those stone walls!'

The man was still laughing in a light-hearted way as he went down the corridor and they heard his voice tell the joke to Tommy at the outer desk. Tommy would then go and tell the joke to the superintendent, and they would both have a good gossip about the various packs of hounds in the county of Cork. Patrick mused for a moment about the comradery that still existed between the remaining Protestants in the city. A thought came to him as he looked through his notes. Yes, he had made a note of the address and telephone number.

'I think, Joe, I'll have a word with the dead man's solicitor,' he said and waited impatiently for Tommy to break off his conversation and condescend to lift the phone.

'Get me Cork 6879, please, Tommy,' he said and added

mentally, *And no need for you to listen in.* He waited, holding the phone, heard Tommy speak to a secretary and then, with his hand over the mouthpiece, communicate in muffled tones with Mr Owen Hearn that 'the inspector was getting onto the solicitor'.

Patrick waited patiently, making a vow that if ever he became superintendent that he would make sure that he had a private line to his office. Once the crisp voice on the other end of the line said, 'Peter Dillon, here, Inspector. How can I help you?'

'Thank you, Tommy,' said Patrick. He deliberately waited until Tommy had replaced his phone before he said, 'It's about the estate of the late Archdeacon Hearn, Mr Dillon. Just a quick question. I have just had the archdeacon's youngest son here and he mentioned that his father was in a partnership in a nursing home business. Perhaps you could fill me in about it,' said Patrick, hoping that not too many legal terms would be heaped upon him and wishing that he could have the conversation in writing so that he could ponder over it.

He listened very intently. Mr Dillon, obviously, had not got around to doing anything about this business. His excuse was that he was waiting to have a word with the heir about it, but he had planned to ask for profit figures and to do an estimate of how much the business was worth and then to ask the remaining partner whether she would like to buy the holding out or whether she would prefer him to advertise for a new partner. 'My knowledge, so far as it goes, Inspector, seems to indicate that this was an immensely profitable business, and it may be that the heir might want to hold onto it and be, like his father before him, a sleeping partner. Otherwise, by the terms of the contract, first preference has to be offered to the surviving owner of the business.'

Patrick said nothing, just waited. It worked, of course. Most of these solicitors were great talkers and few could resist showing how clever they were.

'And my opinion, for what it is worth, Inspector, is that she, the owner of the business, will want to buy us out so as to continue to exercise full control over the running of the nursing home. The late archdeacon told me that he had nothing to do with it. It was, to him, just like an investment in a company. I suspect that the owner would wish to retain full control, but we must wait and see.'

Patrick frowned. 'Would that be correct? If there were any malpractice or a legal case, could the archdeacon deny all responsibility?'

There was a silence and then Mr Dillon's voice flowed as fluently as always. 'Well, of course, in that case . . . but so far as the present circumstances are concerned, that, Inspector Cashman, is the present situation. The lady in charge of the nursing home has been told of the death and the options have been put to her. The heir, the Reverend Adam Hearn, Rector of Midleton parish, has been informed of the circumstance and is willing to await her decision.'

'I see,' said Patrick. 'Thank you, Mr Dillon.' He replaced the phone and turned to Joe. 'Don't know if this brings us any further in our own business,' he said. 'The solicitor implied that the archdeacon shut his eyes to the running of the nursing home and took half of the profits. Presumably, the woman, this nurse, owns a half share in the business and for that she does all the work and then gets the other half of the profits. The solicitor was being very cagey. I suspect he might have heard of a few rumours of dodgy practice – from what Mr Owen Hearn said it almost sounds like a case of blackmail, throwing these unfortunate old women out of their nursing home and dumping them back with relatives. I'm going to keep an eye on that place from now on.'

'The further we go in this case, the more I think that it was a miracle that someone didn't murder that archdeacon years ago,' said Joe cheerfully.

FOURTEEN

Eileen, thought the Reverend Mother, was looking unusually hesitant when she appeared at the convent at the early hour of nine o'clock. Unlike her normal practice, she did not immediately blurt out what had led her to seek the company of an elderly nun when so many exciting New Year events were taking place in the city. She had a look of embarrassment on her face and twisted her fingers as the Reverend Mother wished her a happy new year and added polite wishes to Eileen's mother.

'Something is troubling you, my child,' she observed after Eileen's voice returning the good wishes had died into silence and a glance at the clock showed the Reverend Mother that she had precisely five minutes left before receiving a visit from Sister Mary Immaculate who wished to discuss a more active effort at recruiting novices to their convent. 'Just tell me what it is; and we can put our heads together,' she said briskly.

Eileen made a quick impatient gesture with one hand, as though waving doubts aside. 'I know that I can trust you,' she said, and almost without drawing breath she blurted it all out. 'A girl at the tennis club dance asked me to help her. She asked me, because the fellow who took me to the dance told her that I was from the slums and so . . .'

The Reverend Mother could hear the hurt in the girl's voice and hastened to apply her sovereign remedy. 'Sticks and stones can break my bones, but words can never harm me' the children chanted in the playground, and she always encouraged that attitude. 'Interesting word, "slum", isn't it?' she remarked. 'Not a word used by Dickens though we associate "slum" with his writings. Apparently it originally meant a room, a back room, I seem to remember. It was a favourite word with London cockneys and gradually came to be associated with them. An example of how words seem to change their meaning going down through the centuries, isn't it? I gather that these people are not particular friends of yours.'

'The man is the deacon in the Proddy – I mean in the Church of Ireland cathedral,' said Eileen. 'And the girl is the daughter of their bishop.'

'I see,' said the Reverend Mother placidly. 'And you know these people, do you?'

'Bob Webster is studying for a doctorate in law and philosophy at the university. And the girl, Jacinta is her name, asked him to marry her and he refused and sent her to me – because I lived in the slums and might be able to help her,' said Eileen. She looked at the Reverend Mother in a slightly defiant fashion.

'Well, that's very succinct,' said the Reverend Mother. 'But I do feel that I need a bit more information. How did the interesting word "slums" come to be introduced?'

Eileen bit her lip, but then reluctantly gave a slight giggle. She perched on the windowsill and took out a notebook.

'I must remember that about the origin of the word, slums,' she said after she had scribbled a note. 'It would make a good lead-in for an interesting article in the *Cork Examiner*.' She put away the notebook, hesitated for a moment and then, with a glance at the clock, seemed to remind herself that the Reverend Mother's time was limited, and she visibly drew in a long breath. 'At no time did this Jacinta Thompson ask me to keep a secret and so I feel quite justified in talking to you.'

The Reverend Mother said nothing. She was always cautious about promising secrecy – when it was asked for, she usually replied that she could only promise to do what she felt was right. Eileen had not asked and so she waited to hear what the connection between the word 'slums' and the bishop's daughter was and why the deacon, whom she remembered from Christmas morning as a handsome young man, would have involved Eileen. Deliberately she walked across the room, put a few sods of turf upon the fire and then sat down beside it. 'Come and sit beside the fire,' she said.

Eileen obeyed instantly and that moment while she crossed the room seemed to help to unlock her tongue.

'This Jacinta – she'd be about my age or a bit older – thinks that she is pregnant, and she is terrified to tell anyone and so she wants to get rid of the . . .'

'Of the baby,' said the Reverend Mother placidly. 'Though perhaps she didn't use that word,' she added. 'How does she know that she is pregnant?'

'She has missed three periods and she is sick in the morning,' said Eileen.

'It seems most likely that she is pregnant,' said the Reverend Mother placidly. 'Has she thought about marriage?'

'He's dead,' said Eileen. 'It was the archdeacon, the man who was killed by drinking the poisoned wine on the altar.'

'And what did you say?' enquired the Reverend Mother.

'I told her that I could not help her,' said Eileen stiffly. 'I never even heard of anyone like that, and I have no idea what they do.'

That was probably true, thought the Reverend Mother. It would not have been true of most girls of Eileen's age and from her background, but Eileen's intense ambition meant that she had kept away from the temptation of public houses, and of earning easy money by selling her services down on the quays to sailors and others who could pay. Abortion, according to Dr Scher, was one of the great evils among poverty-stricken girls and women and caused almost as many deaths as disease and malnutrition.

'So, you told her that you could not help her. That was right and good. I suppose you suggested that she get married and she told you that the man responsible for her condition was dead. And how did Mr Webster, the deacon, come into the matter?'

'She had told him that if he would marry her, she would do her best to get her father to appoint him to the position of archdeacon. She seemed to think that her father could pull some strings and get that for him. He's a most ambitious sort of fellow, I think, and apparently the top men in the Church of Ireland get well paid, but the ones on the bottom layer get very poorly paid. Is that right, do you think, Reverend Mother?'

'I must say that I have heard something about that,' confessed the Reverend Mother. 'And what did young Mr Webster say to that proposition?'

Eileen's eyes sparked anger. 'You won't believe this, Reverend Mother, but he told her that he would marry her if she got rid of . . . well, you know. He even said that he wouldn't have another man's b— Well, illegitimate, he meant . . . that he wouldn't have another man's child sitting at his table. Imagine! Someone who is supposed to be a sort of priest! Well, a clergyman, anyway. Imagine him suggesting that she should go off and get an abortion!'

'And so, he suggested that she try you and you turned her down, so what happened next?'

'Well, I was pretty furious, I went off. I was going to go home, but the woman in the cloakroom was making a fuss about me walking to the station and wanting to call a taxi for me and then Joe Duggan, Patrick's sergeant, came out and he persuaded me to come back in. Believe it or not, I had quite a nice time with some of the university crowd, after all,' finished Eileen, looking slightly shame-faced.

'Did Joe know why you wanted to go home?'

'He didn't ask,' said Eileen. 'He probably thought that someone had got fresh with me, or something. He just said someone was looking for me and walked over to the crowd from the university and said, "Here she is." And a fellow called Larry asked me to dance. And so, I sort of pushed it all to the back of my mind.' Eileen bit her lip, looked through the window and then back at the Reverend Mother. Then said, rather slowly, 'I was wondering should I tell Patrick about it. What do you think, Reverend Mother?'

The Reverend Mother thought about the matter for a few seconds. 'Why?' she asked.

Eileen looked slightly taken aback. 'I want to help Patrick,' she said. 'After all, we're friends, were neighbours when we were growing up. These sort of people, well, they despise people like Patrick and me. *Slum dwellers*, both of us,' she finished. There was, thought the Reverend Mother, a hint of anger and of belligerence in the girl's voice. Eileen, she thought, had managed until now to surmount the petty snobbery which was rife in the city of Cork. She had impetuously joined the IRA at the age of sixteen, had been in a house with some university students, male and female, accepted by them, valued for her courage, her quick brain and her sociable disposition and her ability to write eye-catching articles for the local newspaper. And then, when the civil war ended and she tired of the violence, she had worked for a local printer and continued to write for the *Cork Examiner*, had mixed with journalists and radical thinkers, then had been persuaded to go back to her studies and sit for a university scholarship and was now studying law after achieving a first-class honours degree in English. Her friends had been of the sort where origins did not matter, and where people had been valued for brains and courage and a quick tongue. The Reverend Mother was proud of her, but she had seen too much of the class-ridden society in Cork city to believe that Eileen's road would always be an easy one. However, this girl, whom she had known since she was four years old, was resilient and confident and would soon recover from the hurt to her *amour propre*. The other girl was a different matter.

'You are a law student, Eileen,' she said quietly. 'But, of course, you have only had a few months of study. It would be impossible for you to know all the laws that have been passed in this country of Ireland, most of which we have inherited from the British regime, but I will just draw your attention to a law passed in 1861 and still in existence. I think,' added the Reverend Mother watching Eileen's face, 'that the exact words were and still are "procuring a miscarriage is a criminal offence subject to penal servitude for life.".'

'Oh, I wasn't thinking of anything like that! Prison for life! I wouldn't want anything like that to happen to her!' Eileen's voice was horrified, and her cheeks flushed up in a wave of bright red. 'I was just hoping to help Patrick, just to show him what a dreadful man this archdeacon was. I had an idea that the bishop might have, well, I didn't think he would do anything himself, but he might have, well, mentioned it to someone, and perhaps paid someone to get rid of the archdeacon, to punish him, well, I was thinking that he might have given some money to someone like Tom

Hayes, the sexton, thinking that he would get rid of the fellow, not really thinking about how he would do it. But I don't think he would have done it, but someone else. I was in a muddle. I was just going to tell Patrick and let him work it out. I didn't mean any harm to Jacinta. I didn't know . . .' Eileen's voice faded away and she stared miserably at the Reverend Mother with tears in her eyes.

'You have done no harm; you may have done some good,' said the Reverend Mother. 'I am honoured by your trust in me, and you may leave the matter in my hands,' she finished. And then she said gently, 'I have been told that over a hundred women last year were identified as dying, here in Cork, of botched abortions, many others live with permanent ill health. I hope that when you are a lawyer you might help to make the lives of these women an easier one. Now,' she said, rising to her feet, 'give my best wishes to your mother for a happy new year and put the other matter from your mind. Leave it to me to deal with.'

Once Eileen had left the room, the Reverend Mother took her cloak from its hook, laid a sheaf of paper on her desk, checked the locks on its drawers, pocketed the keys and went to the door.

'Ah, Sister Mary Immaculate,' she said as a head emerged from the parlour opposite to her room, 'I fear I have to go out on urgent business. I wonder would you be so kind as to take my place. Deal with phone calls and with any visitors. There is a good fire in here and I have put out some paper so that you could jot down your ideas and when I come back, we will discuss them.'

Having made as much amends for the missed appointment as she could – Sister Mary Immaculate did enjoy sitting in the Reverend Mother's study – she then hastened out of the convent gate and made her way up Bishop Street. When she arrived at the gate of the bishop's palace, she hauled up her watch and opened its lid. Half-past nine of the morning – too early for the bishop to be out, on a day when no religious service was scheduled, and late enough, she hoped, for his lordship to have finished his breakfast.

Several of the tall Georgian windows in the magnificent

house were still shrouded in pale blinds, but she hoped that these were the rooms belonging to his numerous daughters who probably had been celebrating New Year's Eve until early in that morning. She rang the bell and asked for the bishop in a confident manner, telling herself, as she was shown into a parlour, that if he wasn't up yet, he should be sufficiently ashamed of himself to hasten his toilet. In the meantime, she would have time to gather her thoughts and think through a few possible solutions until about ten minutes had elapsed and his lordship appeared.

'Now, you must have some coffee, or tea.' The bishop, she observed, was unusually resolute in his offer of refreshment and so she agreed amiably to have a cup of tea and then changed her mind and chose coffee. It was a treat that she seldom enjoyed but she had a difficult interview ahead of her and it would be just as well if she had all her wits working well. There was, she noticed with amusement, a dish with some small sausages and rolled up rashers of bacon, each pierced with a small toothpick, so that a substantial breakfast could be eaten easily under the guise of a mid-morning snack, and she mentally noted this excellent idea as an interesting piece of gossip to pass onto Dr Scher who was, he had often told her, very fond of sausages. She declined the sausages but accepted a scone. It would be, she decided, only kind to allow Bishop Thompson to fortify the inner man before she dropped her bombshell.

What a pity it was that the man was a widower, she thought impatiently as she watched him eat. Not his fault, perhaps, she had to admit, but the Church of Ireland congregation, she was sure, would have many widows who would have been delighted to marry the bishop of Cork and look after his numerous daughters. Women were so much more practical, more sensible, and so much easier to talk to about delicate matters. Still, the Reverend Mother made a habit of never bewailing what could not be helped and so, once he had made what she considered to be a more than adequate breakfast for an overweight man, she plunged into her story.

'You were telling me that you have a married daughter with a little boy,' she said with a smile. 'What is her name?'

He was relieved that her conversation was not to be about
a dead child and a brutal murder. His face lit up. 'Maria,' he
said, 'yes, she has one little boy. Lovely little fellow,' he said
enthusiastically. 'Maria dotes upon him.'

'And so do you, I'm sure,' said the Reverend Mother with
a kind smile. 'And Jacinta is your next daughter, is that right?'
she went on rapidly. The news had to be broken and the solution discussed. There was no point in delaying matters and
so, before he could answer, she went on. 'It's about Jacinta
that I wished to speak to you. I hope that you will excuse me
for disturbing you so early in the morning.'

He had buttered a piece of toast and smeared it with a thick
layer of marmalade, but now, struck by her tone, he put down
the knife and pushed the plate aside.

'About Jacinta,' he repeated.

'Jacinta is in trouble, I'm afraid,' said the Reverend Mother.
It was a phrase which was often used by girls who came to
see her, came hoping that there might be some escape from a
predicament and in the hopes of borrowing some money to
get the boat to England and find some means of supporting
themselves and their child in a country where more jobs were
available. Jacinta's predicament would not involve destitution
or starvation, but the emotional weight on the family would,
perhaps, be greater. 'She is expecting a baby,' she added.

'What!' His voice rose in an exclamation of disbelief and
horror. 'That's not possible,' he said. His eyes widened and his
cheekbones turned an odd shade of purple. The Reverend
Mother very much regretted the absence of a second wife, of
that convenient widow who might have taken over the care
of an amiable man and his bevy of daughters. She hoped that
he was not going to collapse into some sort of a fit. Perhaps,
she thought, I should have asked Dr Scher to break the news.
At least he would be some use if the man had a stroke or a
heart attack.

'These things happen,' she said in a soothing voice. 'She
is lucky. She has you to care for her and to protect her from
taking desperate measures. Many girls that I have known have
lost their lives by resorting to illicit abortionists.'

That was plain speaking, and she saw him pale and then

that strange colour darkened upon his face again and suffused his cheeks. It was time that she came out with the solution that had occurred to her. She knew the next ten minutes were vital to the success of her plan.

'It is, of course, perfectly possible for a woman to bring up a child on her own,' she said calmly. Face him with an unacceptable solution and then, in the midst of his horror, introduce her advice. 'Hundreds do,' she continued, with a wave of her hand. 'I must say that even in this immediate neighbourhood, I'm afraid that absent or unknown fathers are the norm, and it would be a most unusually lucky young woman who has a father able to support her.'

'But . . .' he said and then he stopped. She could read his mind. All very well for the daughters of the slums, but the daughter of a Church of Ireland bishop could not possibly bring up a child out of wedlock in her father's palace. She searched her mind for a solution and then beamed upon him.

'You said you had a grandson. Your daughter Maria lives in England, is that right?' Couldn't be better, she told herself. The age-old solution. Go to another country.

'The apple of my eye,' he said, and a pleasant smile came over his face. 'Her son is four years old,' he said. 'Tom is his name. A big boy for his age. Learning to read now!'

She looked at him kindly. Such a nice man. So easy to manage. She was sure of that. Her brain worked fast. Four years old and no mention of another child. A problem with fertility, perhaps. Needed a little companion, perhaps. She leaned forward.

'If you and Jacinta were to pay a visit, a new year visit to Maria over in her English home, that would cause no remark. While there, Jacinta could explain her predicament to Maria, could perhaps remain with her sister until the baby is born. And, who knows, it might be possible that Maria would want to bring up the child as a little companion to her son. There is no other child in the family, is that right?'

'No other child,' he repeated. He was thinking hard. 'Maria has been a little sad about that,' he confided. 'Everyone has been at pains to reassure her, to encourage her to believe that there was plenty of time, but . . .'

'I would say nothing,' advised the Reverend Mother. 'It would be quite natural to take Jacinta along as a companion on your little visit. The other girls will be going back to school. Say nothing to Maria. Allow Jacinta to tell her own story and for the sisters to find a solution.'

She watched the despairing look on his face begin to dissipate. She sat very still and did not interrupt his thought process. He was, she guessed, weighing up the personalities of his two oldest daughters, perhaps remembering things from their relationship. Whatever it was, his thoughts were lightening his mood, dissipating the look of near despair that had clouded his face up to a few minutes ago. One of these men who sail through life happily and mostly rely on their womenfolk to sort things out for them. With Dr Thompson, it would have been his wife originally, but when she died, perhaps her place was taken by this Maria. That often happened.

'I suppose,' she said aloud, 'Maria, being the eldest, was a little mother to her sisters after your wife died.'

He smiled ruefully. 'My sister used to tell me that I should have got a governess, but somehow Maria always seemed to know the right thing to do. It was she who decided upon boarding school for them all. She reasoned that she would be there if any of the younger ones suffered homesickness. She insisted on coming with me when I went to see the principal, made sure that the younger ones were with each other in the dormitory, were in beds placed side by side. When they all went off to school, she told me not to worry. That she would make sure to see them all at some time during the day. The school said that she was a mother to them all.' The bishop touched his eyes with his handkerchief. 'I've missed her so much. And yet he is a fine young man. She met him at a dance in Fermoy. Love at first sight. She'll know the right thing to do,' he added in more cheerful tones and pocketed his handkerchief and added, 'Do you think that Jacinta should adopt another name when she is over with her sister?'

The Reverend Mother gave him a sympathetic smile. 'I'm sure that Maria will care for Jacinta and give her good advice about that and other matters.' It was, she thought, none of her business whether Jacinta adopted a married name, but perhaps she could drop him a hint. 'I remember that when I entered the convent and dropped the name Dorothy, a name that I always disliked, and adopted St Thomas Aquinas' name, I felt it to be the beginning of a new life. I see nothing in God's law to prevent someone taking a new name. And, if I may advise, I would recommend that you and Jacinta leave for England as soon as possible. A telephone call to Maria would probably be all that is necessary.'

She rose to her feet. He had not asked the obvious question and she wondered whether he knew who the man was. Once the efficient Maria had gone off to England six or seven years ago, the other girls would have been left to their own devices once they had left school. No doubt he would be guilty about that. Odd that he didn't ask, but perhaps he was one of those men who preferred to avoid embarrassing or distressing subjects. She allowed him to accompany her to the door and even to the gate, listening to his small talk about the weather and about the magnificent holly tree in the side garden of the bishop's palace, but he did not take the opportunity to broach the subject. Nor did he ask for any promises of silence on her part.

And yet it was information that should be conveyed to Patrick.

She puzzled over that until she reached the convent, and then the sight of a shabby old Humber car drawn up outside the convent gate gave her an idea.

FIFTEEN

I t was the following morning when Joe put his head round the door to Patrick's office. 'Well, I've just had a strange phone call,' he said. 'You know how I sent the constable around to every chemist shop in town and nobody could remember selling cyanide for wasps' nests during the last few weeks? Just what I expected, really. August is the time for trouble with wasps, not Christmas.'

Patrick looked up with interest. 'But now someone has remembered something.'

'Better than that,' said Joe. 'It's Fielding's on Patrick Street. We had checked it, of course, checked every chemist shop in the city. I sent the young fellow around. Well, when the constable visited that place, he saw the owner; the old man, himself, a most careful fellow. Told the constable that he always makes a note of the name of anyone purchasing a dangerous substance, interrogates them about why they need it and gives them instructions about not leaving it lying around the house afterwards. And if he is not present, well, the staff have instructions to do the same thing. So, when the constable asked him to look in his book, well, he showed it immediately and said that he had only sold one this year. In June, apparently, and to a man who lives out in Douglas village. That was all. Very wet August if you remember. No trouble with wasps, but . . .' Joe gave a dramatic pause.

'But he was out one day in December . . .' suggested Patrick.

'That's right,' said Joe, 'down with influenza, off work for a fortnight. And so, the son was in charge. Now we come to my phone call. It was a girl. Didn't want to give her name. Said she worked in Fielding's Pharmacy, and she heard what Mr Fielding said to the constable. Didn't like to interfere, but there *was* something sold in December to destroy a wasps' nest. Young Mr Fielding was in charge while his father was ill and apparently a person, a young lady, came in looking for something to kill wasps, middle of December, mark you. The girl who spoke to me said that the customer was a friend of his, the two of them were great friends, according to the shop girl who spoke to me, at least it sounded like a girl, wouldn't give her name, one of those anonymous tip-offs that Cork people love, but said that the pair were great friends, the boss's son and this girl, the customer, chatting about the tennis club.' Joe paused dramatically once more. 'They were on first name terms, also. You'll never guess, but I'll tell you who I think it was – from the description of the girl, blonde hair, very posh accent, and how many girls in the city of Cork do you know with a first name of Jacinta . . .?'

Patrick picked up his pencil. 'Jacinta! The bishop's daughter!' He tapped his lips meditatively with the pencil and then began to think hard. This could be hugely important. Dr Scher had told him of her predicament, had asked for secrecy, but he, a wise man, had not made it a condition, just a suggestion. Patrick thought about the matter and then decided that though Joe was eminently trustworthy, still that piece of information he would keep to himself for the moment. He would have to tell him, of course, sooner rather than later. There was no way that they could work together unless Joe knew all the facts, but still, one matter at a time. The facts from this anonymous phone call had to be recorded.

'When did she buy the stuff?' he asked.

'December the tenth,' said Joe promptly, and then checked his notebook. Patrick had a moment's pride in how well trained his sergeant was, but the satisfaction faded with the realization that this girl was the daughter of the Very Reverend Church of Ireland Bishop of Cork, and that he was going to have to follow up on this matter. And, what was worse, he was going to have to upset Dr Scher and the Reverend Mother.

'December the tenth,' he repeated thoughtfully. 'About a fortnight before the murder. Murders,' he amended. Little Enda must not be forgotten. 'Did your young lady informant tell you why the bishop's daughter wanted cyanide for a wasps' nest in the middle of December?' he asked.

'Yes, indeed,' said Joe. 'Apparently said that a neighbour asked her to get it. The girl in the shop asked her if she was going to use it herself, but she said "no". She said it was for a neighbour, that he had discovered a huge wasps' nest in the attic and wanted to get rid of it before the servants panicked. He was going to attend to it himself.'

'A neighbour,' said Patrick thoughtfully. 'A neighbour to the bishop.'

'Not too many houses on Bishop Street,' said Joe. 'I can only think of one that could be called a neighbour to the bishop, and that is the archdeacon's house which is built just beside his gate. There's a lot of land around the bishop's palace. The other houses on the street are quite a distance away, so that rules the neighbour business out. He's unlikely to have murdered himself. If he wanted to commit suicide, then I can think of easier and pleasanter ways of doing it. Why should he commit suicide? Unless, of course, it was because of his bad relationship with his son, his second son?' Joe put forward the suggestion in a perfunctory fashion and almost immediately added. 'Unlikely. Not the kind. He could have easily remedied that if he felt guilty about it. Just had to change that unfair will. A bit of a bastard, wasn't he? Between ourselves, of course. Plenty of people might have wanted him out of the way, but he wasn't the type to commit suicide.'

'So, if the archdeacon is the only neighbour to the bishop's house, then the tale of a neighbour wanting it sounds like a lie, doesn't it? So why should the bishop's daughter go into a chemist shop and buy cyanide to kill wasps in the middle of December?' Patrick thought about the matter.

'But Jacinta Thompson,' said Joe. 'Why, on earth, should she . . .?' And then, visibly, he stopped, sitting very still and the fingers of his hands, placed upon Patrick's desk, splayed out in a fan-like conformation. He stared over the top of Patrick's head, his eyes fixed upon the window, his lower lip gripped between his teeth.

'Eileen might know something, Patrick,' he said. 'There was something going on at that New Year's Eve dance. The fellow that took Eileen, the deacon – what's his name . . . Bob

Webster – well, he deserted Eileen at one stage, spent ages talking with this Jacinta Thompson, and then Jacinta Thompson went off with Eileen to the ladies' room and there was some sort of row between them. Eileen came back in a blazing temper and went to get her coat. They're very careful of the girls, there, at the tennis club and the woman didn't want her to go off on her own and I came into it and managed to calm Eileen down. Got her in with some of the university crowd. But somehow or other I think it might be interesting to chat with Eileen. Like me to fetch her? She won't have gone out, I'd say. She told me that she usually does some writing in the morning.'

Patrick barely had time to give a reluctant nod before Joe was out of the door. There was the sound of the Ford engine starting up and then the police car, the pride and joy of the superintendent's daily life, slid out and turned up towards the top of the hill. Carefully Patrick removed the telephone receiver from its perch and left it lying on its side on top of the blotter. The superintendent would have been bound to see the car go out and would probably dial Patrick's number to find out where Joe had gone and why a mere sergeant had been granted the use of the police car to go on such a lowly errand.

At the sound of a heavy footstep in the corridor that led to the superintendent's room, he hastily picked up the phone and when the door was pushed open after a perfunctory knock, he was, with the phone clasped to his ear, apparently in the middle of inscribing a dictated note. To his relief his act worked, and the superintendent withdrew hastily and tramped down the corridor to see what he could get out of the duty constable.

Eileen was in good form when she arrived, chatting gaily with Joe about the tennis club dance and laughing at his mimicry of the speech from the club's chairman. 'He missed a treat, didn't he, Joe,' she said with a nod at Patrick. 'Must come next year, mustn't he? I'll tell you what, Patrick, if you ask me now, I'll make a note in my diary. I get very booked up, you know.'

'That would be nice,' said Patrick cautiously. 'I'm sorry to trouble you, Eileen, but the matter is very secret and very confidential so I thought we might be more private here in my office. You don't mind if Joe is present, do you?'

'No, as long as you don't tell him that I was the one who broke the gaslight outside Mrs McGinty's front door,' said Eileen promptly.

'I don't remember that, and who's Mrs McGinty anyway?' said Patrick, and then felt stupid when he saw that they were both laughing.

'This is serious, Eileen,' he said stiffly. 'We have a murder on our hands, and we need to eliminate as many people as possible from our enquiries so as to concentrate on those that might have valuable information for us. Now, you were speaking to the bishop's daughter for a long time on the evening of the tennis club dance . . .'

'You should have a warning sign on you, Joe,' said Eileen. '"*Everything you say or do will be taken down and given to the man behind the desk.*"'

'A man and a small boy have been murdered, Eileen, and I have to do my best to catch the murderer before a third person is killed,' said Patrick angrily. And then he controlled himself and turned back to his notebook and opened it at a fresh page. 'Was there anything said that might lead us towards whoever did such a terrible thing?' he said and looked at her.

Eileen's face had changed, and he knew that she was thinking of Enda. There was a pause. He could see that she was turning over the matter in her mind. When she spoke, he had the impression that she was choosing her words with care.

'Let's say, from what I have picked up from acquaintances, that this archdeacon was a foul, evil man just the type to take advantage of a young girl that he had known since she was a young child. And I wouldn't put it past him to murder a little boy if he thought it would be useful to him,' she said and added, 'now I really must fly. I have a lot to do and a most important essay to write. Come on, Joe! How about letting me drive on the way home?'

That would be that, but he would not let her get her own

way completely. He rose to his feet and held out a hand to Joe for the car keys. 'I'm off to see someone and I'll drop you off on the way,' he said, endeavouring for a note of casual friendliness. 'Thanks, Joe,' he added as he made for the door, grabbing his coat and cap as he went.

'Going out, Inspector?' Old Tommy, as usual, trying to keep up his position of the best-informed person in the office.

'That's right,' said Patrick and having won that small victory, he held the door open for Eileen with as friendly a smile as he could manage.

'If you are going into town, drop me in the South Mall, will you?' she said, once he had cranked up the engine.

He nodded but made no enquiries. He wouldn't give her the satisfaction. She would have no opportunity of snubbing him. She was, he knew, far cleverer than he, and he found himself often resenting that fact.

'It's an annoying case, isn't it?' she said in a casual manner. 'He just seems to be the sort of man that could be a bit of a criminal himself, but it's difficult to find someone who would have murdered him. No one liked him, but murder him? That's another step, isn't it? Don't worry about it, though. Something will crop up and then all will be revealed.'

'Yes,' he said. He endeavoured to speak as carelessly as he could and to sound absent-minded as though he had more on his mind than she could ever realize. This was always the way to deal with Eileen. Ask her a straight question and you got a teasing answer. Convey to her that you did not need her help and she became intrigued. 'Will it be all right if I drop you at the bridge?' he said. 'I'm going straight ahead.' He would not, he thought, tell her that he was going to see the Reverend Mother. It would be hard to make up an excuse and a bit feeble to reveal that he was looking for enlightenment from an elderly nun who had taught him when he was seven years old.

'Going to see the Reverend Mother?' she enquired as she got out of the car. 'That's a good idea. She always knows all of the gossip.'

It was the first day back at school, something he had not realized until he had drawn up in front of the convent and

heard the shrill voices from the playground. The Reverend
Mother was on playground duty and seemed to be surrounded
by a large crowd of children. His arrival caused the gathering
to thin a little, but he himself, and the Garda car, were well-
known to most children and so, after a quick dash to see
whether anyone else was within the car, the majority of the
children immediately returned to the Reverend Mother and
resumed their cross-questioning of her.

It must, he thought, be difficult for her. The younger children
asked the questions, but the older ones hung around on the
outskirts and listened carefully. Like himself at that age, he
thought. Children wanted to know 'how' and 'why'.

The 'why' was explained in simple terms.

'Enda,' said the Reverend Mother, 'might have been asked
to do something bad by someone.'

'Poison the archdeacon,' said one of Enda's neighbours.

'Put poison in the holy wine and he fell down in a fit and
died,' said another and Patrick winced as he realized that
information carefully locked into his desk drawer was common
knowledge among the schoolchildren.

'A bad man gave Enda the poison,' said one of the older
girls. 'He'll go to hell, won't he, Reverend Mother?'

'Might be a "she"!'

'Nah. Women don't do things like that.'

'Yes, they do.'

'No, they don't!'

'Womens allus poisons peoples, 'cos they'se not strong
enough to stick a knife into them.'

'Yes, they are!'

'No, they're not!'

'Do it take long to die of poison, Reverend Mother?'

'He'll go to hell, won't he?'

'A man would've done the climbing hisself. Not bothered
with Enda.'

'Be too big to get through the window, man couldn't get
through that, ye *amadan*.'

'Do you know who dun it, Reverend Mother?'

'Bet you do, don't you, Reverend Mother?'

The Reverend Mother, Patrick noticed, did not attempt to

comment on the numerous guesses, or even, rather surprisingly, attempt to answer the questions which poured out at top speed, mainly from the younger children. She had noticed his arrival with a smile and a nod of her head but said nothing, just allowed the questions and comments to flow until the church bells began to ring.

'Goodness me,' she said. 'Eleven o'clock already. Kitty, go and get the bell. Now, everybody, run as fast as you can, all the way around the playground as many times as you can and stop the second you hear me ring the bell. Let's show Inspector Cashman what very excellent ears that you all have.'

'I'm sorry to keep you waiting, Patrick, but they need to let off steam,' she said to him as he stood and watched the children running wildly around the playground, shouting and laughing.

'Wonder would it do me good to run around the playground; perhaps clear my head?' he said, and she gave him an understanding smile before she rang the bell.

An instant silence fell over the children who stopped in an exaggerated pose of utter statue-like stillness and then the Reverend Mother said, 'There might be a sweet in a few days' time for anyone who tells me what I really said when I told the inspector what good ears you have. Now, line up and show him how excellently behaved you all are.'

'And now, I suppose that they'll all be going around practising the word "excellent" for the next few days,' said Patrick as the children marched into school. 'I remember you telling me that I was a very "persevering" boy and I practised it all the way home so that I could tell my mother.'

'Did I really say that. Well, I must compliment myself because I was right. It has stood by you.'

Patrick smiled a little wryly as he followed her indoors. It would have been handy to have a sprinkle of brains to add sparkle to that word 'persevering' but that was not something that he could do anything about. 'Perseverance' would have to do.

'Eileen said an interesting thing, when I was talking to her this morning,' he remarked as soon as he had closed the door of the Reverend Mother's office behind them. He noted her interest at the name of Eileen and guessed that she thought quite a lot of Eileen's brains and so continued. 'She said that the archdeacon was such an unpleasant person that she could imagine him murdering anyone who got in his way, but she couldn't think who might have murdered him,' he said as he nibbled some of Sister Bernadette's Christmas cake. 'In fact, I think her words were: "He just seems to be the sort of man that could be a criminal himself, but it's difficult to find someone who would have murdered him. No one liked him, but murder him? That's another step, isn't it?" I think that's what she said,' he added hastily as he saw the Reverend Mother smile.

'What a very excellent memory you have, Patrick. It must be a great help to you in your profession,' she said.

'You see, I think that what Eileen meant was that he wasn't a nice man, but there was nothing serious enough to have anyone murder him. I can see why she said that. Joe and I have been all through the notes and there were lots of reasons why he was disliked, but in each case, perhaps, not a strong enough reason for murder.'

'It does depend upon the person, though, doesn't it? Some people may murder more easily than others, just as some worry, become more upset more easily than others. I remember when I was young that a friend of myself and my cousin told us that she was filled with embarrassment and fury because a young man, a great rugby player, told her that she was a terrible dancer and ordered her to step on his very large feet while they waltzed. She did as he asked her, but was filled with fury, said that she felt like killing him for embarrassing her. In fact, I seem to remember that she did say that if she had a knife in her handbag, she would have stuck it into his heart. But my cousin Lucy, Mrs Murphy, who was most confident, then and now, told her that she should just have kicked him in the shins and walked off. So, you see, Patrick, what is a passing annoyance to one person, might be an impetus to murder in someone who feels deeply, who lacks confidence, someone who takes fright easily. There are,' said the Reverend Mother, thoughtfully, 'many reasons why reactions can vary hugely.'

'So, opportunity is probably more important than motive at this stage,' said Patrick. 'I made a list of everyone who had been seen to speak to Enda the day before. I've got it here and the source of my information. Am I keeping you?' he asked politely with a quick glance at the clock.

'No, indeed, in fact, I had pencilled in this time to show my accounts to the bishop's secretary, but he phoned to say that he was too busy to come,' said the Reverend Mother with a quick smile. 'So, you see, this is an empty slot in my calendar, and I can assure you, Patrick, that I feel very strongly that any person who could wantonly poison a small boy should be arrested and have no mercy shown. God may forgive, but I'm afraid that I cannot. Anything I can possibly do to assist, I assure you, as a person who had responsibility to care for Enda . . .' The Reverend Mother paused for a moment and then went on rather sadly, 'I feel that I failed with that child, and my only consolation is that, to quote the Bible, "he knew not what he did". But the man, or woman, who inserted that deadly poison into a child's sweet, knew the consequences of that action, so my reliance is on you, Patrick, to seize that person before another such crime can be committed.'

Patrick bowed his head. 'I have often thought that anyone who possesses secret knowledge about a person, may hold a dangerous power over that person. We found a letter about the precentor, Mr Flewett, in his drawer,' he added, feeling rather uncomfortable.

'Certainly,' said the Reverend Mother swiftly and by the quick, sharp look she threw him, he guessed that she was already aware or had heard rumours of the precentor's fondness for small boys.

'And then there was the matter of the bishop's daughter, his second daughter, Jacinta. Joe tells me that there was a rumour going around the tennis club at Rushbrooke about . . . I might as well tell you since, apparently, most of the members of the tennis club seem to know about it, that she might be pregnant and that there might have been a relationship, a sexual relationship with the archdeacon. If the archdeacon made his daughter pregnant, perhaps the bishop might have wanted to kill him, or the bishop's daughter, herself,' added Patrick, thinking of the small boys who thought a woman was more likely to use poison.

'That's three suspects, so far.'

'Number four and number five go together,' said Patrick hesitantly. 'The two sons of the murdered man.'

The Reverend Mother bowed her head. 'I've heard the story. Very dramatically told by Father O'Flynn. The two wills and one consigned to the fire when young Mr Owen Hearn refused to become a clergyman and wanted to adhere to his own choice of a vocation. Gives them both a motive, perhaps, what do you think, Patrick? The one son filled with fury that he had been left out of his father's will completely and the other might have thought that he would strike while the iron was hot, might have wanted to murder his father before he changed his mind and drew up yet another will, but this time dividing his entire estate between his two sons. What about the others who had the opportunity?'

'Eileen seems to think that the deacon, Mr Bob Webster, might be the ambitious type, so ambitious that he would commit murder to have a chance to become archdeacon. I think that is nonsense myself. I would like to be superintendent, I'd like his pay and I'd like to be able to make decisions myself and not to have to keep explaining what I am doing and why I am doing it, but I don't see myself murdering the man.'

'That's because you have had an excellent and highly moral upbringing,' said the Reverend Mother firmly. 'I wonder whether all murderers are, at heart, spoiled children, persons who feel that their needs and desires have to take precedence over all others. Have you considered who might fit that description?'

Patrick turned that over in his mind. It was an interesting thought. 'They used to tell us, at the training school in Dublin, that private murders were usually committed out of fear. Political murders are a different matter. People feel justified. Quite honourable people will shoot a man on the other side of the argument.'

'So, who was afraid of the archdeacon?'

'The sexton, Tom Hayes, was under his command and according to Mr Bob Webster, the deacon, the man feared the archdeacon. He might have been terrified of being sacked. In a city full of unemployed men, that would be a terrible fear. Everybody sees that long line of the unemployed down the length of George's Quay, all queuing up for a few shillings of dole money to keep them going until the following week.'

The Reverend Mother considered this and shook her head. 'It wouldn't have been a serious fear, not unless they could accuse him of stealing or something like that. Tom Hayes is a hard-working man and I think that they would find it difficult to get as good. He is the son of a farm labourer, he told me once. Most city men wouldn't be as good at looking after these beautiful grounds and at digging graves. These Church of Ireland clergymen have got themselves a bargain and I don't think that the bishop is a man to dismiss a hardworking servant who had done nothing wrong. And even if Tom Hayes was worried by the archdeacon's antagonism, do you really think that he would murder little Enda?'

Patrick hesitated for a moment, but then said, 'If he were thinking of, well, of marrying Mrs O'Sullivan, he might want to get rid of Enda first. I would imagine that no one would want to be responsible for that child. Poor little fellow,' said Patrick compassionately, 'but there's no getting away from the fact that the boy was in trouble most days of the week and shopkeepers would prefer to deal with a man rather than with Mrs O'Sullivan.'

'I rather doubt that Tom Hayes wanted to change anything in his relationship with Mrs O'Sullivan; I think it suited both to leave things as they were,' remarked the Reverend Mother placidly and Patrick delved into his notebook to hide his embarrassment.

'In any case, I think that the precentor, Mr Arthur Flewett, might have much more reason to fear the archdeacon. As I told you, I found something in the archdeacon's desk drawer, something belonging to Mr Flewett, held, perhaps for blackmail purposes. The archdeacon could have threatened to divulge his suspicions to the bishop. He could have destroyed the precentor and to a man like that his job with the choir is probably his whole life.'

'Would you tell me what the archdeacon held?' And then as Patrick hesitated, she nodded decisively. 'You don't need to worry, Patrick. I know a lot about the subject, have had experience in dealing with it and it is a crime that I am always on the look-out for.'

And so, rather awkwardly, Patrick explained about the photograph album in the locked drawer of the deceased archdeacon's desk, taking care to add Joe's explanation about the 'Men Only' swimming place among the rocks in Ballycotton Bay. She listened placidly and then nodded.

'Not enough to convict him, but possibly enough to ensure that he would never again have a job as choirmaster. Not hugely serious in the scale of things. And yet, one can run no risks when it comes to children. I wouldn't have him in my school and, if I had known, I wouldn't have allowed him to have anything to do with Enda – even if I had to go to the bishop himself. I suspect that Father O'Flynn knew something, or at least suspected something and discouraged him from joining his troupe of young Shakespearean players. And the fact that the bishop was not informed, and the man not removed from the choir, is to my mind a grievous sin.'

'Was it enough to give a motive for killing a man,' said Patrick hesitantly. 'I mean that if what the archdeacon held over the head of the choirmaster might have been enough to have him removed from his position.'

'And would deprive him of his livelihood, his self-esteem and his contact with small boys,' said the Reverend Mother decisively. 'Patrick, it is your duty to inform the bishop of this discovery.'

Patrick rose to his feet. 'Thank you, Reverend Mother, it has cleared my mind to talk with you. I will see the bishop and tell him what we found. But before that I will have to see Mr Arthur Flewett and see what explanation he has for the possession of such images.'

SIXTEEN

The choirmaster had an apprehensive look upon his face when Tommy ushered him into Patrick's office. Joe was in his usual position and as soon as Tommy had withdrawn, Patrick took the small photograph book from his attaché case, placed it upon the desk in a position where it could be seen quite clearly by the choirmaster. There was a dead silence and then Patrick said quietly, 'I have a few questions to ask you, Mr Flewett. Would you prefer if the sergeant left the room? The decision is yours.'

'Let him stay!' The man's voice was leaden, and, after one quick glance at the photograph album, his eyes looked straight ahead, staring over Patrick's head and at the wall beyond. He hadn't even glanced at Joe.

Patrick opened the first page, held out the book, hesitated for a moment, waited until the man reluctantly looked at the album and then he continued, quite slowly, turning over each page until he came to the end and shut the book.

'You took these photographs of the boys in your choir?' he asked.

After a moment's pause the word 'yes' was articulated, but nothing further.

'And developed them,' stated Patrick. Joe had noticed the grainy tint of brown and the slight blotches here and there on the pictures, giving the impression of a botched, home-made job.

There was a much longer silence this time. So long that Patrick felt that he should fill it with some words of his own. 'You find the question difficult to answer,' he stated.

'Some questions are easier answered than others.' The answer came slowly and when Patrick didn't respond to it, the choirmaster then said rather quickly, 'I suppose the answer to your question is "yes" and "no", Inspector.'

'Perhaps you could explain.' Patrick was determined to keep his patience. This was a very delicate and tricky matter.

'These pictures, some of these pictures, Inspector, are a deliberate piece of malice and were used to blackmail me.' Suddenly the choirmaster seemed to draw courage and energy from some source. 'Bear with me, Inspector. This may seem a very strange tale, impossible now to prove, but I can swear to you that it is a true story. Yes, every year I take the choir-boys on an outing. The bishop pays for it, and he agrees with me that the boys deserve it after all the hours of practice every week, all the time they give up when they could be playing games or enjoying themselves with a book. And every year I take them to Ballycotton where they have the freedom to swim without the constraint of those awful, knitted swimsuits which hamper the swimming strokes and are icy cold when one emerges from the water. I see nothing wrong in that as it is just a crowd of boys with no girls around,' he finished defiantly.

'And the pictures?'

'The pictures were pictures that any parent could display upon their wall. In fact, after I have printed them out, I offer the boys a choice of one each. And then I put a selection into an album and retain the negatives in case I need to do a second copy of any particular picture. I accidentally left the album and the negatives in the cathedral one night, just beside the organ, and when I went to look for them on the next morning, they had vanished. None of the boys seemed to know anything about it. They had no reason to steal an album; after all they had been offered their choice of picture and if any wanted a second picture, that would have been no problem, since I did my own developing. I'm afraid that I suspected that the sexton might have thrown the package in the bin by accident, but he denied it and so I just went on looking here and there and wondering what had happened. And then one night, after choir practice, just as I was about to lock up the cathedral, the archdeacon appeared with the album in his hand. I was about to thank him, but there was something about him which froze the words upon my lips and then, he opened it, page after page and I . . . well, I felt cold all over. I was shaking. Here and there, throughout the album, there were pictures that I had not taken and that I never would take. I knew what he was about. I expected him to try to blackmail me, but it wasn't money that he wanted, just power.'

Patrick waited, but the choirmaster said no more, just stared at the floor, grinding the knuckles of one hand against the other. After a minute's silence, Patrick said, 'I'm afraid that you will have to explain to me, Mr Flewett. I'm quite ignorant about photography. What did the archdeacon do with your pictures?'

'He took the negative, cut out one tiny portion of the picture, enlarged it to ten times its size and then printed a new picture.' After a moment's silence and a glance at Patrick's bewildered face, the choirmaster gave a bleak smile. 'And so, Inspector, instead of a picture where a boy stood on the rocks beside the swimming pool with the island, a lighthouse and a distant ship all filling nine tenths of the picture, this fiend produced a picture which blotted out all of these things and filled most of the frame with a portion of the boy's anatomy.'

'I see,' said Patrick. He didn't wholly understand but he was prepared to believe that the process was possible, and it would be easy to find out whether it was or not. 'And the archdeacon did not ask for money?'

'No, he asked for nothing, but he did not give me back the album and so it hung over my head. And I feared all the time that he would expose the album and disgrace me. I still don't know why he did it and yet made no use of it. I was left to suffer, and he enjoyed that, perhaps that was it.'

'I see,' said Patrick, rising to his feet. 'Well, thank you for explaining this matter, sir. I'm afraid that I will have to keep the album for the moment.'

The man rose, also, but slowly and reluctantly. He said nothing until Patrick reached out a hand to turn the doorknob, and then he said, 'I hope that you will believe me, Inspector, when I tell you that I would never hurt even a hair on the head of any child.'

'Thank you, sir,' said Patrick, conscious that his voice had a wooden note in it but feeling unable to give any comfort until he had thoroughly investigated the matter. And then, still with his hand on the knob, but making no move to turn it, he said, 'Did you ever think of moving away, sir? Moving away from the archdeacon. Going to another part of the country? You had a skill; every church and cathedral in the country has an organ and a choir.'

'And every church, every cathedral would want a reference and the bishop left all of that sort of thing to the archdeacon,' said the man bleakly and, without waiting for any further comment, he went through the door and swiftly down the corridor.

There was a hearty greeting from Tommy, but no sound of a response from the choirmaster, and a moment later the outer door slammed closed. Patrick turned over the pages of the photograph album and looked across at Joe.

'What did you make of that?' he asked. 'Is it possible to do something like that. This photograph of the boy just looks like an ordinary picture, but it's true that others have much more background in them: sky, waves, island, lighthouse, ship – all the rest of them have one or more of these things. Could the archdeacon have done something like he described; is it possible to mess about with negatives like that?'

'I think so,' said Joe. 'I've no interest in photography myself but one of my brothers is very keen. Persuaded my mother to allow him to make a sort of dark room in one of the attics. Used a couple of old fireside screens and draped an old black curtain across the top. I could ask him, if you like, not tell him anything, of course, but just consult him about possibilities. I'd say, though, that the choirmaster's explanation made sense to me. After all, you can make photographs of a different size and I'm sure it's possible that you can use just one part of the negative. I'd say it sounds complicated, but possible. Strange that there was no attempt at blackmail, wasn't it?'

'So, he said.'

'Had he a reason to lie?'

'I think he had,' said Patrick. 'Just think about it, Joe. If it were just a matter of embarrassment, if the archdeacon were just "teasing" – for want of a better word, teasing him with his knowledge of a hidden vice, well, a good lawyer could make mincemeat of an accusation of murder. Why on earth should the man murder for that reason? Of course, nothing could be proved about the doctoring of the photo. We don't even know, ourselves, whether the choirmaster was the person who enlarged part of a negative of an innocent picture.'

'Do you think that he is a bit, well, you know? That he is a paedophile?' asked Joe.

'I think that it is quite possible,' said Patrick slowly, 'but it is also quite possible that he doesn't do anything wrong. Just like a man can have a yearning for drink but makes sure that he never opens the bottle of whiskey in his cupboard.'

'So, you believed him when he said that he would never hurt a child.'

'I think I did. He sounded very sincere. But I'm not completely sure. What about you?'

'Same here,' said Joe. 'I thought he sounded sincere, also. Of course, paedophiles can fool themselves that they are doing no harm, but then there is the case of the deliberate murder of the little boy, Enda. He couldn't possibly not know that the child would die from one of those poisoned Rolos. If we are making a list of probable murderers, I'd give him a score of ten out of twenty.'

'Not too high, then,' said Patrick. He opened a new page of his notebook and wrote a list. 'I'm just putting titles rather than names,' he said. 'Oddly, that is the way I think of them. Now, how would you rate the bishop?'

'Oh, two out of twenty,' said Joe impatiently. 'He's such a nice old chap. Confirmed me when I was a lad. And why should he kill the archdeacon?'

'The bishop might be a nice old chap, but, according to your tennis club gossip and Eileen's hints, his daughter had been abused, made pregnant by this archdeacon. On the other hand, I really find it hard to think that the bishop would kill Enda. Why should he? After all, he lived so near, he could have crept across the road after midnight and gone into the cathedral. He held the keys, after all. The archdeacon had rounded up all of the keys and had ensured that they were all locked in the bishop's safe. The bishop didn't need to involve the child in the poisoning of the wine. He could have done it himself. No, we'll leave him at two out of twenty. Now, what about the dean?'

'Motive: next on the list to be archdeacon and will get a salary rise. Going to be quite short of money once his eldest son becomes twenty-one and takes over the legacy. Has started a new family and would want to bring them up as little gentlemen or little ladies with nice fat dowries. I think I'd give him ten out of twenty.'

Patrick wrote down the number without comment. It was, he always thought, a mistake to allow personal impressions to interfere with hard facts, especially early in the investigation. Nevertheless, he wasn't happy about the ten out of twenty. The dean, to him, did not appear to be a likely candidate.

'What about our friend the choirmaster, the precentor?' he asked. And then without waiting for an answer, he said, 'I think I am going to give him fifteen out of twenty. He may not have wanted to murder one of his nice, clean, attractive little choirboys, but he may not have felt the same about a filthy little guttersnipe – as he would have regarded Enda. On the other hand, I did believe him when he said that the archdeacon had developed new photos from the negatives. That made sense to me, and I did think he was telling the truth. You'll phone me, won't you, once you've had a chance to talk with your brother. I'll be working late and why don't you go off early? I'd like to get this business straightened out.'

Patrick was alone in the police station with the phone switched through to his office when Joe rang. 'Quite possible, this matter that we discussed,' said Joe. 'My brother thought that it wouldn't be a problem and would need very little special knowledge.'

'Thank you,' said Patrick. It was, he knew, a mistake to ever think that phones were private in this city full of gossips, so he instantly put down the phone. He found that he was glad, although it did not make his job any easier. He got to his feet instantly. He would have to tell the Reverend Mother that his suspicions were probably groundless. This would probably be a good time to drop by. He often visited his mother at this hour in the evening and that would form an excuse for his journey.

But first, he would see the bishop's daughter.

SEVENTEEN

When Patrick arrived at Bishop Street, he did not drive in through the gates of the bishop's palace but parked his car at a discreet distance and then got out and looked around. The bishop's house, or palace, stood well back from the road, isolated, standing within a few acres of gardens around it and encircled with a six-foot wall.

Beside the entrance gate, the small lodge and the avenue leading to the palace, was the archdeacon's house. An enormous three-storey-high house, facing the cathedral. There were also some nice smaller houses on Bishop Street, one of them helpfully had 1901 engraved on a plaque below the chimney. But these were few and the rest of the houses were the usual cabins built at a considerable distance from the stately house which housed the archdeacon. Patrick took out his notebook and double-checked. It was as he had remembered. Of the clergymen connected to the Church of Ireland Cathedral, only two lived in Bishop Street: the bishop, himself; and the archdeacon who lived next door. The rest lived in widely scattered addresses, opting, understandably enough, to forego views of the cathedral for the enjoyment of the clean fresh air available on the hills of Montenotte and Bishopstown, well outside the stench and fogs of the city.

Nevertheless, the chemist's assistant had said that the bishop's daughter was buying the cyanide for a neighbour whose servants had discovered a wasps' nest in the attic. Looking at the situation of the bishop's palace, its most likely neighbour could be said to be the archdeacon.

With a sigh, Patrick got back into the Ford, drove it carefully through the open gates and parked it neatly outside the front door of the bishop's palace.

The bishop was not at home, which meant he would have to make another visit to discuss the matter of the precentor and his fondness for small boys. The story would have to be carefully told and he would have to trust the bishop to deal with it sensitively and to keep an eye on the situation.

However, it might be easier to interview Jacinta without the presence of her father and to his relief it appeared a natural request to the servant once she had declared that she didn't know when the bishop would be back.

A very pretty girl, this Jacinta, he thought when she arrived. He hoped that the rumour of pregnancy might be a false alarm, but there were black shadows under the attractively pale-blue eyes, and she had a tense look about her, with hands that were tightly clenched together and lips that looked bitten and sore. He found himself feeling most sorry for her.

'I'm sorry to trouble you, Miss Thompson,' he said, endeavouring to sound at ease. 'It's just that we had information that you purchased some cyanide from a chemist shop. To deal with a wasps' nest, I understand.'

He left it at that and watched her reaction. She was, he thought, genuinely startled.

'Wasps' nest,' she repeated. 'I think that you must be mistaken, Inspector. What would I have to do with a wasps' nest?'

Now he wasn't so sure that she was telling the truth. There was something a little artificial about her repudiation, almost an effort to put him in his place. *I am the bishop's daughter; what should I have to do with such plebian matters?* she appeared to be saying and, to his annoyance, he felt himself flush.

'You said to the chemist's assistant that you were purchasing it for a neighbour,' he said. 'Perhaps that will jog your memory.'

Now she paled. He could see that. The detail told her that she had been remembered and could probably be identified. She did not reply instantly, though, but watched him narrowly, and he could have sworn that she was weighing up the choices between continuing with a denial or coming up with some plausible explanation. Cyanide, of course, perhaps rang an alarm bell. Perhaps he should have called it 'stuff to kill wasps', he thought.

'I remember now,' she said after a good minute of time had

elapsed. 'Yes, I remember. It was before Christmas. Yes, it was for a neighbour, for the archdeacon.'

She had been watching his face carefully while she said that and perhaps she had observed a measure of incredulity because she started to speak very rapidly, almost too rapidly for his much-practised shorthand skills.

'Yes, I remember. It was the week before Christmas. I hadn't done any proper Christmas shopping and I was in a terrible rush and I had a list a mile long – presents for all of my sisters, and then there are the cousins and my little nephew and my father and then we are always given presents by people from the congregation and my list kept growing and growing and I thought that if I didn't get into Dowdens quickly, it would be full up and I had a lot to get in Roches Stores also and then some cheap things for the servants from Woolworths, my father always wants us to give our own gifts to the servants and then—'

Patrick held up a hand. 'Just tell me what the archdeacon said to you, Miss Thompson.'

'I'm trying to explain that I was in a rush and I didn't really listen to him; I just wrote down "poison for wasps" on my list. I might be able to find the list for you, but no,' she said, almost without drawing breath, 'no, I remember that I burned it. It was something about a wasps' nest in the garden.'

'The young lady in the chemist's shop remembered you saying that the wasps' nest was in the attic,' remarked Patrick.

'I didn't . . .?' she snapped. And then she stopped abruptly. 'Did she? Well, it might have been for a wasps' nest in the attic. I don't remember. I never listened to the archdeacon too much. He was a terrible liar. Don't tell my father that I said that; he'll just be telling me never to speak ill of the dead,' she added hastily.

'And when you came home from your shopping, what did you do then?' asked Patrick. He drew the symbol for the word 'liar' but did not add anything. The accusation was so strange that he would remember what had led up to it. In what way was the archdeacon a liar?

'Well, I got one of the maids to come up to my bedroom and help me wrap up all of the presents.'

'I meant what did you do with the wasp poison?' When she didn't answer immediately, he pressed her. 'It was a most dangerous substance, Miss Thompson. I'm sure that you were told that by the young lady in the chemist shop.'

'No, I don't think so,' she said. There was an unrealistic effort at indifference which was belied by the sharp white teeth which nibbled at the damaged lower lip.

Patrick wrote again. She had not corrected his use of the phrase 'young lady', had not stated that she had been served by her friend from the tennis club, the son of the shop owner. And yet she must remember. The report from Joe's informant had described quite a conversation between the bishop's daughter and young Mr Fielding.

'Let me take you back to that busy morning a week before Christmas when you did your shopping. Archdeacon Hearn asked you to get him some stuff to put upon a wasps' nest. You remembered the errand, went into the chemist's shop, purchased it, and brought it back home with the rest of your shopping. Now, when you parked your car, did you take every-thing up to your bedroom or did you first take the dangerous package of cyanide into the archdeacon's house?'

Again, the lip was bitten, but he had presented her with an easy choice, and she took it. 'I brought it into him,' she said.

'Who opened the door to you?'

'He did,' she replied very quickly. 'He had been standing at the window and saw me coming.'

'Can you remember what he said?'

She looked at him impatiently. 'Well, what do you think he should say? "Thanks", I suppose. What else should he say?'

Patrick looked down at his notebook and then looked across at her. 'I thought that you and he were friends. I would have hoped that you might have had a conversation. I had hoped that you might be able to tell me whether he was worried about something or not.'

The colour flooded into her cheeks, but she pulled herself together with a notable effort. 'Don't be ridiculous, Inspector,' she said shrilly. 'Who told you we were friends? The man was nearly as old as my father – well, he had sons my age. Why on earth should I be friends with him?'

Patrick made no comment but added another note to the bottom of the page. He kept his eyes fixed upon the page, but he knew by the small sounds that she had stirred uneasily in her chair, and he waited to see whether she would say anything more. People usually did overdo matters when they were trying to pull wool over your eyes. That was his experience, and he made some more doodles while waiting patiently for her to boil over.

'I know what it is – someone has been gossiping about me,' she said eventually, and when he looked up at her, he could see that she spoke between gritted teeth. 'It's that sergeant of yours, Joe Whatshisname. He's your little spy, isn't he?'

'Spy?' queried Patrick. 'Do you have any valuable secrets, Miss Thompson?'

'Gossip, then. Everyone knows that the guards pay good money for gossip.'

Patrick ignored that. When he spoke, his voice had a harsh note, even to his own ears.

'Were you friends with the late archdeacon?' he asked. 'It's a simple question, Miss Thompson and my reason for asking it is to find out as much as possible about the dead man. Might he have told you if he were worried about something?' He had begun by feeling sorry for this girl, but then he had remembered little Enda and that pathetic packet of Rolo sweets. There would be, he swore, no mercy in his heart for anyone who planned that death for a seven-year-old child. Nevertheless, he smiled at her. 'Nothing strange about being friends with an older person. I often have friendly conversations with people who are probably three times my own age.'

He thought she might smile at that, but she didn't. Her face remained drawn and her eyes very wide with anxiety, almost terror. Of course, if there was truth in the rumour that said she was pregnant, that could account for anxiety – but terror?

And then she surprised him. 'Cyanide,' she said, and her high-pitched voice made the word come out like a series of squeaks. 'Cyanide! You said cyanide! I didn't know that wasps were killed with cyanide. But that's . . . that's what . . .'

'Killed the archdeacon and the child,' said Patrick, watching her very carefully.

She ignored the bit about the child. 'So, he killed himself,' she said. 'That must have been what happened. It would be just like him not to die in his bed like any ordinary suicide, but to pour poison into the wine and then fall dead on the altar steps just on a day when the cathedral was full of people. He'd like that.'

'You think that the archdeacon sent you to purchase some cyanide so that he could kill himself while conducting the Christmas morning service in the cathedral,' stated Patrick in as neutral a tone of voice as he could muster. He held his pencil poised aloft, ready to write, and watched her face carefully.

Colour had come back into the face, he noticed, and she sat up very straight. 'That's it,' she said, almost jubilantly. 'It was so like him. He always liked to be the one in the forefront. My father didn't care. He's a modest, retiring man, but some of the parishioners used to say to me that the archdeacon behaved as though he were bishop himself. He put on such airs, and he loved to have an audience. That's it, Inspector. The case is solved. It's not a murder, but a suicide.'

'That's interesting,' said Patrick politely. 'Could you tell me why the archdeacon should have committed suicide?'

She smiled at him. Quite a nice smile and he would have sworn that she looked relieved. 'That's for you to find out, Inspector. But I assure you that he was just the sort of man to do something like that. He might have been disappointed in himself. He had high expectations. I bet he thought that by now he would be Primate of all Ireland. Now, Inspector, if you will excuse me, I really must run along. I've so much to do. Glad I could be of use!'

He allowed her to go. He could always summon her to the police barracks if he needed more information, he told himself. She puzzled him, though. That suggestion of suicide – did she really think that he would swallow that?'

The light was still on in Joe's room when Patrick went into the barracks, so, without taking off his coat, he put his head around Joe's door. 'Come in for a minute, Joe,' he said.

Joe was on his feet before Patrick had finished. He swept

some applications for gun licences into a neat pile and then locked them into his drawer. Patrick waited for him. Joe had an excited look, but Patrick only felt near to despair. This case might finish him, he thought as he led the way back into his own office. By the look of the roaring fire, Tommy had alleviated his boredom by leaving his desk by the door at regular intervals and refuelling the fire. Unasked, he was at the door now with a tray bearing a pot of tea and two cups, and a generous portion of biscuits.

'Cold day, Inspector,' he said. And then, almost without drawing breath, he added, 'Terrible thing that murder in our cathedral, isn't it? Everyone talking about it in the pub last night. "I don't know a thing", that's what I said to all the lads,' he added hastily.

'Quite right, too,' said Joe heartily. 'Let me take that tray from you, Tommy. You'll be wanting to get back to the desk quickly in case someone phones the superintendent,' he added in a friendly fashion.

'You have more patience with him than I do,' said Patrick as soon as the door had closed behind the constable.

'Sure, isn't he as old as the hills?' said Joe in a careless fashion. 'Must be way past retirement age. I suppose the superintendent has a bit of a *gra* for him for the sake of the old days, so he puts up with him.'

And because he is a Protestant and used to belong to the Royal Irish Constabulary, thought Patrick, but he said nothing. Joe was also a Protestant and the superintendent had always high praise for him, also. The Protestants in the city were getting fewer and fewer in number and those who remained seemed to stick even more tightly to each other.

Still, he told himself, as he swallowed a gulp of tea, Joe was an excellent fellow, and he was glad that he recommended that he should be moved from the rank of constable to that of sergeant.

'And Jacinta?' queried Joe. 'How did you get on with her?'

'Lady with a poor memory!' said Patrick with an attempt at humour. 'Couldn't remember buying the cyanide at first and then remembered buying it for the archdeacon, himself. You were right. I looked around the street. He was definitely the only real neighbour – I don't suppose that the young lady would think of the lodge keeper as a neighbour to the bishop and his family. And the rest are quite small houses and even little cabins.'

'And had she anything interesting to say?'

'Thinks he committed suicide, thinks it would be typical of him. Thinks that he would love the idea of falling dead on the steps to the altar on Christmas morning with a packed congregation.'

Joe raised an eyebrow. 'And why should the man commit suicide?' he queried.

'"He might have been disappointed in himself. He had high expectations. I bet he thought that by now he would be Primate of all Ireland".' Patrick read from his notebook, took up a biscuit and then put it down again.

'Really! Oh, she can't think that! She can't be that stupid!'

'I think she was frightened,' said Patrick slowly.

Joe nodded. 'Afraid that she would be implicated. I got the impression that she had had far too much to drink that night at the tennis club. Was knocking back Gin Rickeys at a great rate. The trouble with drink is that it makes you talk; I'd say that by the end of the evening most people knew that she was pregnant, and that Bob Webster had turned her down on the grounds of not wanting another man's bastard at his table.'

'Really!' said Patrick. Quite extraordinary, these Protestants! No morals! And a nicely brought-up girl like that. He thought about the matter.

EIGHTEEN

'I must say, Dr Scher,' remarked the Reverend Mother, 'that my acquaintance with you has broadened my mind and enriched my store of knowledge to a degree that would have seemed impossible to me before I met you. No, don't look so startled. Every word of that is true.'

'I am startled,' said Dr Scher. 'Of course, I know it to be true, but I'm just wondering what brought this on. You are not usually so complimentary.'

'I was thinking how you have developed my appreciation of old Cork silver,' explained the Reverend Mother. 'Did you hear a doorbell? I am expecting Patrick. No, don't go away. I think he may be glad of your presence. Just one question before he arrives. Do you think that Bishop Thompson is also knowledgeable about silver?'

'Now that you mention it, and goodness knows why it suddenly came into your head, but the answer is "yes". Knows a surprising amount about it, in fact. I have invited him to come to see my little collection, but he said that it was a pleasure that he had to postpone as he was taking his daughter on a visit to her sister in England.' Dr Scher gave her a shrewd look. 'Your doing, I suppose, was it?'

The Reverend Mother ignored this. 'Here comes Sister Bernadette with the tea trolley. Perhaps you'd be kind enough to open the door for her while I put some turf upon the fire. I feel I have a certain affinity with this fire and that it responds to my touch, so you see to the tea trolley while I see to the fire.'

The fire was burning well, but it caused a little diversion while Dr Scher had his usual bantering conversation with Sister Bernadette. Patrick, she had seen with one quick glance, was not looking well. She suspected that he had slept badly during the last night. He had black shadows under his eyes

and there was an air of weariness and defeat about the way
that his shoulders slumped.

Dr Scher, also, had noticed this and she saw him add
another lump of sugar to Patrick's teacup as he stood over
the young policeman while he downed the sweet drink and
then bullied him into having a slice of Christmas cake. The
Reverend Mother resumed her seat and looked across at her
pupil. He was, she knew, under great pressure. His superintendent, the man who would be submitting monthly
appraisals of his juniors in the Cork barracks to their
superiors in Dublin, would be extremely anxious that the
murder of an archdeacon in the hallowed surroundings of
St Fin Barre's Cathedral should be solved as soon as possible.
Patrick's chance of promotion might depend upon how he
handled this case. The Irish police force might have been
re-christened with the Gaelic name *An Gardai,* but many of
the highest ranking were left over from the old regime, from
the Royal Irish Constabulary, and belonged to the Church of
Ireland. She sat back in her chair and watched him eat as she
mused over this puzzling case.

'You'd imagine that this would be an easy case to solve;
four or five possible suspects, and the victim an unpleasant
man, plenty of motives, lots of clues, I just can't understand
why I haven't solved it yet. I just seem to keep coming up
against a brick wall.' Patrick put down the slice of Christmas
cake and pushed the plate away from him so decisively that
not even Dr Scher tried to persuade him to take it back. 'I'm
almost concluding that it was the choirmaster. I just don't
know why Enda had to be involved, why didn't the man himself
do it in the morning? Would have been easy enough. He would
have been the first into the church in the morning but, on the
other hand, what with the boys and the organ, testing the keys,
testing voices, he would not have had an opportunity to do
something secretly, and it was the sexton who opened the
church. So, the sexton might have spotted him doing something
with the wine. In which case, the overnight business might
make sense. But somehow, I don't think that it was him. If it
were just the archdeacon, I think I would pick him, but I do

think that he was genuinely fond of little Enda. Why involve the boy, especially as it meant the boy's death?'

'So, the precentor, the choirmaster, came into the cathedral after the sexton?' asked the Reverend Mother.

'They came in together. Met in the churchyard.' Patrick's voice had a weary note, as though he had been over and over the matter, had spent wakeful nights over it.

The Reverend Mother bowed her head. 'Of course, the precentor would not have bothered about the altar; his first concern would have been the organ in that underground room,' she said thoughtfully and so low as though she were talking to herself.

'That's right,' said Patrick. 'The sexton said that. He went to fuel the boiler and he heard Mr Flewett pressing the keys of the organ.' He opened his notebook and read out from it. 'Here's what he said: "Mr Flewett was playing the organ, not a tune, just notes." And,' Patrick continued wearily, 'the choirmaster heard Tom Hayes shovelling coal down in the cellar.'

'And who was next into the church?' enquired the Reverend Mother.

'The canon, the Reverend Jack Wilson.'

'Ah, yes, of course, so that was it,' said the Reverend Mother with an air of satisfaction.

'But,' said Patrick. He stopped and looked at her with a puzzled expression. 'Funny, but I would have put him to the bottom of the list. I know that the archdeacon was trying to sue him, but, well, he seems such a nice fellow and . . .'

'And the archdeacon would have been unlikely to have taken matters any further.' The Reverend Mother finished his sentence. 'If necessary, the bishop would have intervened, but I guess that the archdeacon's own common sense would have told him that he would make a fool of himself if he took his colleague to court because of a funny short story, written anonymously and which would probably never have come to his notice if a picture of that beautiful cathedral had not been inserted by an editor. No, I have scant knowledge of Canon Wilson, of course, but I did notice on Christmas morning how he seemed to be quietly taking responsibility for cathedral matters, blowing out the candles, picking up a few prayer books from beneath a seat of one pew and a child's mitten from another. There are people like that, tidy-minded people who automatically check that all is in place and so I am glad to hear that Canon Wilson arrived early, with no specific duty to perform, but that he would be there and would be just the sort of person to notice if something was wrong.'

'Wrong,' repeated Patrick. 'But nothing was wrong. Little Enda's body wasn't discovered until after the archdeacon had fallen dead upon the altar steps.'

'I do feel, very strongly, that our murderer had a poor knowledge of children like Enda and that he expected the child to behave like a well-fed and well-brought-up child, to have put the Rolos in his pocket and to have climbed back out again. I have looked at the back wall of the church and I could see that someone as agile as Enda could easily have done that and certainly the murderer would have relied upon him doing so. And if he had, the chances are that his death, whether it took place upon the street or in his own home, would have gone unnoticed and would never have been connected with the death of a cleric in St Fin Barre's Cathedral,' said the Reverend Mother. And she added, bleakly, 'In this city of ours, children like Enda die easily. Many from rat poison, others from undiagnosed disease; yet more, I regret to say, from starvation and neglect. No, our murderer, I do think, did not reckon upon two bodies to be found within the cathedral and that made the case much more complicated.' She stopped and said, thoughtfully, 'Yes, I see how it happened. It's obvious to me now, but I must say that Dr Scher has been of huge assistance. I do think that it would be quite a puzzle if I had not gone for a walk on Christmas Day, and if Dr Scher had not insisted upon me returning to his house. You see, Patrick, when a person is fanatical about a subject, they tend to introduce that subject on all occasions, no matter what else is being discussed. I must confess that I have introduced the subject of child poverty when our own bishop, Bishop Cohalan, was discussing the Council of Trent and *Ius Novissimum* and so, on Christmas afternoon, while I was eating his housekeeper's excellent Christmas cake, Dr

Scher brought up the fascinating subject of old Cork silver. And,' she continued, with a glance from one puzzled face to another, 'of course, old Cork silver was the solution to our mystery.'

'Well, I'm glad to have been of use to your mighty brain, Reverend Mother,' said Dr Scher, 'but I'm not sure how or why. You must enlighten me.'

'But surely, Dr Scher, you remember remarking to me that the bishop, Dr Thompson, knew a lot about old Cork silver – I confirmed that with you in case my memory was inaccurate. So, we turn to that Christmas Eve night. You've been kind enough to read me your notes about that, Patrick, and I think I have a clear picture of the cathedral. The service is over, the choirboys were pulling out their Christmas presents from a sack held by the choirmaster, some of the clergy were discussing golf, the altar boys – and of course the altar boys are of great importance – were laying out the trays on the tables next to the high altar and to the side altar. The deacon, young Mr Bob Webster, whose job it should have been to supervise them, went off and the others soon followed. And, I think, Patrick, that you mentioned that someone had remarked that they were in a silly mood, very excited as, of course, children would be on the night before Christmas Day.'

The Reverend Mother waited for a moment while Patrick nodded, and Dr Scher repeated over and over to himself, 'Old Cork silver'.

'But next morning,' continued the Reverend Mother, 'on Christmas Day, the choirmaster and the sexton entered the cathedral first and went immediately to their responsibilities, the sexton to the boiler and the choirmaster to the organ. But the third person who arrived, Canon Wilson, had no specific task and so he looked around in the way that a careful, tidy-minded man would do, and he immediately noticed that the silver had been wrongly set out. The little-used, valuable, old, early seventeenth-century chalice and cruet, with the Cork town mark upon it but, of course, bearing the patina of its ancient inheritance, and not looking shiny and smooth as was the more modern silver, was placed by the altar boys in the inferior position, on the table beside the side altar and the shiny, new silver was given to the bishop to celebrate the important service of the day, the main Christmas mass.

'I guess, though this is something that you can check, Patrick – that Canon Wilson instantly spotted the mistake and had the valuable old Cork silver brought back up to the high altar and the modern silver relegated to the side altar.'

The Reverend Mother paused for a few seconds, looking from one face to the other, and then continued.

'But of course, Patrick, the new, modern silver had been beside the high altar all night long and Enda, an intelligent child, had carried out his commission to the letter and had emptied the powder into that shiny, new jug which contained the wine for the high altar. So now, of course, my dear Patrick, you can see that you were trying to solve the wrong mystery. The problem was not who planned to murder the archdeacon – a puzzle to you and rightly so – but who planned to murder the bishop. Interestingly,' she added, 'I remember you telling me that your assistant Joe remarked that "the further we go in this case, the more I think that it was a miracle that someone didn't murder that archdeacon years ago."'

'But who would have wanted to kill the bishop?' began Patrick, and then he stopped.

The Reverend Mother waited. Patrick's mind was slow, but it was methodical and accurate. Given time, he would come to the right conclusion. Dr Scher was muttering to himself about hallmarks and the use of the Cork coat of arms upon the first silver pieces, but Patrick didn't even look in his direction but fixed his attention upon her.

'Do you remember, Reverend Mother,' he asked earnestly, 'that I told you about the canon and his bird-watching activities and how he gave a packet of Rolos to little Enda to reward him for climbing up to report upon the owl's nest. And that when he, the canon, went out to his car, he saw the archdeacon standing at the window looking across at the roof of the cathedral. Of course, I didn't take much notice at the time, but now – well, it all fits in. He saw how quickly and easily the boy climbed up onto the roof. And you see, Reverend Mother, that girl, the bishop's daughter, she bought the cyanide for the archdeacon. I doubted her, thought she was going to poison the archdeacon for what he did to her, but she was telling the truth.'

'Yes, I remember you telling me about that,' said the Reverend Mother with an approving nod. 'Two most significant points. I think you are on the right track, Patrick.' She watched him affectionately. He was growing in confidence, she saw with satisfaction, was becoming more and more sure of himself.

'Of course!' said Patrick, exultantly running his fingers through his dark curls and looking, with his untidy crop of hair, thought the Reverend Mother, rather like the gun-shy, long-haired German pointer that her father had rescued and presented to her for her tenth birthday. 'I've been wasting a lot of time wondering who might have wanted the job of archdeacon, but of course, the job of bishop is the really plum job in the Church of Ireland. Joe told me that. And the archdeacon would have been an almost certainty to get it since everyone knew that he was the one who was managing the diocese.'

The Reverend Mother turned to Dr Scher. 'Did you tell me something that a friend of yours said about the archdeacon, Dr Scher? Something about him being so ambitious, to the degree that he would even stoop to cheating in order to win a mere game of golf. I seem to remember you saying that.'

'Yes, of course,' said Patrick, not allowing Dr Scher time to reply. 'Of course, everything is beginning to add up. The archdeacon was the one to make a fuss about ensuring that no one but bishop had keys to the church. That gave him an alibi but meant that he had to use Enda. He was the first to leave on Christmas Eve night and the last to arrive on Christmas Day morning. Went straight to the side altar once he had put on his vestments. He had nothing more to do if Enda had played his part. He was not friendly with the other clergy so nobody would have noticed if he were tense.'

'I do believe that is an important point,' said the Reverend Mother with another nod of approval.

She watched to see whether anything else occurred to him and was rewarded when he said, 'But, of course, according to Dr Scher, the autopsy proved that he had no breakfast. And the fact that the stove was burning well and had been refuelled probably is a clue to the possibility that he scraped his plate into the stove, then covered the food with fresh pieces of anthracite when his housekeeper had gone back to the kitchen. That is an indication to the fact that he was tense but didn't want to betray the fact. Otherwise, he would have just said that he didn't feel hungry. A lot of people have a hangover on Christmas morning after all those Christmas Eve drinking sessions.'

'But, Patrick, why should the archdeacon kill the bishop? After all, the bishop was a friendly, easy-going person, wasn't he? Not the sort of person who could be disliked by one of his clergy, was he?' asked Dr Scher.

He was, thought the Reverend Mother, a quite unambitious person himself and could not understand the motivation which led to killing a superior.

'Oh, but don't you think that it was ambition?' said Patrick eagerly. 'Do you remember, Reverend Mother, telling me about *Macbeth*, one of Shakespeare's plays? I looked it up in my encyclopaedia that night. He killed a nice old king, just because he wanted to be king, killed him out of ambition. The archdeacon must have wanted to kill the bishop because he wanted to be the top man. In fact,' said Patrick, delving into his notebook, 'I think I have something written down here, something that the bishop himself said to me; I've got it down here in shorthand: "hardworking; so very obliging at deputising for the bishop at meetings in Dublin. The archdeacon took a lot of duties from him; didn't know how he was going to manage without the archdeacon; the man had taken so much off his shoulders." That's what I have written down,' finished Patrick triumphantly. The Reverend Mother nodded approval at him, but said nothing, allowing him the space to think it over and to say after a minute, 'So, the archdeacon wants the bishop's job, but the bishop could live another twenty years. He watched Enda climb up onto the roof with absolute ease and he makes a plan, probably broke the pane of glass in the rose window himself and blamed the sexton for it. Then he told Enda that he had a present for him if he came back after everyone had gone home on Christmas Eve. Even if the child had told that to someone like his mother, it would have meant nothing, it was Christmas Eve, the altar boys had a present from the bishop and the choirboys had a present from the choirmaster. So why shouldn't Enda get a present from the archdeacon? Of course, the boy would come back and of course he would be happy to play a trick. I don't suppose that it meant much to him. And if it didn't work, then the archdeacon could just deny everything. Enda was a terrible little liar. He tumbled a stall in the market once and tried to persuade me that it was a dog that had done it. Even though his mouth was full of cake and his pockets bulging with more cake, he kept on telling me about this dog, a huge, big, black dog, the size of a small calf. That was the way he described it. Swearing that he was telling the truth, "Cross my heart and hope to die!" That's what he kept saying.'

Patrick had a sad look upon his face but then it changed to a look of anger. 'And that man didn't care,' he exploded. 'Just as though Enda were an animal.'

The Reverend Mother shared his anger, though she said nothing. There was something about the callous use of the small boy that made this one of the worst crimes that she had known, in this city full of death from violence and from deprivation.

'And now I suppose that I will be expected to hush it up, to have it classed as an unsolved crime,' said Patrick bitterly. 'The superintendent will have a hundred reasons why it should be buried quietly.'

The Reverend Mother thought about this. There were, she thought, reasons that could be put forward for concealing the truth, but only one, in her mind, had validity. Those of the alien faith and alien blood had never been wholly accepted as friends and neighbours, despite the ceasefire. The revelation that a Protestant archdeacon had poisoned a small boy of the Roman Catholic faith would be enough to cause unrest through the city and even to provoke a full-scale riot. She thought about it for the moment and then raised her head.

'Nevertheless,' she said, 'truth must prevail. The law of God and of man requires it. Our greatest saints endorse it. You cannot allow the stain of suspicion to rest upon those who are innocent. You must tell exactly what you feel has happened to the coroner and the law of the land must take over the responsibility.'

NINETEEN

Eileen sat back in her chair and yawned and then listened. The distant bells from the city churches and cathedrals chimed the hour. She adjusted the paper lever of the typewriter to an open position and then pulled the paper towards her, lifted it from the typewriter and carefully read it through, from the headline to the last word. It was her fifth, and she hoped her last, draft for her space on the *Evening Echo*. The front pages, of course, would be filled with the sensational news from the coroner's court, but she had been promised a space in one of the centre pages. Every word had been counted and every sentence pondered upon.

The Poisoned Chalice

During the Great War between King George V of England and Kaiser Wilhelm of Germany, one million dogs died on the battlefield. It was not their war; the dogs would not profit from it. Their lives were callously thrown away by those who had power over them. They did what went against any instinct in a dog, went out where bombs exploded and, in many cases, they even carried a bomb strapped to their bodies which exploded when they reached enemy lines, killing the dog as well as the German soldiers. That, their trainers had decided, was the only infallible way of achieving the end.

And how were they trained to perform these dangerous errands?

They were trained by being kept hungry, so hungry that when their food was placed in an area where sounds and smells of explosions were simulated, the dogs ignored their instincts and plunged, day after day, week after week, into that dangerous environment. The craving for food overrode all other natural senses of self-preservation.

And, in the same way, on Christmas Eve night, in this city of Cork, a hungry child was bribed with a packet of Rolo sweets to climb into St Fin Barre's Cathedral and pour poison into the communion cup.

A man died.

And the child who could have borne witness, could have condemned the murderer to the scaffold, died also. Poisoned by a sweet which his half-starved body craved.

More than ten years ago, Padraig Pearse, before he lost his life, fighting for his country's freedom, spelled out his dream. He promised to cherish all children of the nation equally.

If we had followed his dream, would a small child in our city have lost his short life for the sake of a packet of chocolate sweets?

Signed: A Patriot.

An hour later, Eileen waited in the tense, excited atmosphere of the upper room of the *Cork Examiner*'s office listening to the thunder of the printing machines in the building next door until the moment when the bundles of newly printed newspapers arrived and the 'Echo Boys' began to call their wares on Patrick Street. Then she snatched up a copy, opened it instantly at the correct page, gloated for a moment over her own words, turned to the front page, and then stuffing the newspaper into her handbag, ran down the stairs and jumped upon her motorbike.

The streets were dense with home-going cyclists, pedestrians, horse and carts and motor cars. The Echo Boys were shouting 'Coroner's Court Verdict' fearlessly standing in the middle of the road handing out copies of the *Evening Echo*, shouting 'Sensational! Horrifying! Shocking! Unbelievable!'

The traffic around South Main Bridge was dense, but Eileen fought her way through, weaving a passage between the Beamish Beer wagons and the market sellers' horse and carts. It was just after six o'clock when she arrived at the Garda barracks. Joe was just leaving. He gave her a friendly wave and pointed towards the door where Tommy was standing with a bunch of keys and a forbidding expression of disapproval on his face.

'Don't mind me,' she said to him, waving a copy of the *Evening Echo*. 'Just popping in to see the boss. I'll let myself out. Just want to show him my article in the *Echo*.'

'He's got it; Joe went out to buy three,' said Tommy, but he stood back to allow her to enter. 'See the bit where the coroner praised the police? The superintendent was ever so pleased about that,' he called after her. And then she heard the door slam shut behind her and the keys turn in the lock.

The place felt empty. The night duty officer had not yet arrived and everyone else seemed to have gone home, judging by the open doors and the quiet hallways. Only Patrick's door was shut, but she opened it without knocking.

He was there. But not frowning over sheets of paper or writing neatly scripted notes. For the first time since seeing him behind that desk, he was doing nothing. His arms were folded upon the desk and his head lay upon them. She moved forward hesitantly and looked down at the tired, white face. Even the closed eyes did not hide the dark shadows that lay beneath them. Tentatively she stretched out her hand and touched the wildly tousled black hair, smoothing it back into its usual ordered neatness. He still did not stir and with a sudden impulse she bent down and kissed him upon the cheek.

'Wake up, Patrick,' she said. 'You and I are going to celebrate. Dinner for two at Mutton Lane Pub!'